Readers love
JOHN INMAN

Dilly and Boz

"If you like your romance with a pinch of gunpowder and a blade then this is one-hundred-percent the book for you."

—Love Bytes

"*Dilly and Boz* is a wonderful romance and a terrifying thriller all rolled into one. I highly recommend it to you."

—Joyfully Jay

Larry Boots, Exterminator

"Those looking for a satisfying love story with both an erotic component and an adrenaline rush won't be disappointed."

—*Publishers Weekly*

"*Larry Boots, Exterminator* was a thoroughly enjoyable read that I'd have no hesitation in recommending."

—*Divine Magazine*

A Party to Murder

"John Inman knew what he was doing when he wrote this book. Definitely a recommended read if you like a good mystery."

—Gay Book Reviews

"I very highly recommend this book to those who are looking for a challenging mystery with romance and the spooky ambiance of a high-energy thunderstorm at night."

—Scattered Thoughts and Rogue Words

By JOHN INMAN

Acting Up
Chasing the Swallows
Dilly and Boz
A Hard Winter Rain
Head-on
The Hike
Hobbled
Jasper's Mountain
Larry Boots, Exterminator
The Last Dance
Laugh Cry Repeat
Love Wanted
Loving Hector
My Busboy
My Dragon, My Knight
Nightfall
A Party to Murder
Paulie
Payback
The Poodle Apocalypse
Ravenous
Scrudge & Barley, Inc.
Shy
Spirit
Strays and Lovers
Sunset Lake
Two Pet Dicks
Words

THE BELLADONNA ARMS
Serenading Stanley
Work in Progress
Coming Back
Ben and Shiloh
Ginger Snaps

Published by DSP Publications
7&7: An Anthology of Virtue
and Vice
The Boys on the Mountain
The Second Son
Willow Man

Published by DREAMSPINNER PRESS
www.dreamspinnerpress.com

JOHN INMAN

RAVENOUS

Published by
DREAMSPINNER PRESS

5032 Capital Circle SW, Suite 2, PMB# 279, Tallahassee, FL 32305-7886 USA
www.dreamspinnerpress.com

Ravenous
© 2020 John Inman

Cover Art
© 2020 L.C. Chase
http://www.lcchase.com
Cover content is for illustrative purposes only and any person depicted on the cover is a model.

Trade Paperback ISBN: 978-1-64405-575-5
Digital ISBN: 978-1-64405-574-8
Library of Congress Control Number: 2019957869
Trade Paperback published June 2020
v. 1.0

Printed in the United States of America

For my readers who asked for horror… enjoy!

Chapter One

TERRY JONES opened his eyes to a bombardment of gentle crystal sounds, clearly orchestrated by Mother Nature herself. The noises were so musical, so unexpected and sweet, they yanked Terry upright in the bed and left him sitting there with an insipid grin on his face. He could sense his eyes bulging out as big as melon balls, and there was some sort of weird little shiver of pleasure crawling up his naked back, which made him wiggle around and damn near laugh out loud.

Holy crap! The sounds on the air were beautiful! No car horns, no wailing ambulances, no beeping garbage trucks warning toddlers on tricycles to get the hell out of the way before they got smashed flat. No earsplitting rumble of skateboards or atonal rap crap blasting from passing automobiles. Not even any kids screaming to high heaven on their way to school. Just the sweet cacophony of birds and the lazy rush and scrape of shifting tree limbs swaying merrily in the morning breeze, tickling the cabin walls. Above his head, a plunk and then a gentle rumble scrambling from left to right told him a pine cone had been knocked loose from the tree outside and sent bouncing across the cabin's roof before tumbling over the edge in what was no doubt a graceful swan dive, to land with a muted thud in the dirt below.

Terry took a second to dig through the blankets to find his sleeping pug, Bruce. Named for Bruce Willis because the dog thought he was hot shit too—and like the real Bruce, sometimes actually was. Bruce was apparently immune to the glorious songs of nature. Terry pulled his limp body out into the morning light and held him up in front of his face to give him a smooch on the belly. Bruce wagged his tail, yawned, snorted a few times in bliss, as pugs are prone to do, then promptly fell fast asleep dangling there in midair.

"Pitiful old guy," Terry crooned, tucking the dog carefully back under the covers.

He gazed around the room, and the second he took in where he was, Terry froze. Memories came flooding back, pelting him like hail. Sharp and icy cold. Horrible memories. *Bloody* memories.

His gaze shot up to the ceiling, and he thought back to the sound he had heard only moments before. The pine cone striking the roof and rolling to the ground. *Or had it been a pine cone at all?*

He shook the covers off his bare legs and stepped onto the cold floor. His cock, which had been standing at morning attention only moments before, was now shriveled and limp. Warily, holding his breath, Terry walked to the upstairs cabin window and pressed his nose against the glass.

The forest surrounding his acre of land was in a furious state of motion—tree branches large and small twitching and swaying in the wind. Tall weeds were bowing to one another on the banks of the ditch that bordered Terry's property in the back. Most of the trees were pine and hickory, with a few towering bridges of honeysuckle draping from one tree to another. Their flowers had not blossomed yet, but the twining vines and leaves of the honeysuckle, as green and vibrant as in high summer, still trembled in the breeze and dripped with morning dew.

Terry stood stock-still at the window. The chilly air seeping through the glass in front of him laid icy fingers across his bare chest and belly. Someday he would have to put in storm windows, but not today. Or anytime soon more than likely. Not while his little neck of the woods was still under siege.

And not when every heartbeat might be his last. As *that* thought struck him, Terry gazed down at himself. At his long fuzzy legs, coated with ginger hair, neatly muscled from years of jogging. At the furry expanse of his chest and abdomen, as lean as his legs, with an added trail of red fuzz leaking down from his navel to lose itself in his nest of coppery pubic hair. His sleeping cock nestled there, one eye peering out at the world as if leery of facing the day.

That little stroke of whimsy almost made him smile. But the smile was short-lived.

Terry held his hands up and surveyed his arms and fingers. Checked around his fingernails for torn skin. He slid those same fingers across his face, up and over his beard to his cheekbones, down his neck, along toward the back of his head. Every couple of seconds, drawing his hands back and studying his fingertips for smears of blood in case he might have scratched himself while he slept.

Nothing. He breathed a sigh of relief.

He gazed back at the bed, where Bruce had poked his nose out of the covers. He was watching Terry for any signs of movement. Preferably movement toward the kitchen where Bruce might find himself being served breakfast.

Terry chuckled watching him, made a motion for the dog to follow, then set off toward the staircase leading down from the cabin's loft where he kept his bed. Bruce flew out from under the blankets in hot pursuit, bright-eyed now but still yawning. His stubby tail wagged in anticipatory bliss while the toenails on his four little feet tippy-tapped across the icy floor.

With a grunt as stiff muscles stretched, Terry poured a bowl of kibbles from the fifty-pound bag under the kitchen sink. He set the bowl on Bruce's blue blankie by the kitchen stove, then refilled Bruce's water dish while the pug burrowed his snout into his food and all but inhaled it to extinction.

With his roomie taken care of, Terry filled a teakettle for instant coffee and placed it on the gas stove, then set about preparing his own breakfast. Eggs over easy and bacon, fried in a skillet on the burner next to the teakettle. He would have liked a baked potato nuked in the microwave and smothered with butter, but he was too lazy to fix it. Instead he made do with cold cereal buried beneath half a cup of sugar for dessert. Terry had a sweet tooth, and donuts were a little hard to come by these days.

While he ate he listened to the mockingbirds who always perched on the chimney above his hearth, sending their voices spilling out across the grate to fill the cabin with song. Of course, the song was one step short of caterwauling, but Terry was used to it. Once in a while, Bruce growled at the racket coming through the flue, but on the whole, Terry figured he was used to it too.

His gaze wandered to the stack of galvanized fence posts piled clumsily against the cabin wall by the back kitchen door. The posts had been glommed from a now defunct home improvement store down the mountain, not too far from the city limits of Spangle, California. Terry's hometown. Since the invasion came, since the beasts had spewed up from the guts of the earth or spilled out of the depths of somebody's fucking nightmare—*wherever* the hell they came from—Spangle had become little more than a deathtrap. A deathtrap Terry Jones had been lucky to escape. So far.

But he wouldn't think about that now.

He nibbled on bacon and soaked up the egg yolk from his plate with the last of the stale bread before returning his gaze to the fence posts in the corner.

The posts were metal, six feet long, perhaps three inches wide and a quarter inch thick. Strong and unbendable. They were pierced with countless holes, intended for the convenient attachment of fencing wire. But Terry wasn't interested in fencing wire. Fencing wire wouldn't fill his needs at all. No, Terry was in the process of using the heavy metal posts to reinforce the outside of the cabin. This included the windows and doors, where he placed the posts like security bars, nailing them two inches apart so he could still see outside but close enough that nothing outside could make its way in. When he was finished with the outside, he would line the walls and ceiling inside as well.

As a second line of defense should the first line fail, Terry was using the metal posts to reinforce the walls downstairs in what he had come to call the blood room. The blood room had once been a fruit cellar, but those days were long gone, Terry told himself with a nasty little smirk aimed at the fence posts in the corner. The blood room was there as a last retreat. A final chance at survival. Sort of like a last-ditch bomb shelter, except nuclear bombs were actually the least of his worries. His and everybody else's in and around Spangle. These days they were more concerned with flying beasts with fangs and claws and an unquenchable thirst for human blood. And who could ever have seen *that* coming?

Terry checked the calendar on the wall beside his chair. He reached over and filled yesterday's square—August 2—with a fat black X, using the Sharpie hanging beside it on a string. There. It was official. He had survived another day and night. Ruffling through the pages of past months, he counted back to May 3. Exactly three months ago. That was the day he hightailed it out of Spangle and entrenched himself here in his and Bobby's vacation cabin on this measly little mountain in the backcountry, three miles out of town. It had always been a refuge before, this cabin. A place for them to relax. Where they could get away from work and spend quality time together, just the two of them. Plus Bruce.

Now, of course, Bobby was no more. He had been taken only hours after they fled the town, as so many fellow residents before them had been taken. On that day, when Bobby was wrenched from Terry's side and swept away in the horror, Terry knew he would never go back to their house in town. Not as long as the horror kept escalating. He had no choice but to carry through with the plans he and Bobby had made to escape the slaughter. So with little more than a broken heart, the clothes on his back, and his beloved little dog, Terry slunk off into oblivion. And now, three months later, here he still was. Hiding out. Cowering, to be more precise. Aching not to be alone anymore, but unable to leave his tiny mountain, the only place he felt safe enough now to call home, and the last place in the world he should really be at all.

He had burglarized a few out-of-business clothing stores since leaving town, sneaking back to replenish his wardrobe. He had looted abandoned grocery stores for canned goods to keep himself alive. But there was little he could do about his broken heart. With time, it had healed a bit. But there were still days—and nights—when Terry all but crumbled under the grief, the weight of missing Bobby. There were so many things he missed. The sound of Bobby's voice across the breakfast table. His gentle snores in the bed at night. The way Bobby inevitably rolled into Terry's arms in the wee hours of each and every morning, his mouth and hands seeking comfort, his sleep-warm skin nestling close until Terry, his own hunger awakened, sought Bobby's warmth as well.

They had been good for each other, him and Bobby. Their love had been real. As real as the creatures that tore Bobby away three months back on this very day. As real as the creatures that would tear *Terry* away *today* if he wasn't careful. If he wasn't diligent.

Once again, Terry searched his hands for any little cut or tear. Any seepage of blood, no matter how minute. He touched his face and checked his fingertips for smears of blood. His beard was getting long, he noticed, since he had stopped shaving. No sense asking for trouble if shaving wasn't necessary. One slip of the razor and they would be on him in a flash. He didn't doubt it for a minute.

Them. Terry shuddered, thinking back. Out of nowhere, filling Terry's mind, was the sound of Bobby's final scream as he was torn to pieces in front of him.

Terry's fork clattered to the floor, and he closed his eyes, trying to squeeze the memory away, to head it off before it took hold of him completely.

It refused to budge, of course. It always did. The memory stayed lodged right behind his eyes, where it always lay in wait. Lurking. Hoping to catch him off guard.

As it just had.

God, Terry missed his old life. And oh sweet Jesus, how he hated that fucking memory!

So he plucked it from behind his eyes with trembling fingers and placed it on a dark shelf at the back of his mind. Tucking it away. Burying it among the flotsam, back where the shadows were deepest. It took every ounce of willpower he possessed, but he managed it.

For now.

Chapter Two

IT WASN'T that cold—this wasn't the Sierras after all. It was only a small 2500-foot peak in the backcountry of San Diego County. But cold was the least of Terry's worries anyway.

While he had only seen the creatures from great distances, swarming high in the sky, since he moved to the mountain three months earlier, it didn't mean they weren't a threat. So he took precautions, as he always did when going outside.

He donned leather gloves to protect his hands and pulled on a thick leather jacket, supple with age, to shield his arms and torso from any accidental scratch or skin tear. To go along with the biker's jacket, he wore heavy blue jeans and boots below the belt. Despite the low temperature, he smeared bug repellant over his face and neck. For all he knew, it would take nothing more than a mosquito bite or a beesting to release into the air the scent of his pheromones or his DNA or whatever the hell the beasts were attracted to in human blood. The simple fact was this: once your scent was out there, once they whiffed your blood and zeroed in on your location, you were as good as dead.

Funny thing, though. Animal blood didn't draw them. He learned that interesting fact on a day shortly after he came to the mountain when Bruce tore his side on a protruding nail. As soon as Terry noticed, he had rushed them both into the fruit cellar, now the blood room—or would be when he finished reinforcing it. He had cowered there waiting for the attack he was sure would come. He sat in the corner in the dark, cradling a terrified Bruce and aiming a shotgun at the stairway leading to the cabin above, hoping to at least blow a few of the fuckers to smithereens before they swarmed through the trapdoor and ripped them to shreds.

Strangely enough, the attack never came.

Terry tried other traps then, other baits, testing to see what blood the beasts found yummy. He shot a squirrel and left its bloody carcass in the yard. Nothing. Back in the days when he could still find fresh meat in the markets in town, he had thrown out raw hamburger to see if that attracted them. It didn't. Once, when the weather was warmer, he ran across a rattlesnake and chopped its head off with a hoe. Nothing.

He thought back to all the attacks he had witnessed in Spangle before he fled. Horrible attacks. Mind-wrenching terror. Violent, bloody moments he knew he would never, ever forget. But not one of them involved any living creature other than a human being. Be it man, woman, or child.

The women between puberty and menopause had the worst of it. For it was those women whose very bodies betrayed them, their menstrual cycles acting like dinner bells.

The creatures had risen up almost six months earlier. As soon as it was understood what triggered the creatures' hunger, women had stayed hidden, aided by their spouses or friends. Safely locked away in basements and windowless garrets, in cupboards, closets, or honest-to-God bomb shelters—what few there were. But now, months later, most of those women—the ones who had not already fled the area completely—had been snatched away. Snatched away because given enough time, the creatures always found a way in. Once they knew where you were, and once they smelled your blood, they never gave up. Ever.

They were large enough and determined enough to burst through glass windows. If swarming in great enough numbers, they could tear and claw and batter their way through doors or ceilings or even walls. If a structure had a weakness, they would sniff it out.

And their hunger never abated. Their fury never calmed. They were endlessly ravenous.

Yet with all their need to feed, with all their endless seeking of human blood, the creatures had their weaknesses too.

For one thing, sound did not attract them. No matter how loud or how strident the noise, it did not draw them. Perhaps they had no organs for hearing at all. Terry didn't know. He had never had a dead specimen to examine, and even if he had, he wouldn't know what to look for. He had no medical training. He wasn't a veterinarian or a zoologist. He was a notary public and a substitute grade-school teacher, for pity's sake. That was his area of expertise. What did he know about impossible creatures from God knows where? How could he be expected to understand what might turn out to be the key to the survival or the extinction of the human race?

Early on, the authorities had tried to force people to leave their homes. Many, including Terry and Bobby, had refused.

Now he supposed there were authorities or experts out there somewhere working on a solution, but he never heard about them. They did not make their studies known to the likes of him. While the power was still on, Terry had destroyed his cell phone, fearing the authorities would use the signal to track him and force him to leave. He didn't have a landline at the cabin. Television reception on the mountain had always been sketchy, and the only radio he had was on his old Jeep, and it was pretty much worthless.

The roads and highways had been sealed off by the town police and by the highway patrol. Terry had seen people in hazmat suits too, but that was early in the game. He hadn't seen any lately. People had been allowed to leave, but no one was allowed back in. Rumor was that Spangle had been quarantined. Cut off from the world entirely. Since they couldn't correct the problem, those in authority seemed to have decided they would simply keep the menace penned up until they could devise a solution. The small backcountry town of Spangle had apparently been sacrificed for the greater good.

For Bobby and Terry, everything they owned or cared about was tied up in Spangle and on the slopes of the tiny mountain nestled next to town. The house on River Street. The cabin in the woods. That was it, their whole world. That was what made them stay. But most importantly, they also had each other. For them, that was enough.

For the second time that morning, while he stood dressing, staring through the cabin's upstairs window, the memory of that day flooded back to swallow Terry whole. The day that Bobby died. The day three months earlier when Bobby was torn to bits. How the creatures swarmed around them both, but only Bobby had been attacked. While Terry sat there helpless and stunned, drenched in his husband's blood. Untouched. And only inches away!

After those few fleeting seconds of unimaginable violence and mind-numbing terror, Bobby's beautiful body had been reduced to little more than a shimmering red mist and a sliver or two of bone twirling through the air. In mere moments, even those were gone.

On that day. On that bloody, horrible day.

Chapter Three

IT HAD been a warm spring then. Over their heads, the Southern California sun spit out heat, raining it down on the earth like a welding torch.

Terry remembered that Bobby had been grinning like a sap that morning. The world was falling apart around them, but the guy could still smile now and then for no reason at all, which made Terry love him all the more. They had legally wed, practically on a whim, almost three years ago to the day, thus the extremely thorough and highly enjoyable anniversary lovemaking that morning. Terry suspected those heart-pumping hours in each other's arms had something to do with the grin on Bobby's face. And the grin on his own face as well.

But Terry quickly learned that having sex that morning had absolutely nothing to do with Bobby's good humor. He had, it seemed, made a decision overnight.

"We're leaving today. Leaving town. We have to escape. Get away from the slaughter. We'll be safe in the cabin," Bobby announced, referring to the mountain cabin they had bought only a year before. "I know we will."

"But the cabin is still in the quarantine zone."

"Yes, but it's secluded. If we lay low, the creatures won't be drawn there. They're used to feeding here. In town. Where food is abundant."

"It's not so abundant anymore," Terry countered. "Most everyone has left. The lucky ones were driven out by the authorities. The not-so-lucky ones were eaten."

"Yes," Bobby said, his fingers clutching at Terry's arms. "And if the creatures move on to better feeding grounds, they'll move to where the people are. They won't fiddle around with our little mountain. They'll head for San Diego. Or maybe Tijuana. A large city would be a smorgasbord for them."

"But what will happen to all the people in *those* places?"

"You know what will happen to them. What we have to do is make sure we're not among them when it happens. Will you go with me?"

"You mean to the mountain? Now? Today?"

"Yes. Right now. The time has come."

"What about our stuff?"

"We'll take food and clothing and Bruce. And anything else we can't live without."

Bobby was right, of course, and Terry knew it. All their friends, in fact most of the town's population still breathing, had already fled. Left Spangle completely, or so he had heard. He and Bobby and maybe a few other stubborn souls were the only ones remaining.

Terry stared down at the little dog at their feet. The mutt had a worried look on his face, as if he knew what they were discussing. Of course, pugs *always* have a worried look.

Bobby pulled Terry close, his eyes desperate, burrowing in. His jaw muscles clenched. Determined. His smile had disappeared. He had made the jump from fuck-happy to deadly serious in ten minutes flat. "Help me pack, Terry. Please. We have to get out of here."

"But why? Why today? What's happened?"

Reluctantly, Bobby tugged him toward the door. As they always did before leaving the house, they examined each other's exposed skin to make sure there were no injuries, no matter how slight. This was the new norm. This was the way everyone lived their lives now. It no longer seemed odd. It was simply what one had to do to survive.

When they were satisfied they were injury free, they stepped outside into the morning light. The silence was deafening. As almost every morning was these days. Spangle had never been a major metropolis. Spanglites were not known for bustling. If they had to move, they ambled. It was almost as if the town had always managed to lag behind when it came to the hurries and complexities of the twenty-first century. Like the residents were stuck in Mayberry in 1955. Calm, unruffled, maybe a little bored. And boring. But still, life went on. Or *had* gone on before the creatures showed up.

Now, of course, the streets were empty but for occasional smears of dried blood on the walkways and roads where kills had been made. Sparkles of shattered glass lay sprinkled beneath punched-out windows. A car was parked sideways in the middle of the street just past the end of their driveway. They had first noticed the vehicle a week ago, its windshield in ruins, the hood coated with blood, congealed to black, where the driver had been pulled through the glass and torn to shreds. The flies had given up on the blood days ago, leaving it to cook in the sun. Neither Bobby nor Terry could bring themselves to push the vehicle out of the street.

"Look," Bobby said, his eyes sad. "Look there."

Turning to where Bobby pointed, Terry realized the house next door had been attacked sometime in the night. Windows broken. Front door sagging from twisted hinges.

Terry stared at the damage. Shocked. A man, a woman, and two children lived there. The Petersons. They were their neighbors. Friends. They had barbecued together. Gone to the county fair together only a few months before. Terry had won the daughter a teddy bear by tossing quarters.

The Petersons, too, had been reluctant to leave the only place they had ever called home.

"Where are they?" Terry asked, a chill settling into his core like he had swallowed a ball of ice.

"They're dead."

Bobby's gaze led Terry's toward a trail of blood drops in the grass.

Terry stared at those drops for the longest time.

There were other items scattered across the Petersons' lawn. An adult's flip-flop, spattered with blood. A shred of cloth from a child's pajama shirt. A foot-long hank of fine blond hair with the rubber band still holding it together at one bloody end. The couple's ten-year-old daughter had worn her blond hair in a ponytail.

Terry didn't understand. "It looks like the creatures took the whole family. I've never seen them do that before. Usually it's one person only. The person with an injury. The person whose blood they smelled. Why would the creatures have taken them all?"

Bobby's eyes were misted over in grief. The Petersons had been like family. "Who knows which one they came for first? But whoever it was, maybe the father and mother fought back. Trying to protect the kids. Or each other. In the melee everyone was injured a little. Blood was drawn from each of them. A little, a lot, who knows? But once it was drawn, it was over. The feeding frenzy escalated. They were torn apart. The whole family. All of them."

Terry spread protective fingers over his throat. A defensive gesture. He squeezed his eyes shut, trying not to think what it must have been like. A tear leaked onto his cheek.

"We're leaving today," Bobby said again. Even more determined this time. He reached over and brushed the tear from Terry's cheek. "We'll mourn later. Help me get our stuff together. Gather up clothes and every ounce of food we have in the house. Don't forget Bruce's dog food." Suddenly he was all business. "Wear your gloves. Wear all the protective clothing you can find."

"And you think we'll be safe at the cabin?" Terry asked, still stunned by the blood trail in the grass. Stunned by what had taken place *right next door* while he and Bobby were either asleep or making love. Right next door! He was so astounded, so *appalled*, he could barely grasp what Bobby was telling him to do. Bobby's announcement had hardly soaked in at all.

"We'll be safer there than we are here," Bobby insisted.

Only then, at that moment, did Terry begin to fully comprehend. "Y-yes," he said. "You're right. We'll go today. Right this minute."

And as simply as that, the decision was made.

Standing there on the front lawn, which was weedy and hadn't been mown in weeks because those things didn't really matter anymore, Bobby pulled Terry close. He wrapped his strong arms around him, and Terry felt comforted there. As he always did. Even with the tiny, voiceless town screaming in silent terror around them.

When a shadow passed over, they tilted their heads up to the sky and observed a black swarm of creatures, like a monstrous flock of crows, only larger, much larger, wheeling away toward the south. Silent but for the sweep and lift of fleshy wings—a percussive pulse of sound that battered at the air around them. In mere moments, the swarm had disappeared, slipping down below the rooftops toward some far-off Spangle street. Toward a soul with only moments left to live. If even that.

Terry pressed his lips to Bobby's ear, whispering softly, his eyes returning to the bloody grass on the lawn next door. He noticed the flick of curtains on a house across the street. Somewhere behind those curtains, a terrified pair of eyes peered out. They were being watched. Not that it mattered. There were terrified eyes watching everywhere you looked these days.

Terrified eyes, or *hungry* eyes.

"We can pick up more food along the way," Bobby said. "There are abandoned stores scattered around. We'll find enough. We'll take the Jeep. It has more storage room than the VW."

"What about the Jeep's canvas roof? The creatures...."

Bobby planted a kiss on Terry's nose. A wicked smile twisted his mouth. "As long as you don't start your period, we'll be safe enough."

Terry rolled his eyes. "Very funny."

But Bobby didn't laugh. He simply went back to the business at hand. Clearly, he had been planning this longer than Terry knew. "All right," he said. "Once we're on the mountain, we can hunt for game if we have to. Rabbits, squirrels. The creatures aren't drawn to animal blood, I hear. Only human."

"How is that possible?" Terry asked. He was disinclined to trust the rumors that ran rampant in the creatures' wake. Not unless he saw it for himself. Bobby shook his head, clearly impatient to get moving. "I don't know, Terry. I don't know. I've already loaded the shotgun in the Jeep. We'll find more shells along the way when we're looking for food. Maybe even more guns. Who knows? And extra gas for the generator at the cabin. It'll be nice to have a backup if the power goes out. I figure it's only a matter of time before the authorities shut the power down to try to get the rest of the people to abandon Spangle. But we'll beat them to it. We're leaving on our own."

Terry stared back at the place where they had once been so happy. The place where they were *still* happy, even if the town was dying around them. "What about the house, Bobby?"

"If we come back, it will still be here. But that's only if we're still alive to come back. On the mountain I think we can survive until this all ends. All right? Are you with me?"

Terry smiled then, because the question was patently ridiculous, and they both knew it. "Of course I'm with you," he answered with sober eyes.

Bobby stared down at Bruce. "Are you with me too?"

Bruce gave a yip that sounded like a yes to Terry.

Five minutes later they were throwing stuff in the back of the Jeep Sahara. Ten minutes after that, they were on the road.

While Bruce slept in the back seat, the streets they drove along were still and silent. Occasionally, in the distance, they would see another automobile, usually a farmer's pickup truck, either crossing the main drag, or veering away to disappear down some side street or other. There were no pedestrians. There were no police cars. Anyone in a position of power had vacated weeks ago. Again, dark smears on the sides of buildings and on the sidewalks showed where the creatures had made their kills. Showed where people had died. The blood sprays and puddles were clotted black now, like blotches of tar, strewn and left to harden in the California sun.

At the same moment, they each spotted a child standing in the gutter at the edge of the street. The child was naked. A boy. No more than six years old. He was sucking his thumb, his great wide eyes staring at the Jeep coming toward him.

"We have to help him," Bobby said, but no sooner had he braked, steering toward the side of the street, than a man came out of a house and raced toward the boy. His father, maybe. He snatched the child into his arms and fled with him back toward the house, his eyes never once leaving the Jeep that had slowed to a stop not fifteen feet away.

"He thinks we want to hurt him," Terry murmured, his heart aching a little to imagine that anyone would suspect them of such a thing.

"At least the boy is safe," Bobby said. And while an odd silence settled between them, he accelerated back onto the street. Bobby continued to watch the man and the child as he drove past. Terry did not do the same. He simply wanted to forget the suspicious look in the man's eyes when he ran from them with the little boy clutched tightly in his arms. He wanted to forget what the man had suspected him and Bobby of wanting to do. As if they were as dangerous as the creatures.

"It's good we're leaving town," Terry said, edging as close to Bobby as he could get with the seat belt holding him back. "I want to be alone with you. I've had it with the human race. Fear has made them… wicked, I think. If they're going to act like animals, maybe they *should* be preyed upon for food."

Bobby nodded dully, an infinite sadness on his face. "Don't think about that man anymore. He didn't understand what we were doing."

Terry didn't speak. He simply sat there, glowering through the windshield.

Bobby sighed and reached over to clutch his hand. "Cut them some slack. People are frightened. They don't think straight when they're frightened."

Terry turned to study the man he loved. "Do you really think that was the boy's father?"

Softly Bobby replied, "I pray to God it was."

After a minute, Terry muttered for his own ears alone, "So do I."

The next few blocks were spent in silence, except for the blatting engine noises and the spurts of wind whipping through the Jeep's removable top, which had never been particularly airtight. The crappy seals on the canvas roof made it kind of pointless to run the air conditioner, but on hot days like this, they always did anyway.

They enjoyed the simple act of motion. The hum of wheels spinning on asphalt beneath them. Trees and buildings zipping past on either side. It was nice to finally be going somewhere. For the first time in months, it felt like they were accomplishing something, that they actually had a plan. They enjoyed the solitude too. It was like the old days, with just the three of them: Bobby, Terry, and Bruce, who was still sawing logs in the back seat. Damn, that dog could snore.

While Bobby drove, Terry fiddled with the radio on what he knew was a hopeless mission to find a station they could hear. All he found was static and white noise. The radio was crap and always had been. Spinning the dial was something to do to pass the time, and Terry knew it.

After passing the sign marking the Spangle city limits, they traveled a winding blacktop road through the rocky backcountry. Out here the traffic was totally nonexistent. They had the road to themselves. At one point, on one of the craggy peaks, Terry spotted a mountain lion sunning itself on a rock. He tried to point it out to Bobby, but by the time he lifted his hand, the cat was gone.

They passed a huge compound of modern new buildings between two mountain peaks, off by themselves, far from the nearest homes or towns. One of the Indian casinos. Before the trouble started, the place would have been packed no matter what time or day it was. Now, of course, it was empty and abandoned, moldering in the heat. Not a car in the vast parking lot. Not a soul strolling through the shopping center alongside. The only movement to be seen was a pack of dogs, scruffy and wild, that were standing in front of the broad casino doors, the glass shattered now, exposing cave-like shadows within.

The dogs watched the Jeep approach. Terry saw one of the dogs, a large German shepherd, lift its lips and snarl. He thought he saw a ripple of tension sweep across its hackled back.

Swallowing hard, Terry tore his eyes from the dogs and studied the buildings as they passed. Even here there were smears of black blood strewn on walls and asphalt. Shattered windows. Remnants of death. Just like in town.

Terry gnawed the inside of his cheek as Bobby accelerated past the silent casino. They weren't far from Spangle here. The casino—or what was left of it—was the only hint of civilization to be seen. Behind them, they knew, ten or fifteen miles beyond their taillights, they would run across the roadblocks quarantining the area. With cops on duty, making sure no one assholed along from the outside to accidentally—or purposely—enter the feeding zone.

Terry had thought, had *hoped,* that once they got past the Spangle town limits there would be fewer signs of the creatures. Like maybe the beasts would be concentrating their efforts on where the most food could be found. In the populated areas. In town. In neighborhoods. In the places where people congregated. Where it would be easiest to find them and take them down.

But if the creatures had attacked the casino, which was only a short distance from Spangle, how safe would he and Bobby really be in the cabin on their tiny mountain? Would they be lucky enough to find that little nook of the world ignored by the creatures because they were off somewhere else seeking more abundant game? Would he and Bobby be safe enough to live out the rest of their lives there, or at least survive long enough for this madness to be finished one way or another? If it ever would?

Bobby drove on, with Terry sitting in silence beside him. Fidgeting. Worrying. In the back, Bruce snored relentlessly on.

They were in the foothills now. Up ahead, Terry spotted a ramshackle roadside market. Back before the world went to shit, they used to come here to buy fresh produce and other necessities from the old Mexican woman who ran the place. Her name was Maria, Terry remembered. They were about twenty minutes from their cabin.

"Let's do some looting," Bobby said with a forced grin.

He pulled in next to the market, raising a billowing cloud of dust from the gravel parking lot. When the dust settled, they looked out on the place. There wasn't a windowpane left intact on the structure. A great hole had been torn in the roof.

When Bobby unleashed his seat belt and reached for the door handle, Terry laid a hand on his arm, holding him back.

"Are you sure it's safe?"

"No," Bobby said. "Of course I'm not sure." And with a tiny devil-may-care grin, he slid his arm from Terry's grasp and stepped outside. Terry followed.

The tiny store lay somnolent in the drowsing heat. The air was dry here. Santa Ana dry. Crinkling the tender linings of the nostrils. A hot breeze was blowing through, weird for December. Terry blinked in surprise to see a tumbleweed roll past and lodge itself under the front bumper of the Jeep. This stretch of blacktop road was as deserted as the streets in town. There were a couple of homes a little farther along, but if there were people around, they were hiding out. Cowering in basements. Hunkered down in the shadows. Waiting, *praying*, for this hell to pass. Trying not to make a sound, although sound did not draw the creatures. Trying not to bleed, because blood was what the creatures craved.

"It's like the Old West. Only spookier," Bobby muttered. He was smiling when he said it. Unflappable, as usual.

As carefree as a tourist, and without so much as peeking around the shadowy doorway first, Bobby strolled inside the store and disappeared. Terry had to hustle to keep up.

Inside they stood side by side while their eyes adjusted to the dark.

When they could finally see, Bobby exclaimed, "Eureka!"

Two minutes later, they were both scraping tinned goods off the shelves and dumping them into one of the rickety shopping carts the store very kindly provided for looters. Nothing uncanned was worth stealing, so they ignored the deli case, which was filled with a swarm of black flies, creating a constant manic *hum* in the background.

Terry looked through the glass at the maelstrom of flies and saw a stack of green pork chops, alive with maggots. Tasting bile and thinking he might actually go the distance and puke up his guts, he quickly turned away.

Bobby was rolling the cart toward the rectangle of daylight that marked the front door. The cart was heavy and had a wobbly wheel and didn't want to roll, filled as it was to the brim with a pretty good assortment of canned stuff that would keep them from starving for a while if things got rough.

Terry hurried to catch up, glad to leave the store behind. Outside, he spotted Bruce peeing on the Jeep's back tire, then turning to watch his masters exit the store, his little tail going a mile a minute in greeting.

Terry clapped his hands and sang out, "Back inside, boy!" and Bruce clambered up through the open Jeep door and hopped onto the back seat. He stared with serious fascination while the two humans unloaded the cart of canned goods, dumping everything into the storage space behind the seat.

Finished, Terry pushed the cart out of the way, and climbed up into the passenger seat. Bobby planted himself behind the steering wheel a moment later, slamming the door shut behind him.

Bobby rolled his side window down, and just then they heard a young voice cry out from beside the store. Looking, they saw a group of three kids, boys, not more than twelve years old. They were barefoot, dressed in rags, and their faces were smeared with dirt.

"Fucking thieves!" one of the kids screamed at the top of his lungs.

Bobby reached for his door handle, as if he thought he might step outside and try to talk to the boys, but Terry grabbed his arm, holding him back.

"Let it go," Terry whispered. "Just drive. Let's get out of here."

Reluctantly, Bobby obeyed. And in the last peaceful moment they would ever share together, Terry and Bobby saw all three boys gather up fistfuls of rocks from the ground and start flinging them at the Jeep.

The stones clanged off the metal hood and door panels, thudded dully on the canvas top. In the back seat, Bruce went ballistic, setting off a panicked round of barking.

"Hurry!" Terry pleaded. "Drive!"

But before Bobby could turn the key in the ignition, a stone flew through the driver's window and struck him above the left eye.

Bobby's head jerked back, and with an astonished expression, more surprise than pain, Bobby brought his hand up to his forehead and wiped away a smear of blood.

Both Terry and Bobby stared at the blood on his fingertips. Stunned.

"No," Terry muttered. A fraction of a second later, he heard the beat of distant wings on the air. Fleshy and meatlike. A ragged shadow passed over the Jeep, and the same word spilled from Terry's mouth again, but this time it came from the depths of a terrified scream, louder than any sound he had ever made in his life.

"*No-o-o-o!*"

And with his scream still echoing in his ears, Terry watched Bobby turn to him and open his mouth to speak, to say, Terry thought, "I'm sorry," but the words were never spoken.

In a flurry of battering wings and rending claws, one of the creatures exploded through the driver's side window, snatching at Bobby's face, Bobby's hair. An instant later, an entire swarm of the creatures tore through the Jeep's canvas roof like it wasn't there. This close, Terry could hear, for the first time, the noises the creatures made. A keening, high-pitched scream, so thin and reedy as to be barely audible, even from only inches away.

Terry lurched sideways, clawing at his door handle to escape. He fell backward off the seat and landed on his ass on the gravel drive, hitting so hard the breath was knocked from his body. Looking up into the interior of the Jeep, he saw Bobby batting his arms, trying to fend the creatures off. The creatures attracted to the tiny smear of blood on Bobby's forehead.

The battle, of course, was hopeless.

Bobby screamed an agonized wail as dozens of razor-sharp teeth tore into him. Face, arms, chest. He had less than seconds to focus his pain-addled eyes on Terry, lying sprawled in the gravel, looking up in horror, his mouth splayed open in a silent scream.

Beyond all hope, Bobby raised his arm. With a bloody hand, he reached out for Terry one last time. But as Terry extended his own arm to make contact with Bobby's trembling, blood-spattered fingers, the creatures covered Bobby completely. In an instant, Bobby was gone, buried beneath a frantic, tearing mass of flesh and wings and snapping jaws.

Batlike, they were, but more terrible than bats. Serrated teeth. Long curving talons. Insane, beady eyes, as black and shiny as onyx, with no compassion in their depths, only hunger. They were unlike any other creatures on the planet that Terry had ever seen. With three-foot wingspans, too large for bats. Too terrible for bats. Too—*bloodthirsty and insanely violent* for bats.

Terry had never been this close to the beasts before. They carried the predator's reek of rotten flesh and putrid blood from past kills lodged in their talons and teeth. Their leathery wings were coated with blood, old and new. Their plump, hairy bodies were drenched in it. Terry gagged at the smell.

At that moment, when the creatures covered Bobby's flailing body completely, with a horrendous squeal of terror and agony, Bobby simply—*rose up*. He was pulled from the seat, lifted high, and torn through the roof. Already in pieces, Bobby's individual shreds of flesh and bone were plucked from the air by grasping claws and snarling jaws and carried off skyward. As he sailed high, still being pulled apart by more than a dozen of the creatures, a last deluge of Bobby's blood sprayed down over Terry's face, spattering his clothes, blinding his eyes. He gasped, blinked hard to clear his vision, and finally closed his mouth, biting back his own scream when he tasted Bobby's blood filling his mouth.

"No," he gasped one last time, choking for air, frantically scooting backward in the gravel, trying to get as far from the Jeep as he could. Far from the blood. Far from the memory of Bobby's screams.

He stared upward, tears mixed with blood streaming down his face. The sky was already empty. Bobby and the beasts were gone. It was as if they had never been there at all.

On trembling legs, Terry pulled himself to his feet and gaped at the carnage inside the Jeep. The interior was coated with blood. The canvas roof hung in tatters where the creatures had clawed their way inside, then pulled Bobby through. Bruce, still cowering, trembled in the back seat. He was covered with blood, his bulging pug eyes wide and terrified. He sat there panicked but miraculously untouched.

"Baby," Terry breathed, tears filling his eyes. Reaching through, he scraped Bruce into his arms and clung to him tight. His little body was slick with Bobby's blood and still trembling with horror.

"He's gone, boy," Terry whispered, still not quite believing what had happened. "Bobby's gone."

Then the anger struck him. He whirled toward the side of the store where the boys had appeared. The boys who threw the rocks. The boys who killed Bobby. He knew it was his turn to kill now. He would rip the little fuckers to pieces, like the creatures had shredded Bobby.

But the boys were already gone.

At that moment, like air from a leaky balloon, the strength and the anger spilled out of him. Terry collapsed to his knees, suddenly too weak to stand. Deflated. A thundering grief settled over him. He clung to Bruce and wept like a child. Slobber and snot dripped off his chin. His breath caught in sobs so powerful it actually hurt to let them go.

Feeling more alone than he had ever felt in his life, Terry slammed the passenger door closed, and clutching the sides of the Jeep so he wouldn't fall on his face, he worked his way around to the other door on legs made of rubber.

The driver's seat was saturated with blood. Bobby's blood. The blood-soaked key was still in the ignition.

He carefully set the bloody dog on the seat beside him and, ignoring the gore as best he could, positioned himself behind the steering wheel and cranked up the engine.

"It's only us now," Terry whispered. "It's only us now, boy."

With a jarring emptiness eating away at his heart, Terry slipped the Jeep into gear. The tires crunched over gravel painted red with Bobby's blood. Dazed, Terry steered the Jeep onto the road and set off once again toward the cabin.

But this time—with the road a teary blur in front of him and with the tattered and bloody canvas roof flapping in the wind above his head— Terry set off alone.

Chapter Four

THE MEMORIES poured over him like an evil, noisome flood. Shaken, as he always was when he failed to stave off thoughts of what had happened, Terry stood in the middle of the bedroom floor, stunned by the power of the images tearing through him. A sheen of sweat lay clammy on his forehead. He collapsed to the edge of the bed and buried his face in his hands until the feelings passed.

A warm tongue licked his ear, and he turned his head to see Bruce's puggy face sniffing at his neck.

Terry swallowed a shuddery breath and dredged up a smile. "Let me guess. If I don't take you outside right this minute, you're going to poop in my slippers and piss on the kitchen table."

Bruce wagged his tail.

"Terrorist," Terry mumbled and pulled himself to his feet.

With Bruce hot on his heels, snorting in anticipatory bliss as always when he was going outside, Terry led the pooch down the stairs and out the front door. Still dressed for the day in gloves and leather and heavy jeans, only Terry's face was left exposed, and the bottom half of that was covered with thick red beard. Happily the weather was cooler now, so the layers of clothing weren't nearly the hardship they might have been.

The air blew briskly, the ground soaked with dew underfoot. A squirrel chittered from a pine branch overhead. Terry was still wrung out from his miserable little trip down memory lane, but he inhaled a great dollop of clean mountain air and tried to put it all behind him, as he had done a thousand—no, a million—times before.

He waited for Bruce to do his business, and when everything was copacetic, they piled into the Jeep and headed off down the mountain lane toward civilization. Or as close to civilization as they planned to get.

The cool morning air washed over them. Terry closed his eyes as much as he could to enjoy it without running into a tree or driving off a cliff. He had kept the Jeep's mangled canvas roof after Bobby's death. It was shredded and offered little or no protection, but psychologically it was a comfort. Even stained as it was with Bobby's dried blood. The Jeep's interior—the seats and floorboards and dash—he had been able to clean, to a point.

Terry still battled with himself now and then about whether or not he should leave the quarantine zone. But somehow his decision always remained the same. He simply couldn't bring himself to confront a world of new faces, strange voices, and unfamiliar smells. Nor did he want to completely abandon his cabin on the mountain. It held too much of his and Bobby's past. He had only agreed to leave their house in town because Bobby had still been with him then. Now that he was alone, Terry's attachment to the cabin had grown exponentially. He was almost desperate to remain secluded within its walls. He knew if his fear of confronting the creatures on his own couldn't shake his determination to stay, then nothing could. Even if he was lonely, even if he was one bloody scratch away from annihilation himself, it would still be his home as long as there were remnants of Bobby's love to be found there, clinging to every surface.

If their roles had been reversed, if Terry was the one who had been killed, Bobby would never have left the cabin either. Terry believed that beyond a shadow of a doubt. He would have been as determined to stay in their mountain hideaway as Terry. Let the world fall apart around them. Let the beasts devour the whole damned planet if they wanted. He and Bobby would have been content to be together, in each other's company, in each other's arms, right there in the tiny cabin until their time ran out.

And now, with Bobby gone and with every action he took still controlled by Bobby's memory, Terry would do no different. And yes, he knew he was being stubborn and maybe even suicidal, but he didn't care.

Bruce didn't appear to care either. He was standing on the passenger seat with his front paws on the Jeep's dash, his fawn-colored ears flapping in the wind, staring out through the windshield at the forest sweeping past. The lane was rough, washboarded and potholed. It was all Bruce could do to keep from tumbling off the seat every time the Jeep hit a particularly nasty bump. Terry took pity on the little guy and slowed down. When a tree limb smacked the rearview mirror on Bruce's side of the Jeep, scattering wet leaves across the interior, the pug gave a furious yip as if mortally offended. Terry grinned and slowed down a little more.

It had been three weeks since he had gone down off the mountain. He was getting low on supplies, and he needed to stock up on firewood now that the weather was growing colder. He could chop his own wood from the deadfall around the cabin, but why risk wielding an ax? Chop off a toe and the beasts would come swarming. Besides, there were lots of supplies to be had if one knew where to look. By now, all of Spangle's businesses were closed, their owners run off to stay with relatives in the city. Or wherever it was people went when the lives they had always known were snatched out from under them and the only choice they had left was to either flee or be eaten.

Wherever they'd retreated to, Terry was pretty sure they wouldn't care if he helped himself to some of the stuff they'd left behind. If they did care, well, they would just have to get over it. Or they could bill him if they thought that would get them anywhere.

That idea was so ridiculous it made Terry snort back a laugh. He couldn't remember the last time he had handled money. Or, God forbid, a credit card. Funny how the Spangle monetary system had petered out really fast when the town started crumbling. It was pretty much the first semblance of society to bite the dust. Poor old skinflint Amos Steinman, the banker, must be depressed as hell about that.

And that thought made Terry grin again.

Halfway down the mountain, he spotted a ragged smear of shadow welling up on the horizon, moving east against the wind, heading straight for him. He braked the Jeep hard, lurching to a stop, and sat holding his breath as the stream of creatures drew closer and closer before slicing across the sky directly above his head. When he was certain they weren't doubling back and coming for him, Terry exhaled and continued to watch them retreat in the distance.

He wondered if they were on their way to feed. Were they homing in on the scent of blood, or had they already fed, their hunger slaked for the time being?

The creatures flew so swiftly that in a matter of seconds they were out of sight, lost in the treetops. They left a sense of dread behind, almost like a film of radioactive dust, eating away at everything wholesome inside Terry's head. When he was a kid, he would have called the way he felt the heebie-jeebies. After all, it was the first time he had seen any of the creatures in the sky for a while. Had he been secretly hoping they had run out the clock on their little attack on humanity? Had they turned on one another and devoured themselves instead, leaving mankind at peace?

Clearly that little exercise in wishful thinking was a bust. Because there they were. Still on the prowl. If anything, by the numbers he had just seen, they might even be moving in greater swarms than they had before.

His heart weighed down with foreboding, Terry eased out the clutch and toed the gas pedal, prodding the Jeep forward, gradually picking up speed. The dust began to billow up behind him again as he followed the winding dirt lane down the side of his little mountain toward the tiny, nearly deserted, blood-spattered town of Spangle.

His first stop was a mom-and-pop gas station he had frequented back in the days when this rustic little neck of the woods had still been operational. Mom and pop were gone now, of course. Gone, as in split, but not eaten, or so Terry hoped. They didn't bother leaving a note on the door when they left. Nor did they lock up the gas pumps before they hightailed it out of town. He knew because he had been stealing gas from them every time he ran low.

He did so again now, topping off the Jeep's gas tank, then filling two five-gallon gas cans and heaving them up against the seat backs where they wouldn't topple over on the bumpy ride home. He and Bruce then headed for what he and Bobby used to laughingly call the commercial center of Spangle. In other words, where a few scattered businesses used to languish in the heat, or the cold, depending on the season. A barbershop straight out of *Mayberry R.F.D.*, where the best you could hope for was to still have two ears when you left the barber chair. Molly's Beauty Emporium, where the latest fashions posted out front were twenty years behind the times anywhere else in the country. A dress shop that catered mostly to old ladies. A thrift store that catered to everyone. Various storefronts touting insurance salesmen, banking outlets, pharmacy supplies. An abandoned factory where nutritional supplements had once been developed but stood vacant now after going bankrupt back in the '80s, or so the story went. There was even a funeral home, whose business one might reasonably expect to be booming, but at this point in the game, it looked as abandoned as the factory. Toss in a handful of other establishments that had been barely eking out a living even before the apocalypse hit, and you had downtown Spangle.

Terry refused to return to the roadside market where Bobby had been killed. He knew he would never go back there again. But there were other sites for him to pillage. Other places to ransack, looking for food. Private homes. An elementary school cafeteria on the outskirts of town where they stored a lot of canned goods, although most of the cans were huge. Various small markets that used to cater to the tourists who passed through Spangle (as quickly as they could) to get to Julian, a true tourist destination, farther up the mountain pass. Julian, Terry knew, was beyond the quarantine zone, so he couldn't go there for supplies. If he left where he was, the authorities would never let him back in.

At the Spangle Hardware Store in the center of town, Terry gathered up a few things he needed for the metal fence posts he was working with—nuts, bolts, nasty-looking metal staples, the biggest nails he could find. While he was at it, he grabbed a new hammer and saw as well as a few other odd tools that might come in handy. These he tossed into the back of the Jeep with a clatter.

At the Target Express next door, Terry walked through the punched-out front windows like he owned the place. He had not caused the damage personally, but he saw no reason not to take advantage of it while he was out and about.

Inside, he browsed up and down the abandoned aisles with one of their handbaskets, collecting this and that. Dry dog food. Chew toys. A couple of extra blankets from the bedding section. Tins of sardines and Spam and Styrofoam cups of instant mashed potatoes, which he loved. On a whim he acquired a two-liter bottle of scotch as well. Bruce padded along at his heels, awkwardly dragging a large teddy bear he had plucked off some shelf or other and claimed for his own when Terry wasn't looking. Seemed they both had their whimsical needs.

When neither he nor the dog could carry any more, they headed back toward the punched-out front windows. Before they got there, they stumbled onto a fresh pool of blood puddled beside the checkout counter at the front of the store. Resting in the blood lay a backpack—used, not new—stuffed with newly gathered food items and ripped to shreds. Alongside the backpack lay a human finger, apparently all that remained of the backpack's owner.

The blood wasn't exactly moist, but it had not congealed to the consistency of tar yet either. The kill was probably less than two days old. A hiker, maybe. Or someone who had finally decided to abandon the town and thought their best hope of doing so was to leave on foot as soon as they stocked up on a few supplies.

Snatching Bruce into his arms, Terry sidestepped the blood and hurried through the broken window to escape the reek of rotting blood. There were memories in that smell he didn't want to contemplate.

He took a last look back at the shattered store window and tossed up a silent prayer to whoever might be listening that the person with the backpack hadn't suffered much. Knowing the creatures were not attracted to sound, Terry still cranked up the engine without too much acceleration and pulled slowly away, keeping his noise to a minimum.

Finding the backpack had rattled him. He thought most of the town's residents had split long before this. And actually, maybe they had. Maybe the backpacker was simply traveling through. He could have bypassed the police cordons at the edge of town by hiking through the woods. Maybe the guy was a thrill-seeker. An adventurer. A nutcase. Who knows? Well, whatever he was, he wasn't one now.

Trying to put the dead backpacker out of his mind, Terry headed for the final place he wanted to hit before heading home. On the very edge of town, secluded off by itself in a copse of Japanese pines, he pulled up next to an unpainted clapboard house that looked about ready to collapse in upon itself. The owner, an ancient character whom everyone in Spangle just called Old Ned, had opted to stay, Terry knew, as he himself had opted to stay.

Unfortunately, Old Ned hadn't stayed long. The creatures got him first. Terry had found his remains weeks ago.

Now, knowing Ned was out of the picture, Terry pulled around to the back of the sagging farmhouse and bumped to a stop next to a head-high stack of firewood Ned had chopped for the masses, as long as the masses were willing to pay for it. Which they always were.

Now, of course, with Ned permanently retired, the wood was free. Terry's for the taking. In fact, he was probably the only customer—or looter—in a twenty-mile radius. Terry was still gentleman enough to feel guilty about it, but not so guilty that he didn't fill every square inch of space left in the Jeep with firewood.

Satisfied he wouldn't have to come back to Spangle for a month or more, Terry positioned Bruce, and Bruce's bear, in his lap, since the passenger seat was now filled with firewood, and headed home.

That evening he sat on his front porch nursing a tall scotch and water. Bruce lay at his feet gnawing on the new teddy bear's ears while Terry dug his bare toes through the dog's coat and watched the sky for streams of shadow. Which, happily, didn't come.

He let the night settle around him, and when the air grew cold and damp and he was just about to go inside and go to bed, he spotted what he had been dreading. A landslide of deeper darkness moving swiftly across the night sky—black against black—blocking out the stars as it went. In the soundless dark, Terry could hear the percussive flutter of countless wings, drumming across the heavens. Bruce, too, lifted his head and gazed skyward. A tiny shiver of fear wrinkled his back. His ears drooped. He tore his eyes from the sky and looked to Terry for comfort. Terry offered it by bending down and laying his hand across the dog's warm back.

"Hush," Terry whispered. "It's okay. They aren't coming here."

He gazed back to the heavens. All the stars were twinkling again. The swarm of creatures had passed. Even the thudding communal beat of their great wings no longer *whumped* on the night air.

But where have they gone? he wondered. *And when will they return?*

He carefully scooped Bruce and the stuffed bear into his arms and carried them into the house. He locked the doors and windows and climbed the stairs to his bedroom loft. Once there, he stared out through the window, watching the treetops in the moonlight, swaying in the wind.

A shudder of familiar loneliness swept through him. He blinked back a longing ache that had Bobby written all over it and turned to get ready for bed.

Thanks to the scotch, which he wasn't used to, his nightmares were horrific. Even worse than they usually were.

Through the long night, Bruce and the bear never left his side. They were a solace, but not enough to silence his dreams. To Terry, the night was endless and empty and screamed constantly of Bobby's absence.

When he woke in the morning, there were tears on his cheeks, and the pillow was damp beneath his head.

Chapter Five

THE BOY and girl were respectively seventeen and sixteen. Their names were Dominic and Grace. The motorcycle they shared as they sneaked onto the mountain was a Suzuki 250cc. Big enough for two people to ride double on, but not big enough to be scary or make an undue amount of noise.

Dominic was a lanky dark-haired boy with what Grace considered to be the sexiest eyes she had ever seen. The rest of him was pretty sexy too. Dominic had taken her virginity only six months earlier. She still considered it to have been the greatest moment of her young life. When she tried—and she didn't have to try very hard—she could still remember how it felt the first time his long cock slid deep inside her, plumbing her depths. Stroking her to orgasm before she could even cry out in ecstatic shame. The gentle way he did it, and the *relentless* way he did it, easing himself deeper and deeper into her very core as she gasped and clutched and pleaded for him not to stop, still made Grace's breath catch thinking about it.

From Dominic's perspective, it wasn't just sex he had found with Grace. It was love. He fully intended to marry her as soon as the school year was over and he graduated from high school. Both their parents would shit bricks, but neither of them cared about that. They only cared about each other.

Grace wore her blond hair long. It framed her face like a flaxen cloud and was only slightly tweaked with bleach to make it just a *smidgeon* lighter than the color nature had supplied, or so she had told Dominic. Not that he cared. Every time he buried his face in that mane of golden softness, it was all he could do not to shoot his rocks even before he got Grace's panties off.

And, oh, how Grace loved it when he did get them off.

Neither of them could quite remember who came up with the idea first. The idea of sneaking into the quarantine zone to catch a glimpse of the creatures everyone was talking about. Grace thought it was Dominic's idea. Dominic thought it was Grace's.

But whoever had the idea first, here they finally were.

They had arrived close to sunset. They knew they weren't alone on the mountain because they heard an automobile not too far away shortly after they arrived. Dominic said it sounded like a Jeep bouncing up one of the mountain paths.

They set up camp below a little knoll blanketed with California poppies. The orange poppies weren't in bloom at this time of year, but the plants were still lush and green and seemed to grow wild everywhere on the mountain. Grace thought it would really be pretty in the spring. Dominic thought it would be a nice place to spend the night screwing. Exploring the mountain for the creatures could wait until tomorrow.

They hadn't brought a tent because neither of them owned one, but they did have a sleeping bag they could share. The sleeping bag zipped up tight to keep the bugs and snakes out, not that there were many bugs or snakes around at this time of year. Still, even with the nights as cold as they were, with their body heat and all the other activities they planned on pursuing, sex being the most anticipated, they knew being cold would be the least of their worries.

And so it turned out.

Bundled up naked in each other's arms with the sleeping bag zipped up tight above their heads, they didn't notice the moon rising over the mountain. The stars came out unwitnessed by them as well. Night fell around them, but they didn't care. Even the cold mountain air did not touch them.

Grace was blissfully aware of only one thing: Dominic's lean body pressed naked to hers. His hardness against her softness. The bristle of his leg hair against the smoothness of her shins. The way he squirmed in low and slid his lips across her belly made her chew on her bottom lip, it felt so good. The heaviness of his long cock pushing against her thigh, inches from where she really wanted it to be, was perhaps the best part of cuddling naked with a boy in a sleeping bag made for one.

She gasped as he took her nipple into his mouth. The pain was so exquisite she had to gently push him away.

"I-I'm sorry. It's too sensitive," she murmured.

Dominic lifted his head to gaze at her through the inky darkness inside the bag. Even without seeing him, she knew he was smiling in disbelief. "You always liked it before," he breathed, his voice weak with need. As he whispered, he slid his cock a little higher up her thigh. Teasing her. Teasing her because he knew how much she really wanted it.

Grace's fingers played through the little patch of hair at the base of Dominic's spine, right where the rise of his ass began.

When he stooped to take her nipple into his mouth again, she bucked hard, and pushed him away with more determination this time.

He huffed in annoyance and gazed up at her again. "What the hell is wrong with you? You only act like this when you're starting your period. Sensitive, cranky, first you want it, and then you don't want it. What's going on?"

She snuggled closer to him, even as he tried to edge away, annoyed. She wrapped her warm fingers around his penis. It was still as hard as stone, and it twitched and swelled in her hand when she gripped it. A rush of desire crashed through her that almost took her breath away.

She lifted one leg and straddled him, rising up and settling over his chest, her mouth at his throat. With her fingers, she guided him inside her.

He wasn't fighting anymore, but she heard him chuckling beneath her as his cock slid deep.

"You've never been this wet before. Holy shit, you're really turned on!"

Grace cried out when the first waves of orgasm took her. She clutched Dominic against her and pulled him in as far as he would go. She felt hot liquid spill down over her perineum. It surprised her. *My God, did I come that much? Did* Dominic *come?*

She slipped her hand between them and dragged her fingertips over the tender skin beneath her vulva. The liquid was everywhere. Hot and sticky.

She smelled it in the darkness and instantly knew the truth.

"Oh no," she hissed. "It's my period."

Dominic stopped pumping, his cock stood stiff inside her, piercingly deep, buried to the hilt, filling her every crevice.

For the first time, she heard honest-to-God fear in his voice. "You can't have your period here. We talked about this! The monsters are drawn to the smell of blood. You know that."

She fought to speak, the tears already welling up. Fear rose up too, even while desire still clamored around inside her. "I must be early! It's never happened before!" But still she didn't want him to stop.

She clutched at his thighs and pulled him ever deeper inside herself. Something about her period, and the fear too—something about how it sensitized her body—made her beg him not to stop.

"Please, oh please," she pleaded, arching her back, dragging him closer. "Don't stop. Finish it, Dom. Finish it! We're sealed up inside this bag. The creatures won't know about the blood."

Dominic had begun to respond in spite of himself—in spite of his fears—when he heard the first of the sounds.

The percussive *hwump* of wingbeats on the air. The cracking of tree limbs as something large crashed through the pines looming over them. The whisper and thud of needles and pine cones sprinkling the earth and peppering the sleeping bag above their heads.

"Listen!" she gasped, freezing in spite of herself.

"Oh no," he muttered, wrapping his arms tightly around Grace's slim body, burying his face between her breasts, listening hard to the terrified pounding of Grace's heart. And to his own. His cock shrinking and his hunger for her drifting away even as she continued to tremble beneath him. Not with need now, but with a growing, mindless terror.

They both sensed—they both *knew*—they were no longer alone.

Dominic opened his mouth to hiss, "Lie still. Don't move."

But the words never came because the creatures came first.

In a haze of tattered nylon and white cotton batting, the sleeping bag exploded around them, pulled apart by grabbing claws and scissor-like teeth. A thundering heartbeat later, the creatures tore through the flesh beneath.

Dominic and Grace were dead before the moonlight touched them.

Chapter Six

THE DAY was warmer than the days before. A hint of coming summer, maybe. Terry sweltered under the biker's jacket and the heavy gloves while he spent the morning nailing more fence posts to the inner walls of the cabin. The windows and doors were already covered, but he knew that would do little more than slow the creatures if they took it into their heads to attack. To really protect himself and Bruce, he needed to fully shield the entire structure.

The blood room had been finished for a couple of weeks now. Walls, ceiling, floor. When the trapdoor was closed at the top of the cellar stairs, Terry had rigged two sliding beams of steel made from galvanized fence posts that locked the drop-down door in place and made it impossible for anyone or *anything* to batter their way inside.

Terry had stocked the blood room with boxes of canned goods and cases upon cases of bottled water he had borrowed—well, *looted*—from the businesses in town. If he needed to hide away from the creatures for any amount of time, he and Bruce at least wouldn't starve.

As he worked, he continually wondered if he was acting a fool. Why not flee the quarantine zone entirely? Take Bruce and the Jeep and get the hell out of Dodge? As far as he knew, he was one of the very few who had not left already. Since Terry had seen only a handful of people in weeks, most or all of the Spangle residents must have either deserted the town and surrounding affected area, or else the creatures had already had them for dinner and Terry was one of the last ones standing.

A depressing thought.

Giving a soft whistle, he called Bruce to his side, and taking up his old shotgun from where it stood by the front door, Terry left the cabin in search of game. He was sick of Spam and canned tuna, and he craved fresher meat. Rabbit, maybe, or a nice young squirrel. His back was sore from working with the heavy steel posts, and a walk in the woods would do him good. Bruce was looking a little pudgy around the middle, so a nice walk wouldn't hurt him either.

About a mile back in the woods was a small meadow where, in the summer, wild blackberries grew. Bobby used to gather them when they visited the cabin and serve the berries up with cream and sugar, since they were a little sour on their own. They had laughed like hyenas once when Terry tried to bake a blackberry cobbler and mucked it up so badly that even Bruce wouldn't eat it. And Bruce would eat anything.

Terry smiled now, thinking back on that day. When his memory began to edge toward another day—the day in front of the roadside store when Bobby's life was lost—Terry steeled his heart and pushed the memory away. He was becoming such a master of burying memories he didn't want to think about, he almost succeeded.

Almost.

He stepped from the trees onto the blackberry meadow now. Looking up, he stumbled to a stop so quickly that Bruce walked into the back of his foot. The day before, Terry had set a wire snare along a small game trail that wound its way across the meadow, hoping to bag a rabbit for tonight's dinner.

He allowed himself a brief glance skyward to make sure there were no creatures winging across the heavens, not that he should draw their attention even if there were, since so far he had managed to survive the day with all his blood on the inside. Satisfied he was safe, he let his eyes fall back to the snare. It was not only empty, but the peg had been pulled from the ground, and the whole contraption tossed into the weeds at the side of the trail.

Bending low, Terry examined a torn-up patch of earth with uprooted clumps of grass and mud clods scattered around where a rabbit had clearly tried to escape the wire. There were fluffs of gray fur still wafting about and specks of blood here and there on the grass stems. But the rabbit was gone.

Terry stood, scratching his chin while Bruce sniffed around the crime scene looking befuddled. The pug sniffed up a puff of rabbit fur and sneezed when it clung to his nose. Terry smiled down at him; then his eyes wandered back to the snare where it lay coiled at the side of the trail. It had rained a couple of days earlier and the ground was soft. Terry bent low and studied the torn-up patch of earth, trying to find something that would identify the culprit who stole his dinner. A fox, maybe. Or a wild dog. Even a mountain lion might have done it, he supposed, but that was the biggest predator he could think of since there weren't any bears on this mountain.

He walked a grid like they did on the cop shows, angling back and forth across the ground, searching for footprints. Since his mind was focused on trying to find a small print, he didn't see the big one until he almost passed it by. When the truth hit him, he whirled back around and practically jumped out of his shoes.

What the fuck?

The print was human.

Terry stared at the pattern of a hiking boot in the soft dirt. He could plainly see the design of the shoe's sole etched into the mud. He placed his foot next to the print, thinking it might be his own. It wasn't. It was smaller by a couple of sizes. He lifted his foot and studied the sole of his own hiking boot to compare its tread with the one on the ground. That didn't match either. So no way in hell had he made the footprint.

Which meant Terry wasn't as alone on this mountain as he'd thought he was.

It took him a minute to decide how he felt about that. He supposed it wasn't altogether a bad thing. The creatures were the enemy, not his fellow humans. Of course, this particular human had a nasty habit of stealing snared bunny rabbits, but maybe the guy was starving, so Terry was willing to cut him a little slack for swiping his dinner.

Still, Terry had been on the mountain for months and hadn't seen a soul. By now even the town of Spangle appeared to be mostly deserted. So what was someone doing here so close to Terry's cabin? Did he work for the government, maybe? That was assuming the government was trying to solve the problem at all, which Terry had seen no sign of. The only thing the authorities had done was seal off the area and leave the creatures in charge. Containment seemed to be their major goal, not extermination. And wouldn't Terry Jones love to know which asshole came up with *that* boneheaded plan?

But putting all these considerations aside, at the moment Terry was more concerned with the immediate problem of having his dinner hijacked.

A movement from Bruce caught his attention. The pug was sitting in the grass, nose high, snuffling into the breeze. When Terry lifted his own nose and sniffed the air, he thought he detected a whiff of woodsmoke.

And buried in the whiff of woodsmoke, was the tantalizing aroma of cooked rabbit.

His rabbit, no doubt.

"Nervy bastard!" Terry hissed and took off through the trees at the edge of the glade where he thought the scents were originating from. He wove his way through the underbrush with Bruce panting and snorting along behind him in an effort to keep up on his stubby little legs. The deeper Terry got into the trees, the stronger the smell grew, and after a while, a haze of gray smoke became visible on the air.

The moment he spotted the smoke, he also glimpsed a splash of orange between the trees. Like a hunter's vest. Moving slower now, more carefully, Terry crept closer. He eased a few low-hanging branches quietly out of his way until he had a clear view of the area ahead.

The splash of orange was a hunter's vest, all right. Tucked inside the hunter's vest was a tall, slim man with a mop of dark hair. He was sitting on the edge of a boulder watching Terry's dinner brown on a spit over a well-laid campfire. Behind the man stood a green tent with a camp chair parked in front of it. Beside the chair lay a backpack, a couple of books scattered around, and—most incongruously, Terry thought—an old portable typewriter with a page of white paper fluttering up from the carriage, rattling in the wind. Since everybody used computers these days, Terry hadn't seen a portable typewriter in ages.

All this was most interesting, but Terry's eyes kept going back to his stolen rabbit, which was smelling pretty damn good at the moment.

He cleared his throat and announced grandly, "That's *my* rabbit you're cooking!"

If he had been trying to startle the man, he couldn't have been more successful. The poor guy was so surprised he almost fell backward off his rock. He scrambled to his feet and whirled to face his accuser. The moment he did, it was all Terry could do not to suck in a startled breath of oxygen.

The guy was gorgeous!

Apparently, Bruce thought so too. Without waiting for permission, the pug slipped between Terry's legs and made a mad rush toward the stranger. His little tail was a blur, his tongue was hanging out, and the grin on his doggie face, which pugs get when they're excited, was pretty much unmistakable.

The stranger cast an apologetic glance in Terry's direction, then folded up his long legs and knelt down on the ground, arms out to accept the dog's hello. But Bruce wasn't there to say hello. He passed the stranger right by and headed straight for the rabbit on the spit.

The man looked so surprised at being so thoroughly snubbed, Terry had to bite back a laugh. When the stranger lifted his eyes to see Terry grinning at him, the stranger smiled too. Heaving himself off the ground, he strode forward on those long legs with his hand out in front of him, preparing to shake as if determined not to be snubbed a second time.

"Jonas James," he said, in a mellow baritone that made the hair on the back of Terry's neck stand on end. Later Terry would try to analyze whether he got a chill because it was the first human voice he had heard in months or because this particular human voice was just so damned sexy.

"Terry Jones," Terry stammered. "And that really is my rabbit, you know."

Jonas James was courteous enough to look guilty. He stepped forward the last few feet and grasped Terry's hand, pumping it up and down whether Terry wanted him to or not.

"In that case," Jonas said, "maybe I can invite you to share dinner with me. I do believe your rabbit's about done."

Terry hooked a chin toward the fire. "That's assuming my dog doesn't claim it first."

Jonas looked where he was pointing and jumped like he'd been stuck with a pin. Rushing forward, he snatched the rabbit away from Bruce's outstretched fangs, and waved the stick with the rabbit impaled on it back and forth to cool it off before tossing it on the camp chair by the tent.

"Hot," he growled, blowing his fingers.

Charmed in spite of himself, Terry tried his best not to look it. "You know, this isn't the safest place in the world to be right now. Who the hell are you, and what are you doing on my mountain?"

Jonas James pooched up his lips and took a stab at glowering as if he didn't appreciate the tone. "First off, I already told you my name."

"Yes," Terry interrupted, "but who *are you*? What are you doing here? How did you get past the quarantine barrier?"

Jonas stood upright, tense as a post, as if deciding whether to answer or not. Finally, he allowed his obvious dislike at being cross-examined to wilt a bit from his face. Still, he didn't look ready to explain himself quite yet. "What makes you say it's your mountain? Do you own it?"

Terry hedged and tried not to shuffle his feet. "Well, no. I don't *own* it. Well, not all of it anyway. I do own a cabin and an acre of land back that way about a mile through the trees."

Jonas stuck his fists in his hips. "So it's *not* your mountain, then."

"Well, not technically but—"

"So you have no right to demand why I'm here at all."

"No, I suppose I don't, but—"

"Why haven't *you* evacuated?" Jonas asked. "Are you here to study the creatures?"

"No!" Terry snapped. "I live here! And just because everyone else has left, it doesn't mean I'm required to do the same." He paused long enough to blink. "Why? Is that why *you're* here? To study the creatures?"

It was Jonas James's turn to shuffle his feet. "Well, not exactly to *study* them. No."

"Then back to my original question," Terry snarled. "Who are you and why are you here?" Jonas's eyes slid toward the camp chair. His eyebrows shot up into his hairline.

"Where the hell's our dinner?" Jonas demanded. "And where's your dog?"

Terry spun around and stared at the empty camp chair. There was nothing on it but a little blob of grease and an empty wooden spit. The rotisseried bunny—and Bruce—were gone.

Terry heaved a dramatic sigh. "Well, now it looks like I owe *you* dinner." And a moment later, he added with a guilty frown, "I hope you like Spam."

Chapter Seven

JONAS JAMES stared at the man who had accused him of trespassing and decided he liked him anyway. It hadn't taken long to arrive at that decision either. Something about the redheaded giant with the full crimson beard and green eyes appealed to him. The man's slim hips, exquisitely muscled arms covered with a pelt of very appealing ginger hair, and a pair of shoulders that went on for days and days didn't annoy Jonas much either. And oh, how he'd always loved redheads.

"You should be wearing more clothes," Terry observed, eyeing him up and down.

Jonas molded his face into a vaudevillian scowl. "See, now. I hate it when a handsome man tells me that." He chuckled under his breath, amused when Terry Jones blushed.

"I was being serious," Terry grumbled.

"So was I," Jonas shot back, only half kidding. Then he relented. "But you're right. The next time I go into town, I'll try to find a leather jacket and heavy gloves. Maybe a motorcycle helmet to protect my head."

"Good idea!" Terry exclaimed, as if the idea of a helmet had not occurred to him before. "We'll both get a helmet. There's a Suzuki dealership on the outskirts of town. I'll drive us there."

"Do you pay for stuff or just steal whatever you want?"

Terry shrugged. "I prefer to think of it as requisitioning for the common cause."

"Good enough. Requisitioning it is," Jonas stated happily, slurping down another slice of Spam. He couldn't make a sandwich because there wasn't any bread.

Jonas was sitting at his new acquaintance's kitchen table. Along with the Spam, they were dining on canned spaghetti. A gourmet meal it wasn't. The man's pug, Bruce, was curled up on a blanket in the corner, snoring away and belching occasionally, having already consumed Jonas's intended dinner. Fresh rabbit. While Jonas ate the canned Spam, he studied the patchwork of galvanized fence posts attached to the cabin's walls. They didn't fully enclose the structure, but Terry had clearly been working on it. Tools, boxes of nails, big metal staples, and stacks of fence posts lay scattered all over the floor.

"Why don't you simply find a brick building to live in?" Jonas asked. "I'm pretty sure the creatures can't burrow through brick."

Terry eyed him with pity, as if wondering how anyone could be so stupid. "Because a brick building wouldn't be home, would it? This cabin is my home. If I'm going to make a last stand, it'll be from here."

The cabin seemed to be one large room on the ground floor with a staircase leading up to a loft above and another staircase under a trapdoor, currently open, leading to a cellar below. Trying not to appear to be snooping, he glanced around at the framed photos cluttering every surface. He took in all the homey touches. Bedraggled doggie toys scattered everywhere. A dog bed by the fireplace that looked rarely slept in. Books overflowing bookshelves under the reinforced living room window. A half-empty bottle of scotch with a shot glass beside it sitting on an end table by a recliner.

Jonas's gaze traveled back to the framed photographs. Snapshots of Terry Jones and a good-looking guy who was well represented in most, if not all, the other photos. Usually arm in arm with Terry.

"You two were… close?" Jonas quietly asked.

Terry clearly didn't have to turn around to see what Jonas was staring at. "If you must know, yes. The creatures took him three months ago. On the day we left Spangle to take up residence here, as a matter of fact. I made it. Bobby didn't. So much for being close."

Jonas sighed. "I'm sorry."

Terry glanced at him from under hooded eyelids. A spark of fire flared up in his eyes and just as quickly faded out. "Finish your dinner," Terry said more kindly. "It's actually good to see another face. Not sure why I'm being so defensive. Especially after my dog ate your dinner."

Jonas smiled. "The dinner I stole from *you*."

"Well, yeah, there's that."

They shared a glance. Terry finally relaxed a bit, and Jonas was glad to see it. He knew they had gotten off on the wrong foot, what with him stealing the guy's rabbit and everything, and Jonas was diligently trying to correct that first impression.

"This canned spaghetti isn't half-bad," he ventured.

"It sucks," Terry answered.

"Well, yeah," Jonas agreed, and they shared their second friendly glance.

Terry cleared his throat after wiping his mouth with a paper napkin and setting his fork aside. "All kidding aside. Why are you here? Why are you on this mountain?"

Jonas set his own spoon aside and leaned forward, propping his elbows on the table. "I'm a writer. Sometimes a freelance reporter. I'm here to learn what I can about the creatures and possibly write a book about them."

Terry appeared unimpressed. "Would you like me to tell you everything I know about the creatures?"

Jonas leaned closer, all ears. "Certainly. Tell me."

"They eat people," Terry said quietly, and immediately fell silent.

Jonas blinked. "That's it?"

Terry shrugged. "Once they smell your blood, you've got maybe five seconds tops to get your affairs in order. That's pretty much all you need to know, don't you think?"

Jonas dropped back in his chair. "Yeah, I suppose it is. Not quite enough to fill up a book, though. Where do they live?"

"I don't know. In a cave somewhere, I suppose. There are a few caves scattered around. Some are little more than holes in the rock. Others go on forever. This mountain was formed by volcanic eruptions more than a million years ago. Thus the caverns."

"So. The creatures are like bats, then," Jonas said.

"Yes and no. Mostly no. The true bats around here are gentle animals. And the indigenous bat species only come out between dusk and dawn to eat insects. These creatures are far bigger and scarier than bats. They hunt and feed in packs. And they hunt whenever the hell they want, day or night. And more to the point, it's not bugs they chase down. It's humans. They move so swiftly you don't even see them coming. They home in on the scent of blood, and wherever they *do* live, it must be close, because they can reach you in moments. There is no fighting them. Once you've drawn their attention, you're as good as dead. They swoop down and tear into you like buzz saws."

Jonas swallowed. "That's... horrifying."

Soberly, Terry nodded. "Yes, it is."

Jonas's eyes burned with eagerness as he stared at the man in front of him. Enthusiasm welled up in his gut, as it always did when he considered the creatures he had come here to find. Sometimes he wondered if his interest really sprang from a need to write about them or if it was his own inherent nosiness that made him want to learn everything he could about the fuckers.

Jonas fiddled with his napkin while he spoke. "I'm not a geologist, but I did get my hands on a US Geological Survey map of the area. Entrances to two of the larger caves are clearly identified on the map. There are other scars on the face of the mountain that simply show up as shadows on the prints. Fracture zones. Openings to underground rivers and lakes, maybe. Geological gaps in the crust, some small and tight, others endless, which, as you say, probably go on for miles. There are other caverns that have been sealed up tight by the movement of the mountain over time, either as it rose up in millennia past or eroded down to what it is today. Those I don't suppose we need to worry about."

Jonas let his enthusiasm trail away when he noticed Terry's apparent lack of interest in what he was saying. "You don't think this stuff is important?"

Terry drew in a long, deep breath and stared out through the metal slats covering the cabin window. It was early afternoon. There were house finches playing on the firewood stacked up outside. Finally his attention returned to Jonas. "Rather than wondering where they live," he said, "I think the more important question is how did these creatures evolve at all? What force of nature set them on the track they're on? There has never been an animal quite like this in the zoological records."

"Pteranodons?" Jonas ventured. "Flight capability. Carnivorous. They were far bigger, I know, but—"

Terry shrugged, interrupting. "There's a resemblance, maybe. But pteranodons were nowhere close to the monsters we have here. These things can whiff blood on the air like sharks sense it underwater. From miles away. And once they smell it, there is no stopping them. In mere seconds, they swoop in and tear you apart." He leaned closer, his gaze burning into Jonas's, "And when they tear you apart, *they leave nothing behind. Nothing.*"

"You've witnessed them feeding?" Jonas asked.

Terry's gaze slid to the pictures on the windowsill. The pictures of Terry and the man Jonas assumed had been his lover. Photographs of the man whom Terry said died the day they were coming here to ride out the storm.

"Yes," Terry said, his voice firm but muted in sadness. His fists lay clenched on the tabletop as a flush rose to his cheeks under his pale skin. Those cheeks clearly weren't reddened by embarrassment this time. But by fury. And infinite grief. "Yes, Jonas," he repeated quietly, clearing his throat. "I've seen them feed." Terry pushed his plate away and settled back in his chair. He wiggled around sideways and stretched out his long blue-jean-clad legs. In another place and another time, the big lumberjacky-looking guy would probably have pulled out a pipe and lit up. Now, of course, he simply shook out a couple of mints from a tin in his shirt pocket and popped them in his mouth.

He stared into the fire on the grate for a moment before asking, "So tell me, Jonas. What is the government doing to correct the situation?"

Jonas blinked, not sure quite how to answer. Then he decided the best bet would be to simply tell the truth. "As far as I can tell, they aren't doing anything."

It was Terry's turn to dumbly blink. "*Nothing?*"

Jonas tried to look apologetic when he said, "They seem to think the best thing to do is sit back and hope for the best. Maybe the creatures will die out on their own. Or maybe they'll annihilate one another. To tell you the truth, I think the closest thing the government has to actual game plan is to simply wait and see."

"That's amazing. Not exactly proactive, is it?"

"No. No, it isn't."

Terry's eyes were glued to one of the photographs on the wall. An eight-by-ten blowup of Terry and his former boyfriend hiking through a pine forest, probably on this very mountain. They looked happy and young and very much in love, Jonas thought.

When he spoke, Terry's voice came out as barely a whisper, fragile but with an underlying tension that put a sharp edge to his words, like a knife honed to the point of shattering. "I can't believe they're doing nothing. What about the people that have died? Are they going to simply write them off as fodder?"

Jonas leaned forward. "It might be worse than that. There are activists out there who want to protect the creatures. Keep them here on your mountain and around the remains of Spangle, using the land as a sanctuary. They want to give evolution a chance to set things right. They're calling what's happening here a genetic anomaly."

There was a fire burning deep in Terry's green eyes. "You're joking. It's not an anomaly, it's a smorgasbord. Or was, back before most of the residents were eaten."

Jonas sighed, forcing himself not to glance at the photos on the wall. "They think this is nature's way of fighting back, Terry. Against what's happening in the world. Against the latest round of mass extinctions that have started to decimate the planet. The pinheads want to see how nature runs with this disaster. Give nature a chance to correct its own mistakes. They figure as long as the infected area is relatively small, nature has a better chance of solving the situation on its own."

"It's also the best time for the government to send some troops in here and blow the fuckers out of the sky, don't you think? While there aren't that many creatures here? Before they have a chance to spread?"

Jonas rapped his knuckles on the wooden table, and his fork fell out of his empty bowl. He picked it up and put it back.

"There are people aching to do that too. Soldiers. The military. They are lined up along the quarantine line beside the scientists right now. Each of them trying to get their way before the other one does."

"So what's *your* plan, then?" Terry asked, eyeing him cagily, as if now they had come to the moment of truth, and it was time for Jonas to put up or shut up. "What exactly do you think *you* can do? Like you said, you're not a geologist. Listening to you, it doesn't sound like you're much of a scientist either. In fact, if I had to make an educated guess, I'd say you aren't any sort of *ist* at all. So what's your plan, Mr. Writer-With-A-Portable-Typewriter?" he asked again. "What is it you want to accomplish?"

Jonas settled back in his chair and crossed his ankles, staring into the fire. He tried not to look worried but suspected he did anyway.

In a voice far calmer than his statement warranted, he said, softly but firmly, "After seeing what they did to your town—and to the people here—I think there's only one thing we can do. We have to find them. And then we have to side with the military and wipe the fuckers out."

As if drawn against his will, Jonas's gaze fell on the photograph by the window. The one with Terry and the young man hiking through the trees.

Terry must have seen where he was looking. "His name was Bobby," he said. "Or did I tell you that already?"

Jonas nodded, unsure how to respond. To his surprise, Terry continued, "You can stay here with me if you want. While you're figuring out where their lair is. It's not the Ritz, but it's shelter. It's the safest place on the mountain, or will be when I finish fortifying the cabin."

Jonas's eyes bounced back to the man across the table from him. "Really? I can stay here?"

"Yes. On one condition."

Jonas took a second to chew on the lining of his cheek, as if thinking it over. "And what condition might that be?" he finally asked.

Terry narrowed his eyes and drummed his fingers across the tabletop. "That you let me help you wipe them out."

Jonas sat motionless for a moment. He paused only a second or two before extending his hand across the table. He didn't allow himself a smile until Terry extended his own hand in return, slipping it like a warm glove over Jonas's fist.

"It's a deal," Jonas said, enjoying the touch of Terry's strong hand surrounding his. Probably more than he should. Then a smile crept over his face, and before he could stop it, he was grinning like a fool.

"Partners," he said.

And with a little less jubilation, Terry answered, "Partners."

"Friends?" Jonas prodded coyly. "Or is that too much to ask?"

Terry grunted and rolled his eyes. "Let's say friend... *ly.* But don't let it go to your head."

In the corner, between snores, Bruce farted.

At that, the two men, hands still clasped, shared their first laugh.

Chapter Eight

LATER THAT night, they shared their first drink together. Scotch. Neat. In little souvenir shot glasses with Spangle, California, printed on the sides. While they sipped, they watched the sparks from the fire shoot up into the flue. The wind had picked up, and occasionally a pine cone would go bouncing down the slope of the roof to land with a dainty thud in the mulch outside.

It was the first night in a long while that Terry did not dread the coming darkness. The first night in months that loneliness had not sat down beside him while the mountain's shadows closed in.

"It's good to have someone else here," he said with his lips still on the shot glass. Startled by his own courage in admitting the truth, Terry tossed the rest of the whiskey down his throat as if to burn any further declarations from his system before he could utter them too.

"Careful." Jonas grinned, eyeing him closely. "Next thing you know, you'll be telling me how you really feel." The guy was starting to get a little drunk, Terry thought. Maybe his houseguest wasn't used to undiluted scotch. As far as that went, neither was he.

Terry worked up a smile. "Are you saying I don't know how to open up?"

Jonas held the shot glass up to the light coming off the fire and read the writing on the side. "No, but I will say your glassware sucks. Not exactly Waterford, is it?"

Terry eyed his own shot glass. "These are for guests who pop in without warning."

"Ouch."

"All the other glasses in the house are from Smucker's. Want to complain about them too?"

"No. Actually so are most of mine."

Jonas reached over, snatched the whiskey bottle off the little table between their chairs, and poured them each another shot, prompting Terry to snipe, "I love it when a houseguest feels comfortable enough to steal my dinner, then make fun of my crystal before proceeding to dole out my booze like he's the one who looted it instead of me. Glad you feel at home."

Bruce was on the floor on his blue blankie, licking his butt. He was really going to town. Both men scrutinized him for a minute. Terry was tempted to joke "Golly, I wish I could do that" but thought better of it. That tiny glimmer of self-control told him he probably wasn't as drunk as he thought he was. It also set a host of other thoughts scampering through his head concerning his houseguest, most of them inappropriate.

Since they were no longer tossing digs at each other, Terry burrowed down in his chair and studied Jonas clandestinely from under his drooping eyelids.

Jonas James, he decided, was a very attractive man. He was as tall as Terry but without the muscled bulk. His legs were long and graceful, his hands large and expressive. Most of the time when he talked, his hands were fluttering around his head like startled birds. His eyes were golden amber, the color of cognac. They lay buried beneath long lashes, as dark as kohl, that swept up and down gracefully when he blinked. His hair was dark, not quite as black as his lashes, but not light enough to be called brown either. He clearly hadn't shaved for a while, whether because he was growing a beard to protect his skin from injury like Terry or because he simply hadn't got around to it.

The most interesting facet of Jonas's appearance, Terry thought, really had nothing to do with how he looked at all. It was the timbre of his voice. Rich and mellow. Like a perfectly tuned and expertly played reed instrument. Well modulated and soothing. An oboe, maybe. Or the low notes of a clarinet.

On the other hand, there was also a wise-guy aspect to Jonas that Terry didn't know if he appreciated or not. Here they were, always a heartbeat from death, smack-dab in the middle of what could very well be the opening salvo of the end of man's dominance on the planet, and the hunk in front of him was cracking jokes about the stemware. Even more confusing, it had prompted Terry to toss jokes right back.

Honest to God, Terry couldn't remember the last time he had joked about *anything*.

As if the ambivalence he felt about Jonas wasn't confusing enough, now he had gone and extended an open-ended invitation to him to stay with Terry here at the cabin. While the guy was clearly gay—to judge by some of the clever little asides he had tossed out here and there—Terry really didn't think that would be an issue. But what exactly were the ground rules for living together going to be? Aside from the upstairs loft where Terry slept, the cabin only had one room, other than a tiny bathroom with a shower back by the kitchen and the blood room downstairs. That was it.

Terry gradually began to realize he was being stared at. He turned to find Jonas's eyes on him. Those eyes were not only very attractive, but they were also crinkled in amusement.

"You're worrying about the sleeping arrangements, aren't you?" Jonas asked, a tiny dimple dotting one cheek, which seemed to indicate he was trying not to grin. Terry had learned that much about Jonas already.

"No, I—"

"It's not like we're teenagers, you know. How old are you? Thirty-seven, thirty-eight?"

Terry glowered. "Thanks a lot. I'm thirty-three."

"Hmm. Must be the beard. Anyway, let's say we're both well into the age of reason. So don't fret, kind sir." Jonas tilted his head toward the far wall. "I'll take the couch right there. You and the mongrel can continue sharing your hopefully nonconnubial bed upstairs, where you won't be bothered by little old me."

Terry got huffy. "I had already decided you would take the couch."

"Good. Then it won't be a problem."

"What I was really worried about," Terry said, pointing to the iPhone poking out of Jonas's pack, "is *that*. They can track us through cell phones, you know."

"The creatures?"

"No. The authorities. You'll have to disable it if you're going to stay here. If they decide to chase everybody off this mountain, I don't intend to be included in their plans. I'm not leaving."

"Neither am I," Jonas said.

"Then killing the phone won't be a problem."

"No," Jonas said. "It won't." With that, he rose and crossed the room to pluck his phone out of the pack. Without hesitation, he tossed it into the fire. Turning back with a grin, he asked, "Disabled enough?"

Terry shook his head incredulously. "Yeah, I suppose that ought to do it."

A silence settled over them then. This time, to fill the quiet, it was Terry's turn to dole out a couple more shots of scotch, prompting Jonas to ask, "Do you always drink like this?"

"Only when I'm annoyed," Terry answered. When Jonas barked out a laugh, Terry allowed himself a grin too. Jesus, he really was getting drunk.

He licked around the lip of his shot glass and studied Jonas over the smoky liquid. The amusement that had found Terry moments earlier disappeared quickly enough when a question occurred to him. "Will anyone be wondering where you are? Family? Friends? A lover?"

Jonas smiled sadly and shook his head. "No family to speak of. What friends I had aren't really friends at all, I've lately decided. Just work cronies and acquaintances more than anything else."

"And what about romantic entanglements? You're a good-looking guy. You must have a few of those."

Again, Jonas cast a sad little glance his way. "No lover" was all he said. The moment the words were out of his mouth, Terry saw his gaze return to the photographs by the window. He especially seemed to be entranced by the snapshot of Terry and Bobby hiking on this very mountain.

"You and your husband were very happy, weren't you?" Jonas asked out of the blue.

Terry tried not to show his surprise. "Yes. But how did you know we were actually married."

Instead of answering, Jonas gazed down to Terry's hand resting on the chair arm. Terry lifted it and stared at the silver wedding ring on his fourth finger. "Oh yeah."

Jonas was already eyeballing the photograph again. "I'm sorry you lost him like you did," he said. "That must have been… *debilitating.*"

Terry almost smiled at that. "Odd choice of words," he said. Then, on second thought, he decided the word was excruciatingly perfect. Made a little breathless by Jonas's unexpected perception, Terry softly echoed the word he had just heard. "Debilitating. Yes. That's exactly right. That's exactly what it was. Sometimes I think I'm still trying to pull myself out of it."

"I really am sorry," Jonas said again, eyeing him closely. Then, as if realizing he was perhaps prying, he turned his head toward the fire and brought his shot glass up to his lips.

Terry considered him for a few seconds, and then, as if the words came from someone else, he heard himself mumble, "Thank you, Jonas. That's the first word of sympathy I've heard about Bobby's death. I appreciate it."

Without speaking, Jonas simply nodded.

Bruce was snoring again, curled up in the arms of his teddy bear, which had grown more ragged and worn as the days slipped by. Not six inches from his head, the fire was crackling on the grate, mostly embers now. A single thread of smoke was being pulled upward through the flue toward the mountain sky outside. If one of those smoking embers should explode, it would probably set the pug on fire. Bruce seemed willing to take the risk.

"I know of a cave," Terry said, watching the fire die away. "The opening is very small. I doubt if it's on your map. I can take you there one of these days."

As if Jonas hadn't heard, he turned to Terry and said quietly, "I lost my lover too. In a car wreck. More than a year ago. I just wanted you to know."

"Oh. I'm sorry," Terry stammered, surprised and touched that Jonas would share this information with him.

Jonas nodded. Terry could see the reflection of the embers in his eyes. For the first time since he had met the man, he also saw sadness there.

"I wanted you to know you're not the only one who's suffered a loss," Jonas said. "And if we don't find a way to stop these creatures, I fear the whole world will come to understand loss. They won't stay here, you know. Your little beasties. On this tiny mountain. In your tiny hometown. They'll spread out. Maybe they're working themselves up to it already, now that the food supply is growing thin. A few soldiers and scientists and highway patrol guys manning roadblocks and keeping people out won't stop these things from migrating. They have the whole sky to travel in. If they choose to leave at night, no one would even know. We have to find them and kill them before they do."

Terry reached out to pour another shot, then stayed his hand. He'd had enough. He firmly placed the bottle back on the table.

"You make it sound so easy," he said. "How exactly do you plan on killing them?"

Jonas shrugged. He was getting bleary-eyed. He looked like he'd had enough to drink as well. "We have to find their nest first, Terry. Then we'll figure out how to kill them."

Terry's gaze traveled around the cabin. At the work he had done to reinforce the place. He had accomplished a lot, but there was still a lot more to do. Perhaps two-thirds of the inner walls were covered with the galvanized fence posts, nailed in place an inch or two apart, lined up one right after the other. Then, on the walls and parts of the ceiling that were finished, he had strung wire between the posts, strengthening the walls even more. When he was finished, he was pretty sure nothing would be able to get inside. The entire cabin would be as safe as the blood room already was.

Terry turned to study Jonas, who was staring into the fire, looking melancholy. Terry wondered if it was the mention of his dead lover that made him feel that way.

"We have to finish the cabin first," Terry quietly said. "You help me do that, and I'll help you find the creatures and kill them."

Jonas lifted his eyes, surveying the walls already done. "Do you have enough posts to finish?"

"No. We'll need to go into town and commandeer some more. There are hundreds of them at a home improvement store on the outskirts of town. I can only carry so many in my Jeep, but two more trips into town should do it. Will you help?"

Jonas dredged up a smile. He didn't look quite as bleary-eyed as he had a minute ago. Maybe he could hold his liquor after all.

"Yes," he said. "I'll help. We'll finish the cabin before we do anything else. That way we'll have a safe refuge if shit starts hitting the fan. Agreed?"

Terry dipped his head. "Agreed."

He groaned his way out of his chair and screwed the cap on the whiskey bottle before crossing the room and setting it on the kitchen counter. Bruce had lifted his head and was watching him as if he knew it was time for bed.

"There are spare blankets and pillows in that closet there," Terry said. "You know where the bathroom is. If you decide to go outside for a stroll, don't. Leave the doors and windows closed and locked."

"All right."

Jonas was already unbuttoning his shirt. Terry stood at the foot of the stairs, cradling Bruce and watching him. Without any show of self-consciousness, Jonas shrugged out of the plaid work shirt and tossed it on the chair he had been sitting in. He kicked off his boots and peeled his socks away. Standing now in nothing but blue jeans, the fly of which was already half-unzipped, he moved toward the closet and dug around for bedding.

Terry held his breath, observing him. Jonas James was indeed beautiful. His skin was tanned and flawless, the hair on his chest dark. The veins in his lean arms bulged beneath the skin. When he bent into the closet to retrieve the bedding, the top of his jeans pulled down to show the cleavage of his ass and the smooth, pale skin surrounding it. At the base of his spine was a small patch of dark hair that Terry found mesmerizing. Somehow he knew in that moment exactly how Jonas's skin would feel beneath his fingertips. And more importantly, how it would taste against his lips.

As if suddenly aware he was being watched, Jonas took a peek backward under his outstretched arm to see Terry there behind him, ogling. He straightened and turned to face him. The jeans he wore had lost a little more of their battle with gravity while he was poking around inside the closet. A trail of dark hair had become visible, sweeping down from his belly button to the beginning of a bush of black pubic hair and just a hint of the fleshy base of what looked to be a rather substantial cock resting inside it.

Terry's own cock twitched at the sight. With cheeks suddenly burning hot, Terry gulped and turned away.

Behind him, Jonas called out, "Have a good night, roomie!"

Somehow Terry knew the bastard was grinning when he said it.

Chapter Nine

TERRY AND Jonas spent the morning reinforcing the walls and ceiling of the loft where Terry slept. With the metal posts slotted across the windows and blocking a lot of the light, the room was left in dusklike gloom, even while the noontime sun burned bright outside.

They had been at it nonstop for four days now. Working and living close together, they had learned a lot about each other, and an easy friendship seemed to be taking hold. It wasn't only friendship, though. Sexual tension had been building too. At least it was building on Terry's end. How Jonas saw their budding relationship, Terry wasn't sure. And he was afraid to ask.

Jonas cracked a sardonic smile while checking out what they had accomplished. "At least the bars over the windows are spaced far enough apart that you can peek outside and see what's trying to kill you."

Terry offered a wry grimace in return. "Always a consideration when you're about to get eaten."

"It'll be hot in the summer with no breeze to speak of," Jonas noted, looking doubtful as he reexamined the nailed-over windows.

"That's assuming we survive till summer," Terry said, knowing full well his comment was likely to put a damper on the conversation.

"You're a cheerful guy," Jonas said, but there was no humor in his eyes. The truth of Terry's words was obvious to both of them.

"Back to work?" Terry groaned, rubbing his back.

"Back to work."

They slaved for a couple more hours, arranging the last of the galvanized fence posts across the loft's ceiling, fixing them to the walls with fat nails, then attaching the final few yards of baling wire Terry used to strengthen his barricade. They only quit when they ran out of material.

Terry eyed Jonas as they both threw down their tools and heaved sighs of relief. It was getting hot in the closed-off loft, and they were both sweating buckets. During the course of the long hours, they had shed their shirts to ward off heatstroke. At least that's what Terry kept telling himself.

He was working in a pair of battered cargo shorts with tools hanging off every belt loop and nails bulging the pockets. Jonas had donned a pair of sweatpants with the legs cut at the knees. Terry had to fight to tear his eyes away from Jonas's bare torso long enough not to smash his thumb with the hammer at least once every two minutes.

With the last of the posts attached inside the loft, they stood side by side and studied their handiwork. Jonas slung a companionable arm across Terry's shoulder. The skin-on-skin nearness impacted Terry more than it probably should have. Images flashed inside his head of the first night Jonas spent in the cabin. Jonas standing shirtless by the closet door with his jeans dragging down around his ass. His skin so perfect in the glimmer of embers burning on the grate. His strong bare feet poking out from under his pant cuffs, with little wisps of dark hair sprinkling his toes. Every inch of the man sexy as hell.

After that, Terry had made it a point to be upstairs and away from temptation when Jonas undressed for the night.

That first night with Jonas standing half naked in the light of the fire still made a nice memory, though. Of course, it didn't hold a candle to looking at Jonas now with his chest all sweaty and his dick bobbing around under the thin fabric of the sweatpants he had on. Sometimes when Jonas stood just right, Terry could see the outline of his cockhead pressing against the fabric. At times like that, it was all Terry could do not to gawk. Clearly the guy didn't believe in underwear.

"We should go to town," Jonas said, blithely unaware that Terry was staring at his crotch. Or at least pretending to be. "We've used up all the posts except for those three over there in the corner. We'll need a lot more to finish up that last wall downstairs."

"We'll also need to pick up more baling wire." Terry sighed. "It's a pain in the ass, but it strengthens the walls. There's not much afternoon left. Before the sun goes down, we'll drive into Spangle and pick up what we need. I don't like to be out after dark."

"All right. Dinner first?"

Terry wiped his sweaty brow. "Yeah," he said. "Dinner first. I'm starving."

They gathered a few odds and ends from the kitchen—canned corn, which they could eat cold from the container since they weren't that picky, tuna, a couple of tins of fruit cocktail, three or four candy bars that were already getting stale—and toted it all out to the porch. Plunking a can of Alpo into a bowl for Bruce, the three of them settled in.

Jonas studied the blisters on his fingers. "When I first saw all the work you'd done on the cabin, I didn't realize how hard it must have been for you. Working alone, I mean. How long have you been at it?"

Terry shrugged. "The idea came to me about a month ago. Actually it wasn't so bad. It gave me something to do to pass the time. I hadn't realized how lonely it would be, out here on this mountain all by myself. For the first couple of months, I was pretty much a basket case. Still trying to decide if I should stay or leave. Missing Bobby. Grieving. Trying not to let myself fall apart."

"I'm sorry about your husband," Jonas said, his mouth turned down, watching Terry through hooded eyes.

Terry turned to him then. He forced a smile when he saw the pity on Jonas's face. "You don't have to keep apologizing every time I mention Bobby's death. It wasn't your fault. Maybe I shouldn't talk about him so much, but it's hard not to. When he was alive, he was such a huge part of my life. With him gone it's like I'm left with a big empty place where he used to be. If I didn't talk or think about Bobby, my mind would be a blank hole filled with nothing."

"I know," Jonas said, his eyes taking on a sadness of their own. "Loss leaves us kind of fractured and incomplete. I still reach out sometimes in the middle of the night and run my hand through the bedclothes, searching for Martin." Jonas stared out into the trees, the can of fruit cocktail resting forgotten in his hand. The highest branches of the pines were rustling softly, tossed by a gentle breeze blowing up from the desert foothills.

They were seated side by side on the front step with Bruce at their feet. He had finished his Alpo and lay napping now with his little puggy chin resting on his front paws. His ear did a flip when an ant crawled across it, and the ant went flying.

Feeling self-conscious about it, but doing it anyway, Terry laid his hand on Jonas's arm. The dark hair there bristled against the palm of his hand. For the first time, he let himself enjoy the warmth of Jonas's skin beneath his fingertips. The feeling was electric. In a voice barely loud enough to carry, he said, "It gets better, don't you think? The missing? The incompleteness? It goes away a little bit more each day."

Jonas looked down at Terry's hand on his arm; then he lifted his eyes to Terry's face. "I suppose so," he said. "The missing does get easier. The loneliness doesn't, though."

"No," Terry said, an old familiar melancholy burrowing through him. "The loneliness doesn't change much at all. No matter how much time passes."

The air was getting cooler as the afternoon waned. Terry supposed they would be putting their shirts on soon, and he dreaded that. The two of them sitting half-dressed was a definite turn-on. No two ways about it.

As if Jonas had read his mind, he reached over and dragged his fingers through the hair on Terry's chest. Terry froze.

"You look like a lumberjack," Jonas said, smiling, his strong fingers massaging Terry's breast. "A big furry lumberjack. I've never seen so many muscles and so much ginger fuzz on one human being in all my life."

Terry frowned, but his eyes crinkled with amusement at the same time. "You make me sound like a redheaded Yeti. Not sure if that's a compliment or an insult."

"Trust me," Jonas said, "it's a compliment." His fingers flexed outward, moving more slowly over Terry's chest now, as if gauging the suppleness of the flesh beneath his hand. When their eyes met, that one damned dimple flickered on Jonas's cheek.

Terry edged a millimeter away, because Jonas's touch was making him feel uncomfortable. Jonas took the hint and withdrew his hand. The humor in his eyes didn't fade much, however. Terry got the impression Jonas was amused by Terry's wariness when they made the least show of getting to know each other better. Especially if it involved physical contact. Jonas always backed off, though, whenever Terry sent out those vibes. Just as he did now. To make everything a little more confusing for Terry, he couldn't decide if he was happy to be left alone at times like that or annoyed that Jonas would give up so easily.

He gazed down at his hands, trying to think of something to say to make the moment less awkward. "Do you think it will be enough? What we're doing to protect the cabin? Do you think it will keep the creatures out?"

Jonas took a moment to study Terry's face before glancing back at the open door behind him. Dust motes still hung in the air inside the cabin from all the hammering and banging they had been doing. Jonas was evidently giving the question serious thought. To Terry's disappointment, when Jonas finally answered, he didn't look convinced.

"I think there's more you can do," he said.

Terry blinked. He hadn't expected that. He'd mostly asked the question for something to say to get past the moment when Jonas had laid his hand to his chest. That he might not be doing everything he could do to seal off the cabin truly had not occurred to him.

"Like what?" he asked. "What else can we do?"

Jonas's gaze turned shifty and his dimple reappeared. "You can wire all that metal up to the generator. Then if an attack comes, and if those fuckers so much as touch the cabin, you can burn them out of the sky."

Terry sat frozen in concentration, considering what Jonas had said. "Like a big bug zapper," he breathed. He realized right off that it wouldn't be that hard to do. With only one drawback. "We'd have to bring the generator inside. Right now it's sitting at the back of the cabin under a little overhang of roof. We'd have to move it inside so we wouldn't need to leave the cabin to crank it up."

Jonas shot him a wink. "And how hard can that be?"

Terry tried not to groan. "What I don't know about electricity is a lot. If it was left up to me, I'd probably either leave us permanently in the dark or fry the cabin right off the map."

"Luckily," Jonas said, "I know a few things about electrical work that maybe you don't. It shouldn't be that big of a job. Just unhook the generator outside, drag it in, and rehook it to the wires at the first junction inside."

"The generator runs on gas," Terry said. "What about exhaust fumes?"

Jonas tapped his chin, thinking about it. "We'll have to drill a hole big enough for the exhaust pipe to disperse the fumes outside so they won't asphyxiate us."

Terry had to agree with that. "Not being killed by fumes would be good."

"Yeah. Plus, we wouldn't want to deprive the creatures of killing us first."

They smiled at each other briefly.

Terry squeezed one eye shut, considering their plan. "If we're inside when we juice up the walls, won't it juice us up too?"

"Not if we stay on the wooden floor and away from the metal posts."

Terry considered that. "Will it kill them?"

"The creatures? Probably not. But it might give them incentive to think twice if they decide to attack the cabin a second time."

"So basically what it will probably do is piss them off."

"Yeah. It'll be fun."

They stared at each other with dawning grins.

"I like the way you think," Terry said, tossing out a wink.

Jonas winked back. He pushed himself off the front step and gathered up his trash. "Thanks. Let's go to town."

Chapter Ten

MORE WORK was involved in thoroughly securing the cabin from the predatory creatures than either man expected. Another week passed and many trips into town ensued. Still they weren't finished.

On one foray, they raided the Suzuki dealership and acquired motorcycle helmets with drop-down face masks. They took to wearing them every time they left the cabin, since even an injury as minor as a bug bite might be all that was needed to throw the creatures into a frenzy. Also, while the helmet wouldn't prevent an attack, it might afford a few extra seconds before the smell of blood leaked out from an unintentional head wound or nosebleed, giving Terry or Jonas time to reach safety.

With the passage of time, a routine began to unfold. They worked hard, they ate together, and yet their conversations were sparse. Jonas never quite felt comfortable around Terry. Not because he didn't like him, but for the opposite reason. He suspected he liked him too much. Especially the physical aspect of the man. Terry Jones was a big, hulking, bushy-bearded redhead with muscles galore and sweet green eyes that stopped Jonas in his tracks every time they homed in on him. In the world of gay men and gay relationships, Jonas had been around the block a few times, and he knew what he liked. If he could ever break through the barrier they had erected between them, Jonas knew he wouldn't mind exploring that world again. With Terry.

But their first priority was survival. Without that, relationships or *possible* relationships, didn't matter much, did they?

Over the course of the next two weeks, they worked continually on reinforcing the cabin. The chore of moving the generator inside occupied a lot of that time. It required days on end, through endless rounds of trial and error, but eventually they were able to hook it up to the wiring inside so it could be started up without anyone needing to go outside. They had to hold off on electrifying the metal lining until they finished sealing the cabin completely, but in the meantime, Jonas succeeded in using a length of plumber's pipe to run the exhaust fumes through a hole in the cabin wall to be released outside.

When all that was finished to their satisfaction, they continued making supply runs in Terry's Jeep to stockpile food and salvage what they could from the stores in town. A few more fence posts to finish lining the cabin walls. Spare clothing. More guns. Anything they thought might come in handy if they were forced to lay low in the cabin for any length of time.

With every trip into town, Jonas expected cops to pop up and arrest them for looting. Or worse yet, simply start shooting and not bother arresting them at all. But Spangle was a ghost town. Or close to it. At first appearance as uninhabited as the mountain.

On one trip back up the lonely mountainside after a food run, not long after Jonas arrived, they spotted a splash of color in the bushes off to the right of the unpaved road that wound a path through the trees. Terry braked, and they both got out to investigate. Curious to see what was going on, Bruce padded along at their heels.

It had rained the night before, and the forest was muddy. They squelched downhill beneath the sodden pines, hopping logs and roots while the ground got boggier and squelchier the farther they descended. The air was thick with the earthy stench of mold and rot. Creamy-headed mushrooms had popped up overnight in the crevices at the base of plants and stones. Moisture still dripped from the trees. As the weather had cooled off considerably since Jonas first arrived, they both knew cooler weather was moving in. Thus the big rush to stock up on supplies.

"It was around here somewhere," Jonas muttered, out of breath from tromping through the underbrush. He was sweating like a pig under the leather jacket, and with the frigging helmet with the Suzuki emblem wrapped around his head, he felt like his noggin was stuck in a bucket. Not a wisp of air touched his skin, and he knew Terry was in the same boat. They were both sweltering in what couldn't be more than sixty degrees.

"It was red and green," Terry added. "The flash of color I saw. Sort of like a tartan kilt."

"Great," Jonas grumbled with forced glee. "Maybe we'll find a cute Irishman down here among the pussy willows. I wouldn't mind stocking up on one of those if we get the chance."

Terry muttered, "Asshole," and Jonas snickered, unrepentant.

A few feet farther on, their joking ended.

"There," Terry said.

Jonas followed where Terry was pointing. In a patch of California poppies, their blossoms long gone, he spotted a clump of padded cloth. Or nylon, maybe. It lay wadded up, shiny with moisture and sprinkled with pine needles and mud, yet the colors were still vibrant. Scattered around the clump of shiny material, other items could be glimpsed in and out of the undergrowth. Two backpacks, torn and faded, lying side by side. Empty soda cans, shimmering like silver. Shreds of clothing. A pair of men's hiking boots, and another boot with pink laces that clearly belonged to a woman. The matching boot must have been carried off. Perhaps when the body was taken.

Jonas realized he was staring down at the remnants of a campsite. A ring of stones with muddy ashes in the middle showed where a fire had been set. Maybe for warmth. Maybe to heat the food tins, which they could see tossed around in the undergrowth, the labels washed away by either rain or the deterioration that comes from lying in the weeds for however long they had been there.

The glimpse of tartan Terry thought he had seen was what remained of a sleeping bag. "So I guess it wasn't an Irishman after all." Jonas sighed dramatically, not really trying to be funny, but hopefully lightening the mood a little, since he had a really bad feeling about what he was looking at here.

When he didn't get an answer, he glanced back and saw Terry standing well away from the debris field. He had Bruce clutched tightly in his arms. The little dog was squirming to get down, but Terry wouldn't let him.

Their eyes met through their helmet shields, but Terry didn't say anything. There was such hurt in the redhead's eyes that Jonas's heart constricted.

"You're as silent as a cloud," Jonas softly said. "What are you thinking?"

"I'm thinking it's been a long time since we saw a living person."

"Do you think we're the last on the mountain?"

"Maybe. But there are still a few people in town, I think."

Jonas blinked, considering that. Then he turned away and knelt beside one of the backpacks. Using a stick to poke around, he wedged it open and peeked inside. A moment later, he pulled out a small digital camera. The camera looked shiny-new and dry.

"I wonder...," Jonas murmured. He flipped the device open. Taking a moment to study its workings, he pressed a tiny switch on the side. A small screen at the back of the camera burst to life. A young couple's faces appeared. They looked little more than kids. A blond girl and a handsome dark-haired boy. Jonas scrolled through a dozen photos. Some selfies taken by the girl, another of the boy lying naked on the very sleeping bag now lying tattered on the forest floor. In that photograph, his eyes were sexually bright, his legs spread wide, teasing the photographer with an unhindered view of his erect cock.

Jonas sensed a presence edging up close behind him. It was Terry, eyeing the photographs over his shoulder. Jonas continued scrolling through the rest of the shots. They were all of the young couple, many of the pictures sexual in nature, others sweetly innocent. Each of them was clearly snapped here, at this very spot on Terry's mountain. It was the last piece of real estate the young couple would ever see.

When the final photo had scrolled past, Jonas heaved a long sigh. "Hikers," he said. "They look like high schoolers. Teenagers. Probably came here on a dare. Or just for a thrill. They were lovers, I guess." And with that last observation, Jonas fell silent as a rush of sadness tightened his throat.

"They died here," Terry said quietly behind him. "They were torn apart, and like everybody else who's died on this mountain or down in town, they didn't stand a chance."

"You don't know...."

Terry looked down at the scattered remains of the teenagers' campsite. "I know," he said. "And so do you."

Gently, Jonas tucked the camera back inside the backpack and left it where he'd found it. He rose to his feet and stepped back from what must have been the kill zone. "They never knew what hit them, did they?"

"I hope not," Terry said. He lifted his eyes to the sky. "Daylight's dwindling. It'll be dark soon. We should get back."

Jonas knew he was right. Darkness fell fast on the mountain— one minute dusk, the next minute pitch-black. He could almost feel the coolness of the coming darkness pressing on his skin, which was of course impossible, since he didn't have any skin exposed, wrapped up as he was in bikers' leather, heavy denim, and with the bigass helmet encapsulating his fucking head. Just like Terry.

Jonas took a step back and bumped into Terry. He expected Terry to quickly step away since he had been so hesitant to make physical contact lately, but this time Terry surprised him. Almost tenderly, Terry rested a hand on Jonas's shoulder, then slid his other arm lightly across Jonas's chest, pulling him close. Their helmets clunked together, Terry's broad chest splayed against Jonas's back. Neither man tried to step away from the other. After seeing what they had just seen, Jonas suspected they needed the closeness.

Jonas stood rooted to the ground, not sure what to expect, while Terry held him close and spoke softly in his ear through his face mask. Inside the helmet, Terry's voice echoed, deep and solemn.

"I think it's time we started searching for the lair. We have enough food and bottled water and fuel for the generator and wood for the fireplace to last us for months if we're careful. It'll be getting cold soon. Occasionally, we get snow up here this time of year. Not always, and not much usually, but sometimes enough to cover the ground. Maybe the creatures will slow down in the colder weather. Maybe they'll even hibernate if it gets cold enough. The truth is, we don't know what they'll do."

"Do bats hibernate?" Jonas asked.

Terry shrugged. "Some do. Others migrate to warmer climates. Some even do both. But don't forget, these aren't bats, these aren't even *close* to being bats, so we don't know what to expect."

Jonas considered all that. "I'm rooting for hibernation. With luck, they'll burrow deep into their cave and go to sleep for a few months. Give us time to sniff them out. The last thing we want is for them to take off for parts unknown. As long as they're on your mountain, we at least have a chance of finding them and wiping them out."

"*Our* mountain," Terry said.

Jonas tensed in Terry's arms. "What did you say?"

Terry didn't release his hold. In fact he tightened it. "I said it's our mountain now. Since we're the only ones left, it must be ours."

Jonas let those words sink in. He took a moment to enjoy this new closeness Terry seemed to be offering him. The massive hand on his shoulder, the muscled arm across his chest, the whispered words in his ear, gruff but gentle.

Knowing he was probably making a major tactical error, but knowing too that he really had no control over the matter, he slipped around in Terry's embrace and faced him head-on. Their helmets were inches apart when Jonas reached up and flipped Terry's visor to the top of his head. When he could peer inside, he pushed his own visor back and out of the way.

Terry's hand was still on his shoulder, his arm splayed across his back now instead of his chest. His breath was warm on Jonas's face. Terry's eyes opened wider, studying him. Jonas's heart gave a tiny kick when he realized Terry wasn't trying to pull away. In fact, Jonas was determined the opposite was about to happen.

"I'm going to kiss you now," Jonas whispered, his voice catching in a nervous flutter.

Terry's voice, equally nervous and just as fluttery, whispered back, "All right." The moment those two little words were out, he licked his lips.

That tiny glimpse of tongue gave Jonas courage. He closed his eyes and carefully leaned forward. The brims of their helmets plunked together, and the next thing he knew his lips were on Terry's mouth. The kiss was soft at first, almost virginal. Ten seconds into it, Terry's feet nudged up closer to Jonas's. Then his lips parted slightly, opening up to the kiss. When Terry's hand came to lay across Jonas's cheek, Jonas's stiffening cock went crawling down his pant leg like a gopher. He gave a gasp, which he suspected was somewhere between a laugh and the prelude to an orgasm.

Something started squirming around against his chest, and he realized it was Bruce, still gripped in the crook of Terry's arm. He was trying not to get squished between the two of them.

Jonas arched his back enough to give the dog some breathing space, but even as he did that, he kept his lips on Terry's mouth. The fuzzy red beard was tickling his nose, his dick was throbbing like a toothache, and he wanted nothing more than to tear Terry's clothes off right there on the side of his—*their*—dumbass mountain.

But all he did was stand there trembling, boner pulsing, knees knocking, continuing to hold Terry close and let the kiss go on and on and on.

It was Terry who finally eased away. He looked deadly serious. Jonas saw his own reflection staring back from Terry's somber green eyes. The green shimmering there seemed to be part of the surrounding forest. Another clump of foliage. Another bush.

Jonas swallowed hard, gazing back. "I've wanted to do that for a long time," he managed to sputter, licking the taste of Terry's kiss from his lips.

"I'm not sure I'm ready for this," Terry said, his cheeks flushed, two little worry lines entrenched between his eyes.

"Please be ready," Jonas murmured. Then trying not to look desperate, he amended his statement. "Or don't be ready, Terry. Respond the way you want to respond."

"I'm not sure I want to respond at all."

Jonas pressed his erection against Terry's leg. Both men were hard now, and both men knew it. A playful grin touched Jonas's mouth. "Judging by what I'm feeling in your pants, I think you already responded."

Terry made a feeble gesture to pull himself away, but Jonas wouldn't let him go. "I'm sorry. I shouldn't have made a joke. I know this is hard for you."

Terry rolled his eyes. "Was that *another* joke?"

Jonas laughed out loud. "No! I swear it wasn't!" He molded his face into what he hoped was a more acceptable expression of concern. "Look," he said softly, "I know you don't want to let me into your structured little existence, but do it anyway. It isn't cheating on Bobby. Bobby's gone. And unless I'm reading all the signals wrong, I think you're wanting me as much as I'm wanting you."

Terry dropped his forehead to Jonas's shoulder. Jonas could sense him closing his eyes and wishing he was somewhere else. Maybe.

To Jonas's surprise, Terry muttered softly, "I do want you." And with that, Terry shuddered in his arms. "I guess this means you won't be sleeping on the couch tonight, right?"

"I'm pretty sure it means I won't be sleeping at all. And neither will you." Jonas grinned.

Terry found his own smile then. He even lifted his head and shared it. "I guess I can live with that."

As quickly as his smile came, it dropped away. In the thud of a single heartbeat, both men stiffened and cast their gazes skyward. Terry's face paled. Jonas's breath was snatched from his body. He pulled Terry closer, and both men dropped to their knees in the weeds. Bruce whimpered in

Terry's arms. He was watching the sky too, just like his masters, and his bulging puggy eyes were as big as silver dollars.

The acoustic pattering of wingbeats filled the air. The thrum of meaty downstrokes pounded overhead, drawing closer by the second. The sounds intensified. Jonas continued to hold Terry close, as much to protect Terry as to protect himself.

"What's happening?" Jonas breathed.

Their eyes skittered to each other's faces, looking for injuries, looking for blood. Jonas saw none on Terry, and he knew by the confused look in Terry's eyes, that he had seen none on Jonas. Their gazes parted and swiveled back to the sky.

While they had been kissing, the beginning of night had slipped over the mountain. It wasn't totally dark yet, but the world was filled with shadow now, and the air was cooler than it had been only minutes before.

A shiver of fear crawled up Jonas's back as the wingbeats drew nearer. The percussive pounding of fleshy wings drumming across the sky grew louder with every passing second.

Still clutching Bruce between them, both men cowered on the ground, making as small a target as they could. Breathless with terror now. Their kiss forgotten. *Everything* forgotten but that one horrifying sound filling the air, echoing between the trees, showering them with fear.

Then, in an explosion of sound, the wingbeats grew even louder. Jonas tensed. He could feel the air moving over him, rustling the foliage. Or was Jonas imagining that? Bruce whimpered in their arms, and both men clutched him tighter, shushing him to silence.

In the middle of a deepening dusk filled with bottomless dread, they held their breath. Waiting. All three of them, frozen in fear as the wings drew ever closer.

And suddenly they were there! The creatures! The drumbeat of their flapping wings flooded over their heads, pressing both men to the ground in terror and dread. Again, Bruce whimpered, and together they held the little dog even closer to keep him quiet.

As quickly as the creatures came, they just as quickly withdrew. Sliding past. Invisible in the darkness. Only the thrumming of their wings gave the creatures' location away. They were swooping past, mere feet above the heads of the men cowering below.

And then they were gone. A blessed quiet descended as the wingbeats swept over them, disappearing through the trees, moving off to the horizon, thankfully out of sight now, out of earshot. Headed to other feeding grounds. To other poor souls who perhaps did not yet know they were under attack. But very soon would.

Jonas and Terry remained crouched in stunned silence, still wrapped in each other's arms, cradling Bruce between them. They listened, eyes wide, while the last murmur of wingbeats faded away in the distance. The sounds of the forest rolled back in. The chitter of insects. The flutter of starlings in the underbrush, daring to come out now, as if they too had been frozen with fear by the creatures that passed above.

To his amazement, Jonas realized Terry's warm hand was still on his cheek where the kiss had brought it. When Terry moved his fingers across Jonas's stubble of beard, Jonas twisted his head to press his mouth into Terry's palm. He closed his eyes, relieved beyond his wildest imagination that the danger had passed and he was still crouching there in Terry's arms. Alive.

Terry watched him, his eyes relit, full of longing. "They've gone," he whispered.

"Then let's go back to the cabin," Jonas whispered back. "Quickly. There's something I want to do."

"I'll bet there is," Terry answered with a wicked glint in his eye. With a laugh bubbling somewhere inside his frizzled red beard, Terry yanked Jonas to his feet and raced him to the Jeep.

Chapter Eleven

"OH JESUS," Jonas panted. Sweat and a hot splash of Terry's come sparkled on his face.

They were sprawled out next to each other in opposite directions on Terry's bed at the top of the stairs. Naked. Still trembling. Not wanting it to end quite yet, Terry gave a tiny lurch forward, easing his satiated cock deeper into Jonas's mouth.

Jonas accepted him happily. At the same time, he slipped his own rock-hard dick unerringly past Terry's beard and into the delicious heat of his mouth. Terry laughed and swallowed him whole.

Then, with a cry that surprised them both, it was Jonas's turn to come. Terry clutched his bucking hips and worshipped his spewing cock until the last drop was spilled.

After that, they lay in stunned silence and simply clung to each other. Soon, Jonas's hands began roaming again. Exploring Terry's furry ass. Outlining the vertebra in Terry's muscled back. At the same time, Terry wrapped his own arms, still weak from release, tightly around Jonas's slim waist. Relishing the heat and smell of the man. Not ready to let him go.

Terry enjoyed the sensation of Jonas's warm cock softening inside his mouth. The taste of Jonas's juices still burning on his tongue. The way Jonas's heavy balls rested atop his chin. He opened his eyes and brought his own hand around to stroke the flat belly in front of him. Somewhere inside the man he was holding, he heard the pounding of a frenzied heartbeat, slowly winding down.

He let Jonas's cock slide from between his lips and, lifting his head, sought out the face at the other end of that long, beautiful torso. He found Jonas staring back at him, and as he gazed at him, Jonas released the pressure of his lips around Terry's dick and let it slide free as well, smiling as he did.

"When you come," Jonas panted, his voice puffily content and breathless from exertion, "you really, really come."

Even with everything they had experienced, Terry felt a blush burning his cheeks. *Thank God for the beard,* he thought, embarrassed by his own embarrassment. "I could say the same for you," he breathed.

As soon as the words were out, he planted a kiss in the damp nest of dark pubic hair billowing beneath his chin. Jonas's hips rose up to meet him, and both men gave another delicious shudder. Jonas's long fingers traveled along the back of Terry's legs, massaging the muscles, stroking idly through the pelt of red hair that coated his long thighs.

"You're beautiful in all your fuzziness," Jonas murmured, his mouth teasing Terry's stomach.

Terry wasn't crazy about the fuzzy remark, but still it was all he could do not to purr like a cat. Deciding not to quibble about it, he dragged a kiss over Jonas's rib cage as he slid upward in the bed. Jonas scooted down to meet him, and Terry laid his lips to Jonas's come-smeared mouth. He tasted his own release in the kiss, and the eroticism of that simple act caused his heart to set off at a gallop inside his chest. The dimple in Jonas's cheek appeared, signaling a grin about to erupt. But when their lips came together, Terry closed his eyes, and when he opened them again, the grin had disappeared. Jonas broke the kiss long enough to twist around in the bed to face the same direction as Terry. He nestled close and buried his face in the furry mat of Terry's chest. Their long legs twined together down below.

Terry squeezed his eyes shut once more, relishing the feel of Jonas's lean body resting in his arms. Their soft cocks snuggled one against the other, and their hands continued to idly explore the newly discovered terrain beneath their fingertips.

"It's a long time since I've been with anyone," Jonas murmured, his lips nibbling at the hair on Terry's chest, tugging playfully at it with his teeth while he spoke.

"Same here," Terry managed to say. And the moment the words were out, a vision of Bobby came flooding into his head, filling up every corner, pushing out all the recent wonders Terry had experienced with Jonas. "Well, not that long ago, I guess," Terry amended sadly.

"It's been months since your husband died," Jonas whispered, lifting his head to study Terry's face. A pained look must have entered Terry's eyes when he gazed back, judging by Jonas's sudden frown. Voice deepening with concern, Jonas said, "Please don't feel guilty about what we just did. Bobby's gone, Terry. You didn't do anything to hurt him. Living like a monk for the rest of your life would only hurt you, not him. Nothing we do together can ever change what the two of you shared. I would never want it to."

Terry allowed himself to be swallowed up in the depths of Jonas's cognac-colored eyes. Eyes that could be gentle and kind, then turn around and snap with sarcasm, if that's how Jonas was feeling. But no sarcasm shone in them now. There was only kindness and compassion.

Terry nodded, clearing his throat to find his voice. "I'm not feeling guilty." It was a lie and he knew it. He *did* feel guilty. He felt guilty as hell. Still he had no desire whatsoever to pull himself from Jonas's arms. It was too delectable, holding on to someone again. Not feeling alone for the first time in months. Not lying here all by himself and having no one to reach out to. And having no one to reach out for him. Someone to press himself against. To coax into orgasm, then experience the thrill of that person coaxing the same from him.

"Think of it as a wartime love affair," Jonas whispered, scooting down in the bed again, burrowing his face into Terry's belly. "We could both be dead tomorrow. We should take advantage of each other while we can. Enjoyable moments for both of us have been few and far between lately."

Terry smiled then. He dragged Jonas back up to eye level. When he had him where he wanted him, he wrapped him even more tightly in his arms. "Thanks for explaining it to me. Let me see if I've got this right. We're fuck buddies in a foxhole, trying to get our rocks off one last time before a SCUD missile zooms in and blows us to smithereens. Is that the plan?"

Jonas snorted. "Well, that wasn't *exactly* what I meant, but if it works for you, I'm willing to accept that premise." He stiffened in Terry's arms and whispered, "Listen. What's that thumping sound?"

Terry laughed. "Don't worry. It's only Bruce. He's downstairs scratching."

"Jesus, he sounds like a three-hundred-pound woodpecker banging on a tree."

"It's the little guy's hind leg banging against the floor. You'll get used to it."

Jonas twiddled a clump of Terry's long fiery beard, winding it around his forefinger. "Maybe I will at that. Big hunky redheads always make me feel content. When they have dogs, it's even better."

"Did you and your lover have a dog?"

"No, we had a cat."

"Was your lover a redhead?"

"No, he was bald. I like bald men too."

"Is there any sort of man you *don't* like?"

"None that come to mind. Dog owner, cat owner, bald as a cantaloupe or hairy as a Wookie, it's all the same to me. I guess that makes me a slut."

Terry grinned. "I guess it does."

They burrowed closer, grinning now. Terry decided to let himself enjoy the release of tension, the easy exchanges of friendship.

A flurry of pattering at the window not six inches from their heads told Terry it had started to rain. Soon it began to come down harder. He could hear the rain thrumming across the roof and cascading through the downspout. A flash of distant lightning faintly lit the room, and long seconds later, a lazy boom of thunder grumbled through the cabin.

"When I was a kid," Jonas said, his voice lazy and reflective, "I used to count off the seconds between the lightning and the thunder. That one was about two miles away."

Terry eased his beard from around Jonas's finger. He rose on one elbow and stared at the window in the dark. "Listen. The rain is really starting to fall. The storm is getting closer."

"It's getting colder too." Jonas reached down and dragged the covers over their naked bodies. Terry snuggled happily beneath them, relishing Jonas's warmth, enjoying the cozy clatter of raindrops on the roof above their heads.

They lay in silence for a while, listening to the storm. A candle burned on the nightstand. Occasional flashes of lightning and the muted glow of embers on the grate downstairs cast an orange glow on the cabin walls. They were the only lights visible.

"We need to make one more trip into town for metal posts. That should supply enough to finish fortifying the cabin."

"What happens then?" Jonas quietly asked. He had burrowed all the way under the covers. He lay there now, his cheek to Terry's chest, his fingers gently kneading Terry's abdomen like a drowsing cat's paws.

Terry tucked his head under the covers too. He buried his lips in Jonas's hair because he liked the sensation of having that dark mass of curls covering his face. He cleared his throat, seeking his voice. "I think it's finally time we start searching the caverns. Maybe we can study your maps in the morning. Lay out a plan. When we go into town for posts, we can pick up some gear for spelunking too. Ropes. Cleated boots, if we can find them. Better flashlights. I need a holster for my pistol. Some light food we can carry with us."

Jonas lay quiet, as if letting it sink in. "According to the maps, there are only two caves on the mountain. One isn't very big. The other appears massive. You said you knew about a third."

"Yes. It isn't far from the cabin. Opens up inside a tumble of boulders where there must have been a massive geological upheaval about a gazillion years ago. I saw a mountain lion sunning himself at the opening once a couple of years back, so it may be occupied."

"A mountain lion doesn't worry me," Jonas noted. "Considering what we're really looking for, a mountain lion seems pretty tame."

"Still, we'll have to be careful when we're exploring."

He could sense Jonas smiling in the dark. "Exploring is my favorite pastime."

As if to prove it, Jonas's fingers began to move more urgently over Terry's flesh. He gently prodded Terry's legs apart, then scooped his balls into the palm of his hand. Squirming down in the bed, he pressed his mouth to the silky flesh and laughed when Terry lifted his hips off the bed in response.

"You like that," Jonas growled. He nestled his cheek alongside Terry's cock, trailing kisses up the length of it. When he reached the tip, already swollen yet again with desire, he didn't hesitate to slip it into his mouth.

Terry arched his back and squeezed his eyes shut, lost already in Jonas's attentions.

"It's going to be a long night, isn't it?" he managed to sputter.

"Let's hope so," Jonas mumbled, his tongue stroking Terry's cock. Terry swept the blankets aside again. And in the candle's flickering flame, he rolled closer to better enjoy the beautiful man beside him.

Later, when the rain had stopped and their own desires had been quenched once more, they lay in each other's arms. Spent. Terry barely noticed when Bruce came crawling onto the bed to tuck himself between them.

Outside, in the night sky over the still dripping forest, ravenous creatures crisscrossed the sky in growing desperation. Hungrier, now, because their food supply was dwindling.

No one in the cabin noticed.

Chapter Twelve

JONAS FUMBLED his way out of bed at first light. Terry was already gone.

He tugged on jeans from the day before and, gathering up his shirt and socks and shoes, padded barefoot down the stairs. He found Terry at the kitchen counter, prepping a pot of coffee.

Dumping his shirt and shoes on the kitchen table, he draped his arms around Terry, just as Terry turned to greet him.

After a brief stiffening of surprise, Terry allowed himself to be hugged. When Jonas pulled back enough to see what was going on, Terry stepped backward, dropping his arms.

"What's wrong?" Jonas asked. "I thought...." He let that last sentence fade away unfinished, because frankly, he didn't know what he thought, and whatever it was, he knew it was too early to worry about it anyway.

Terry's gaze dropped to the floor. He turned away long enough to hit the On switch for the Mr. Coffee machine, then leaned back against the counter—facing Jonas again, but still not quite looking at him. He crossed his arms in a protective stance that Jonas didn't care for at all.

He asked again, "What's wrong, Terry? What the hell happened between last night and this morning to turn you off like this?"

To his amazement, a shimmer of tears blurred Terry's green eyes. They weren't heavy enough to fall, but they were there all the same. It nearly broke Jonas's heart to see them.

As Terry struggled to find his voice, his face grew stern. Jonas could see him licking his lips through his bushy beard, doing everything he could to build up the courage to get the words out. To free himself of whatever it was he was trying to say.

Then Jonas knew. Before Terry even spoke, Jonas already knew.

"I'm not ready for this...," Terry stammered. "...this fooling around. Our lives are on the line here. We have no business starting something that can only end in heartbreak. My world has fallen apart enough already. I'm too susceptible to all this fresh emotion. I don't think I could stand any more hurt dropping into the middle of my life right now."

Jonas knew Terry didn't want to be touched—his very posture screamed it. But he didn't care. He reached out and laid his hand on Terry's chest anyway. "Why do you think I'm going to hurt you?" he asked softly. "Why do you think I would even *try* to hurt you? I'm in the same boat you're in, you know. Neither one of us has much of a future waiting for us."

Terry gave his head a tiny shake. His eyebrows scrunched together. Suddenly he looked even more upset than he had a moment ago. "That's not what I mean," he mumbled into his beard, his eyes still on the floor.

Terry tightened his arms over his chest, and even though he didn't try to pull away from Jonas's touch, Jonas knew he was feeling uncomfortable. Vulnerable. Cornered. But Jonas didn't care about that either. If he had to corner the guy to make him listen, that's what he would do. He was determined to break through this stupid wall Terry had suddenly thrown up between them. He couldn't let it stand. He *wouldn't*. Last night had been too incredible to let it all end like this. In that rumpled bed upstairs, he had been given a glimpse of something he had not seen in a long, long time. A hope for the end of loneliness, maybe. Possibly even a shot at real happiness, if the two of them didn't ruin it before it got started.

Like they were doing right now.

Jonas took a step closer. Close enough for their belt buckles to clink together. Terry's looming hulk seemed to shrink the closer Jonas got. Still Jonas wouldn't relent. He was feeling as stubborn as Terry now. He had something to say, and he was damn well going to say it. Terry would simply have to stand there and listen.

"You don't have to be afraid of me, Terry. I'm not here to break your heart. I'm not here to do anything you don't want me to do. I wouldn't have crawled into your bed last night if I hadn't thought you were ready. Or if I hadn't thought you wanted me there."

Terry expelled a shuddery breath while his gaze remained on the floor. Jonas could barely hear the words when Terry muttered, "I did want you there."

At that, Jonas caught the first speck of light at the end of the tunnel. A shimmer of hope. He let a tiny smile escape to welcome it in. Tucking a finger under Terry's chin, he lifted his face so they could look into each other's eyes. Terry's eyes, as green as the forest outside, were dry now. Jonas was pretty sure that was a step in the right direction. The last thing in the world he wanted was for Terry to feel bad about what had taken place between the two of them during the night. Especially when Jonas had found only happiness in it. And such unexpected possibilities.

"I enjoyed making love to you, Terry. I haven't enjoyed myself that much in a long time. And I'm insecure enough to be standing here hoping you enjoyed it too."

Jonas watched as Terry's lips twitched into a smile. He kept most of it hidden away inside that bushyass beard of his, but Jonas knew it was there. He could see it in Terry's stance. In the way Terry's body relaxed a wee little bit. But mostly in the way those wondrous eyes didn't look so wounded anymore.

"Terry, listen to me. If you want to go back to how we were before last night, then I understand. I won't pester you over it. While I want nothing more than to get your naked ass back into that bed right this fucking minute, I also don't want you to do anything you don't want to do. I realize we aren't exactly in a situation here where a shot at romance could be considered a viable option. Hell, we're lucky to survive from one sunrise to the next. And every day that does pass with us still standing upright in the middle of it only means one thing. It means that by sheer good fortune we squeaked through another twenty-four hours without getting eaten."

Terry wasn't fighting him anymore. Jonas could sense it. Terry's eyes were drilling into his. He appeared to be seeking out every nuance of whatever the hell he thought Jonas was trying to say.

"What?" Jonas asked, slightly perturbed at being silently interrogated when he didn't really understand what it was that Terry was finding so confusing. "*What?*"

Terry's face softened. "Did you say romance?"

Jonas froze. *Had* he said that? Yes, he supposed he had. Still annoyed, and suddenly slightly rebellious, he stammered, "Well, yeah, I guess I did. Romance. So what the hell is wrong with that?"

Terry gave his head another shake, then leaned forward and rested his forehead on Jonas's bare shoulder. It was so unexpected that Jonas forgot what he was about to say next. Instead, he slipped his arms around Terry's broad, warm back and tugged him closer, holding him in place.

"I don't understand what you're thinking," he whispered in Terry's ear. "I don't understand what it is you're so afraid of. If something happens between the two of us, then I say we go for it. If all that happens is we spend a few enjoyable hours making love, then I have no problem with that either."

Terry exuded a rumble as he tried to clear his throat. He gave his head another tiny shake while still not lifting his forehead from Jonas's shoulder.

Jonas slipped his fingers in the rat's nest of Terry's red hair and pressed a kiss into the middle of it. "Yeti," he whispered around a smile, and this time he felt a returning smile pressed against his collarbone.

"Am I driving you crazy?" Terry asked without lifting his head from Jonas's shoulder.

Since he figured lying wouldn't get him anywhere, and saying the wrong thing would be even worse, Jonas took the coward's way out and offered a simple grunt in return.

"I think I'm feeling guilty," Terry murmured, another smile touching Jonas's skin, as if he knew why Jonas hadn't answered. "I-I didn't expect to be with anyone again. Let alone have sex with them inside this very cabin in my very own bed. I wasn't sure I'd even *see* anyone again after stashing myself away on this frigging mountain. It's simply all too mind-boggling for me to get my head around, this sudden rush of feelings. Feelings I never thought I'd have again. Feelings I thought I'd never *want* to have again."

Jonas snuggled close, pressing his lips to Terry's ear, massaging Terry's smooth back. He lowered his voice, barely uttering his words loud enough to be heard. Thinking it was more personal that way. Thinking it would be less frightening for Terry. Less threatening.

"I would never try to make you forget Bobby, if that's what you're worried about. You believe me, right? If what happened last night between us ever manages to go any further, it won't mean you loved Bobby any less. It will only mean that your heart is big enough and brave enough to care about someone else as well."

"I never said I cared about you," Terry said.

At that surprising statement, Jonas took a moment to chew on his lower lip while he formulated a response. Finally, he said, "I never said I cared for you either. I do enjoy sucking your dick, though."

This time the smile that brushed against Jonas's shoulder had some teeth in it.

"You old smoothie, you," Terry quipped. He lifted his head and gazed into Jonas's eyes. Jonas was happy to note that the worry trenches in his forehead had evaporated. Most of the angst seemed to have been erased from his face as well. To his surprise, what Jonas did see was a sudden burst of concern light Terry's expression. The expression deepened when Terry's fingers came up and brushed across Jonas's cheek.

"What happened to your face?" he asked.

Jonas blinked. Confused. "Why? What's wrong with my face?"

Terry reached behind him and snatched up the stainless steel toaster, holding it in front of Jonas's face. "Your skin is raw. You look like you've been sandblasted."

Jonas studied his own reflection. Terry was right. His cheeks, nose, and chin shone bright red. Even his lips, buried as they were inside his sprouting beard, which was about thirty-six hours beyond a five-o'clock shadow but nowhere near as bushy as Terry's, appeared red and swollen.

He realized what it was at the same time Terry did.

"It's rug burn from my beard," Terry said. "I scraped half your face off when we were kissing."

Jonas grinned, staring back. "I wonder if there's a rug burn on my crotch. That's where you spent most of the night rooting around."

Terry frowned. "Not funny."

Jonas's smile didn't falter. "It's a little funny."

They stood silently considering each other. Both men still grinning. Both men as red as beets. Jonas from beard burn, Terry from embarrassment.

Terry lifted his hands and laid them to each of Jonas's fiery cheeks, gently caressing the redness there. "Your skin feels hot," he said.

"I'm hot all over," Jonas answered, his single dimple popping unexpectedly into view.

Terry's hands slid from his face and forged a trail along the length of Jonas's warm chest and belly. They came to rest at the waistband of Jonas's jeans, and as if working under a single purpose, both hands converged on Jonas's belt buckle.

With a wicked gleam in his eye, Terry lowered himself to his knees and unclipped Jonas's belt. When it was out of the way, he popped the buttons on Jonas's jeans and with one quick yank, tugged them all the way down to his ankles. Jonas's cock sprang up and bopped him on the chin like a billy club.

"Well, hello there," Terry growled, as if surprised by what he'd found.

Jonas dug his fingers deep into Terry's mop of red hair and coaxed him closer to his dick. Terry didn't put up much of a fight.

"I guess your internal concerns have been resolved, then," Jonas muttered, his voice weak, his knees beginning to knock.

"I guess they have," Terry muttered back, grinning with anticipation.

Chapter Thirteen

JONAS HAD been ready for twenty minutes while Terry had been holed up in the cabin's tiny bathroom since breakfast. It left Jonas with nothing to do but twiddle his thumbs and slurp at his sixth cup of coffee, which was about three cups too many. He was starting to vibrate from the caffeine.

As impatient as he was, he still managed to drift away every now and then in a dreamy trance, thinking about him and Terry sprawled naked in each other's arms. After their first night together, things got sidetracked at breakfast the next day, starting with a blowjob on the kitchen floor. From there, matters spiraled into total chaos—sexually speaking—and they ended up spending the rest of the day and the next night together in bed all over again.

Today, twenty-four hours later, Jonas was so stiff he could barely walk. He couldn't imagine what was taking Terry so long in the bathroom. This was the day they had chosen to scope out the first of the three caverns scattered beneath the surface of Terry's mountain. The plans had been made while they were rooting around in the middle of the night in each other's crotches, not to mention more daring locales, happily dehydrating themselves. They had the day all mapped out. *So what's the holdup?*

"What the hell are you doing in there?" Jonas bellowed. "If you're beating off and leaving me out of the loop while you do it, I'm going to be really upset!"

From behind the bathroom door he heard a bearlike growl, not from Terry but from Bruce. The pug was in there with him. He also heard a familiar human voice mumble something that sounded like "Slut."

Jonas grinned at that. He settled back in the wooden chair, fully dressed in leather and denim and gloves. The only thing he hadn't donned was the motorcycle helmet, which he cradled in his lap. He was tapping an impatient riff across the top of the helmet with his fingernails while the words to "You Light Up My Life," echoed around inside his head.

He wasn't sure why. He hated that fucking song. He slurped down a little more coffee and stretched his legs out so he could prop his boot-clad feet on the kitchen table.

He was seriously considering battering down the bathroom door when he at long last heard it creak open behind him. Jonas scraped his boots off the edge of the table and dragged himself to his feet.

"It's about time," he snarled good-naturedly. Then his eyes popped open wide, and he stood there stiff in amazement. He took a step forward. Then he took a step back. He cupped his chin and cocked his head first one way, then the other, trying to analyze what he was seeing. Finally he decided to just stand still and stare. Slowly, a sweeping smile began to spread across his face. He couldn't have hidden it if he wanted to. It was the Ebola of smiles. Unstoppable, uncurable. Flashing a myriad of teeth he barked out an astonished laugh. "Holy shit, Terry! What have you done?"

Terry ran a hand over his freshly shaved cheeks. He looked deeply uncertain all of a sudden. "Is it that bad?" he asked shyly.

Jonas gawked. He ran a hand over his own cheeks in reaction to what he was seeing. Then, seeing the doubt in Terry's eyes, he forced himself to snap out of it. He stepped forward until their faces were inches apart. He stroked the back of his fingers along the smooth expanse of Terry's newly mown cheek; then he used his other hand to explore the other cheek. While he was there, he slid his thumb along Terry's bottom lip, enjoying the fact that he could see the man's gorgeous mouth in all its beauty for the first time without it being buried under a truckload of grizzled facial hair.

"You handsome dog," he said around that same dawning smile. "You did this for me, didn't you?"

"You were getting a facial peel every time we had sex. I had to do something."

"We could have simply stopped kissing."

"That wasn't an option."

Jonas really liked that. He batted his eyes. "Aww." Impossibly, his smile broadened even more. His jaws were starting to ache. "You've got a dimple in your chin I didn't know was there."

Terry grinned. "I'd almost forgotten about it myself." He opened his mouth and clamped his teeth gently around Jonas's thumb. "So do I still look like a Yeti?"

Jonas laughed. "No. Your Yeti days are over. Now you're just a big, burly, clean-shaven redheaded hunk of lumberjacking manhood."

"Oh, goodie. I always wanted to be one of those."

Jonas heard a sneeze, and they both turned to look through the bathroom door where Bruce was sniffing at a pile of red curly hair that had fallen to the floor in front of the sink.

"Wow, look at all that!" Jonas bawled, impressed. "It's like you shaved an orangutan."

"Imagine how much hair there'd be if I shaved my ass."

Jonas grabbed him by the shoulders and gave him a shake. "Don't you dare," he snarled. Then he laid his lips over Terry's mouth and kissed him long and hard. Not having to chew his way through Terry's beard made the kiss a totally different experience. And infinitely more enjoyable.

"Thank you," Jonas muttered, stepping back and licking the kiss from his lips.

Terry blushed, but he looked pleased too. "You're welcome. And thank you for the last thirty-six hours of nonstop sex."

It was Jonas's turn to blush. "Are you as sore as I am?"

"Stiff as a board," Terry said. "And this time not in a good way." Both men arched an eyebrow in sardonic agreement.

Jonas slipped his motorcycle helmet over his head and handed the other one to Terry. Before putting it on, Terry turned to Bruce who had fallen asleep atop the pile of hair on the bathroom floor.

"You stay here," Terry said, wagging an admonishing finger at the pug. "Where we're going, you won't be safe."

"Because of the creatures?" Jonas asked, gathering his stuff together. Hiking pole. Terry's holstered Smith & Wesson 5-shot .38, which Terry told him he probably couldn't hit the broad side of a barn with, but he was welcome to wear anyway if he promised not to shoot himself in the foot. A coil of strong rope he draped over his shoulder. Snacks and potable water and a couple of large Maglite flashlights with extra batteries they shared between them. The Maglites had been stolen from the sporting goods store in town the last time they were there. Except for the shotgun, which Terry planned on carrying, the bulk of the equipment was stowed inside two new backpacks, also commandeered from the sporting goods store.

"No," Terry said. "Not because of the creatures. Because of the cave. It would be too easy to lose Bruce in there. He could disappear down a crack, and we'd never see him again."

They were headed for the one cave not on Jonas's map.

"So you know this cave pretty well?" Jonas asked.

"I don't imagine anyone knows it very well. I've been in it a couple of times. Bobby and I explored it once. And I explored it once by myself. But that was before the creatures showed up. God knows how far back the cave goes underneath the mountain. Both times I entered, I didn't go very far inside. It's too creepy. And I didn't have any equipment. I was afraid I'd get lost."

Terry worked his arms through the straps of his backpack and positioned it comfortably across his shoulders. Before he could pull his helmet over his head, Jonas caught his arm and stopped him, just long enough to stroke his fingers down Terry's freshly shaved cheek one last time.

"You really do look handsome," he said softly.

Terry's eyes crinkled up around a shy smile. "Thanks. I was half-afraid I'd scare you off when you saw the real me."

"Fat chance." He cast a glance through the kitchen window, then gazed longingly at the staircase. "The day's still young. We could pop up to the loft for a few minutes before we leave."

Terry struck a pose and cupped his hand behind his ear, listening.

Jonas stiffened. His gaze shot skyward. "What is it? What do you hear?"

Terry laughed. "My dick. It's pleading for mercy."

"So I guess that's a no, then." Jonas groaned, breathing a sigh of relief even while batting comically wounded eyes. He leaned in for a final kiss before slapping his face guard down to hide his grin.

"Got everything?" Terry asked, donning his own helmet and patting himself all over, checking his equipment, making sure he had everything he needed to take.

"The cave is close?" Jonas asked, adjusting his backpack.

Terry nodded. "This one is, yeah. We can walk."

At the door, Jonas cast a last glance back at Bruce, still sleeping on the bathroom floor. As quietly as he could, he latched the door behind them, and he and Terry set off through the trees. The sky was overcast from the recent rain, the air brisk and cool and clean. The smell of evergreens lay sweetly pungent on the air. Above their heads, birds were singing a spirited concerto and chasing one another through the branches, happy the rain was over.

They weren't twenty feet into the woods when Terry slipped his gloved hand around Jonas's. The way he did it, without a hint of embarrassment, made Jonas's heart swell.

"I'm glad I'm not alone anymore," Terry said, pushing damp branches out of their way. "It's good to have someone to talk to again. And do other stuff with too." He made the statement calmly, like he was commenting on the weather. But Jonas heard the ardor with which the words were spoken. And again his heart responded.

Rather than speak in return or make a sly comment about the "other stuff" Terry had mentioned, he simply squeezed Terry's hand and edged closer so their shoulders touched as they walked.

He smiled behind his faceplate, enjoying the nearness, as the trees slid past around them.

To his surprise, Terry wasn't finished saying what he wanted to say. He tugged on Jonas's hand and pulled him to a stop under the low-hanging fronds of a towering sugar pine. Fat cones, sodden with rain, hung from the tree and lay scattered across the forest floor at their feet.

Both men lifted their visors so they could see each other's eyes.

As soon as their gazes connected, Terry said, "I think Bobby would understand about us. I don't think he would hate me for what we're doing."

Jonas pulled Terry closer until they stood inches apart. "I'm sure he wouldn't hate either one of us."

They stood quietly then, ears cocked, while the birds trilled above their heads. "Listen. It almost sounds like nothing is wrong, doesn't it?" Terry asked. "Like it's just another day."

"Was it always this quiet?" Jonas asked in a hushed voice. "Your little mountain?"

Terry stared up into the pine boughs draped above them. At the mockingbirds and the starlings playing among the needles and cones. At the glimpse of blue sky peeking through dripping limbs.

"No," Terry said in a sleepy, lazy voice. "There used to be more sounds on the mountain. Traffic sometimes carried up from the highway below. On still mornings you might hear the wail of a car alarm from somewhere in town. Hikers could be glimpsed now and then through the trees, laughing and fooling around. Down the trail in the other direction, there's another cabin where a family used to come to spend their weekends. We used to see them laughing and traipsing about. I haven't seen them since the trouble started. They may be dead for all I know."

"Let's hope not," Jonas whispered.

"Yes," Terry agreed. "Let's hope not."

By silent agreement, they lowered their face masks and continued their trek through the trees, still hand in hand. Jonas decided it would have been a pleasant walk if they hadn't been so overdressed. The leather jacket chafed his armpits, and the helmet seemed to cut off all the air. He longed to rip them both off and fling them into the bushes. Even the shotgun was annoying the hell out of him, getting heavier and heavier as he carried it with the stock tucked under his armpit and the barrel aimed down at the ground in front of him.

The trees opened up, exposing them to the sky. They clambered up a steep hillside meadow dotted red with Indian paintbrush. Bees were everywhere, gathering pollen. Honeybees. Yellow jackets. Fat black-and-gold bumblebees. Jonas was a city boy and not that fond of bees. Suddenly he was glad for the leather jacket and crash helmet after all.

Cresting the hill, Jonas released Terry's hand. He followed in Terry's footsteps as they waded single file through the waist-high carpet of Indian paintbrush and descended the other side.

At a spot where a jumble of boulders lay scattered in a gully at the bottom of a rise, Terry pointed and said, "This is it."

Jonas peeked over Terry's shoulder and saw nothing but a pile of rocks. "I don't see a cave."

A rumble of laughter erupted from inside Terry's helmet. "That's because it's hidden," he said.

Dropping to his knees, Terry crawled through a clump of blackberry briars and instantly disappeared.

"What?" Jonas cried out. "Wait! Where'd you go?"

When he didn't get an answer, he reluctantly dropped to his hands and knees and followed Terry into the prickly brush.

Chapter Fourteen

TERRY CREPT forward on his hands and knees, continually plucking his clothing free from the barbs of the blackberry vines he was crawling through. A moment later, darkness began to swallow him up as he entered the small entrance tunnel that led to a larger cavern inside. Jonas bumped along at his heels, grumbling and grunting, touching Terry's calf now and then as if he needed to reassure himself with human contact. Six feet into the shadows, the tunnel opened up around Terry. He stumbled to his feet and brushed the muck off his hands and knees.

"We're there," he announced as Jonas clambered to his feet behind him. "Just watch your head. The ceiling's a little low."

Jonas reached up and took a fistful of Terry's leather jacket to pull himself up with, rather like a panic-stricken drowning man clutching the life vest of the poor guy floundering in the waves beside him.

Terry covered Jonas's hand with his own and gave it a pat. "Easy there, tiger. It's just a little darkness, is all. We're not even fully inside yet."

Jonas sounded tense. "I thought you said we were there."

"We will be in a minute. You got your flashlight? If you do, this might be a good time to turn it on." Terry flicked the switch on his own Maglite, and the enclosed space they were standing in burst to life around them.

Jonas fumbled around for his flashlight, and a second or two later, with two Maglites shooting off beams of light in every direction, the tiny cavern was lit up like a crime scene. Some sort of large bug or spider, spanning six inches across, went scurrying off between their boots and ducked under a shelf of rock to the left. "Holy shit!" Jonas barked as he broke into a nervous tap dance, hopping from one foot to the other and spinning around, looking for more spiders. Finally he swiveled the flashlight forward and shot the beam directly into Terry's face, blinding him.

Terry batted it aside none too gently.

"Oh. Sorry," Jonas stammered.

"It's okay. You're not claustrophobic, are you?" Terry asked.

"I wasn't yesterday," Jonas feebly joked, his voice quivering in the dark. "Don't like bugs, though. Especially ones as big as dinner plates." He pushed the visor up on his helmet and sucked in a deep breath of cold cavern air.

"I'd keep that closed if I were you," Terry said, indicating his face mask. "God knows what else is down here. We don't want the scent of blood leaking out if one of those plate-size bugs drops down from the ceiling and bites you on the nose."

"Oh yeah," Jonas muttered, flipping his face guard closed. He seemed to suddenly realize he had a death grip on Terry's jacket, so he forced himself to let go with evident reluctance.

Terry grinned and gave him a hip bump. "It'll be okay," he said. "Just stay close to me."

"Oh gee, must I?" Jonas snapped, dribbling sarcasm. "I thought I'd take off exploring on my own!" Then he mumbled, "Dumbass," and huffed out a breath of air, clearly trying to calm himself down.

Following their flashlight beams, they scoped the place out. The opening in the earth was little more than a slit in the face of the mountain. Where they stood, the cave was less than three feet across and maybe five feet high. They had to continually duck so they wouldn't bang their head on the rocky ceiling.

It had been almost a year since Terry was inside the cave. He had been there with Bobby.

"Wait a minute," Jonas said. "Is this all there is?"

"No," Terry said, his voice hushed in the darkness. "We have to go deeper in. Then the cave opens up. Like I told you before, I don't know how far back it goes. Maybe not far at all. I'm not sure."

Jonas tucked his hand into Terry's jacket pocket and left it there. It seemed to give him courage, so Terry didn't say anything. Truth was, he liked the connection. Terry wasn't much more thrilled to be in this black hole than Jonas was.

"Maybe that's why this cave isn't on my geological survey map. It isn't big enough to be measurable."

"Maybe," Terry said. "I don't know. I'm not a geologist. You ready to go deeper?"

Jonas didn't hesitate. "Nope. Not ready. Not ready at all. I'll never be ready. Ready and me aren't getting along right now. Ready took a hike, I think. Off to Tucson, maybe. Or Guatemala."

Terry snorted back a laugh. "Good. Glad you're on board. Let's go deeper, then."

"Perhaps you misunderstood…."

Terry sidled forward, slipping between the stone walls, which quickly closed in as he moved deeper into the crevice. Jonas edged his way along behind him, grumbling under his breath. At a place where the rock narrowed to such a point that it touched both Terry's chest and his back at the same time, he felt Jonas stiffen up like he'd been tased. The hand in Terry's jacket pocket knotted up into a fist.

"Don't worry," Terry whispered. "You won't get stuck. We're almost there. It opens up in a minute." He wasn't sure why he was whispering. Well, yes, he was. The place was creepy as hell, and Jonas's fear seemed to be contagious, burrowing its way into Terry the same way the two of them were burrowing between the rocks.

As Terry promised, a few feet farther in, the walls opened up. Terry stretched his shoulders wide and breathed a sigh of relief. The air was colder here, seeping under his clothes even through the leather he wore, brittle and windless and utterly frigid. It was like stepping into a walk-in freezer. The darkness closed in around them, hand in hand with the cold. The shadows were so thick and dense, he imagined them spilling over his skin like a slathering of black paint.

He reached behind him and clutched Jonas's arm. "It's okay," he whispered. "We're in. Turn your flashlight off."

Jonas clearly didn't like that idea. "Are you nuts? Why?"

"I want to show you something."

"No."

"Do it!"

Jonas growled, but he switched his light off.

Terry did the same, and suddenly the shadows seemed to recede a little bit. The ceiling had opened up above them, stretching as high as they could see. Sparks of what looked like foxfire appeared along the cavern walls, undulating in seams of speckled light, trailing off into the distance.

Jonas sucked in his breath. "It looks like stars. Galaxies."

Terry pressed himself to Jonas's side, pulling him close. Deep inside, he suffered a tiny spasm of guilt knowing he had shared this sight with only one other person in his life.

"It's some kind of fungus," he explained. "It's bioluminescent somehow. Glows in the dark. But when you aim a light at it, it blinks out. Bobby and I discovered it a couple of years ago. Isn't it beautiful?"

The beauty seemed to be lost on Jonas. He switched his flashlight back on and sent the beam shooting around the cavern floor looking for more spiders. "It's so cold! Does anything live in here?"

Terry paused before answering. "I guess that's what we're here to find out."

Terry switched his Maglite back on, and the shimmer of fungus on the cavern walls disappeared. "Listen," he hissed.

Jonas tensed beside him as they both leaned forward listening to a trickling sound up ahead.

"Water!" Jonas said.

"Yeah. It seeps through the rocks and forms a little pool back there. Bobby and I found that too. The water is clean and clear. The fungus forms a ring around the pool, making a luminous circle along the edge of the water when the lights are off. Bobby always thought it was the fungus that cleansed the water."

"What's on the other side of the pool?"

"I don't know. The pool is as far as we went."

Jonas still sounded nervous. "Did you see bats when you were here before?"

"No. But we didn't stay long."

"Should we go deeper?"

Terry was curious now. They had come all this way. All their efforts would be wasted if they turned back now. And too, there was a twinge of bravado tickling away at his ego. He didn't want Jonas to think he was a total wuss.

"We'll go a little past the pool. How's that? As long as we can hear the water, we won't get lost. I promise."

Jonas didn't sound entirely convinced. "Well, if you're sure."

"I'm sure," Terry lied, and taking Jonas's hand, he moved deeper into the shadowy cave. For the heck of it, they stopped a few feet in and switched off their lights again. The fungus was thicker here, and where the pool lay in front of them, it formed a donut-shaped circle of light around it.

Jonas sucked in his breath. "It's beautiful!"

"I know," Terry whispered back.

Their Maglites blinked on, and the light around the pool disappeared. They moved forward again to circle around the side of the pool, which was about four feet in diameter. As they passed it, something white splashed in the water, showing itself for a split second in the glare of their flashlight beams. A fish or some sort of amphibian. Frog, maybe. Pigmentless. As pale as milk. Creepy.

Jonas's hand tightened around Terry's. "I saw its face. It didn't have any eyes. This place is like a horror movie," he hissed.

Terry smiled in the dark. "I thought you said it was beautiful."

Jonas huffed in annoyance. "So I hate animals without eyeballs. I'm fickle. Sue me."

They eased their way past the pool. The floor was uneven beneath their feet. Loose scree and stones clattered as they walked. In other places, clumps of muddy clay squelched beneath their boots. They had to choose their steps carefully.

"You've seen these creatures up close," Jonas whispered. "The ones that kill people. How big are they? Crow size?"

"Bigger."

"Owl size?"

"Bigger."

He heard Jonas gulp in the darkness. "Eagle size?"

Terry considered his answer. He didn't want to exaggerate. The truth was horrible enough without exaggeration. He chewed on the inside of his cheek for a minute, thinking. Finally he said, "Bigger than an eagle, smaller than a condor. And meaner than either. But with shorter wings."

"Do they flit like bats?" Jonas asked.

Terry gave a grim chuckle. "Does a freight train flit? No. These guys just barrel in. They barrel in en masse from high in the sky and rip you to shreds. Flitting is the last thing they do."

"You've seen them feed," Jonas said, his voice a reverent hush. It wasn't a question, because Jonas knew the truth as well as Terry did. They had talked about it before. Bobby's death. All of that.

A flash of memory seared through Terry's brain. It was a memory he had been battling against for months, and a memory he could never seem to shake. The memory was brief and brutal. It brought into clear focus Bobby's last seconds on earth before he was yanked through the canvas roof of the Jeep and pulled apart in front of him. Shredded in midair. All of his beautiful humanity reduced in a heartbeat to strings of flesh and tendon in an exploding mist of blood.

"Yes," Terry quietly answered as a familiar pain dug at his heart. "I've seen them feed." *The understatement of the century.*

Jonas's hand came out and stroked his back. "I'm sorry," he said. "I shouldn't have brought it up."

Terry shook the apology aside. He turned and faced Jonas, holding his flashlight beam down so it wouldn't blind him, but leaving it high enough that Jonas could see his face. Hoping Jonas could see the truth of what he was about to tell him as they stood together here in this miserable black hole in the mountain. It was a struggle to keep his voice calm. It was a struggle not to grab Jonas's arms and shake him into understanding.

"I know what you're getting at, Jonas. You want to know if they feed like vampire bats. Well, they don't. They don't feed like anything on the planet. They're monsters, okay? So don't be lulled into comparing them to bats. Bats are sweet. Harmless."

Jonas looked unconvinced. "What about vampire bats? Maybe they—"

Terry waved him silent. "Even vampires, Jonas. These things fly during the day. Vampire bats don't do that. They soar high in the sky. Vampire bats rarely fly higher than a meter off the ground. Vampires drink blood, yes, but they don't consume the flesh of the animals they drink from. They don't tear their host to shreds. Vampires sip from teeny tiny slits they make in their prey's skin. These things don't sip, they devour. Blood, flesh, even the bones are torn to splinters. They're strong, Jonas. Vampire bats aren't strong like that. Plus vampires are tiny. Before they feed they weigh about two ounces. True vampires have a wingspan of seven inches. *Seven inches.* The wings on these things are four feet across at least, maybe five, and God knows how much they weigh! Ten pounds maybe? Fifteen? Twenty? While these creatures may vaguely resemble bats, you can't compare them to bats in any conceivable way. You have to take my word on that."

"You've thought about this. You've done your research."

Terry gripped his flashlight tighter. "Yes, I've done my research. And trust me, these creatures are unique to the animal kingdom. There's nothing else like them. They are fast, and they are ruthless. And when they smell your blood, Jonas, trust me, there's no way to stop them. They'll swoop in and kill you before you even have time to scream. That's all you need to know. All right?"

Jonas hitched in his breath and, without answering, pulled Terry to him, holding him close. "I'm sorry," he said again, pressing his mouth to Terry's shoulder.

Terry eased himself from Jonas's arms. "It's okay. Let's just be careful. We don't want any surprises." He took Jonas's hand and, in a voice still wobbly with emotion, said, "Let's keep going and get this over with. A few more yards in and we'll call it a day."

Jonas nodded. He looked humbled and fearful again in the beam of Terry's light. "Okay."

They turned together to face the deeper bowels of the cavern, and that's when they heard the sounds. The faint click and clatter of tiny nails scrabbling at rock. The gentle swat of fleshy wings fluttering against plump bodies. The cry of tiny voices, chittering in the dark, somewhere high above their heads, near the unseen ceiling.

Jonas yanked him to a stop. "Listen!" he hissed. "It's them!"

Spurred by the sound of Jonas's startled voice, the cave suddenly erupted around them. Small black specks, like living scraps of ash, exploded to life, swirling through the air. Tiny wings flapped against their face plates, blocking what little light they had left to see by. Jonas and Terry slapped the beasts away from their helmets. Their flashlight beams bounced all over the place, stirring the specks of black into a frenzy. High-pitched voices of outrage, each as piercing and sharp as a pinprick, peppered the air around them like a million tiny fingernails scraping at a million tiny blackboards.

Again, Terry flapped his hands in front of his face, and in that one strobe-like moment, he saw in his flashlight beam the clear outline of what it was they were flailing against. A benign face hovering in midair, peering in through his mask with delicate black eyes.

He grabbed Jonas's arm and cried out, "Stop! Stand still. They won't hurt you."

It took Jonas a moment to comply, but when he did, Terry could tell he was beginning to understand. He edged closer to Terry and lowered his arms, no longer trying to swat the creatures away.

The black swarm continued to tornado around their heads, spinning, whirling, still screaming curious cries in their chittering, birdlike voices.

"Turn off the lights!" Terry cried. "Turn off the lights!"

Terry and Jonas both switched off their flashlights, and within the thundering whirlwind of wings that circled maniacally around them, a sudden hush began to grow. Startled wings, as fragile as a child's fingertips, stopped slapping against their helmets, ceased sweeping across their face masks. Small furred bodies brushed more gently against their backs and arms now, some landing, then quickly taking off again. No longer attacking. No longer terrified but judging the threat and finding it minimal. Relinquishing their fear and replacing it with curiosity.

Terry stood in the dark and listened as the maelstrom slowly abated. Jonas remained close beside him, trembling in the dark. He seemed calmer now. As Terry was. As the animals were.

"These really are bats," Terry said softly, so as not to frighten the tiny creatures any more than they were already. "These aren't monsters, Jonas. These are just bats. Mexican free-tailed bats, maybe. I think we scared them more than they scared us."

"Not sure you're right about *that*," Jonas groused, his voice still pitched as high as the bats around them.

Terry groped for Jonas's hand in the dark and gave it a squeeze. When Jonas squeezed back, he knew everything was all right. They stood motionless, hand in hand. For long minutes they waited while the mass of tiny creatures swirling around them began to thin out and eventually fade away altogether, melting back into the shadows from wherever it was they came.

Edging backward through the cave they had just explored, Terry nudged Jonas along in front of him. When the trickling of the pool became loud enough that he knew they were close, Terry switched his Maglite back on and took the lead.

"Let's get out of here," he whispered, feeling like an interloper and hoping not to stir the bats up again. "These animals are harmless. We've disturbed them enough."

They eased their way through old familiar shadows to the growing dot of light that showed them where the real world lay waiting for their return.

As they crawled into the sunlight and burrowed their way through the briars, Terry was happy as hell to be out of the cave and away from the dark. But he wasn't nearly as happy as Jonas.

Jonas was mumbling to himself as he crawled along at Terry's feet, "That's enough exploring for one day. It's back to the cabin for me. Yessireebob."

"Need a drink?" Terry asked with a grin.

"Yes!" Jonas snapped back. "And I might need to change my underwear."

Chapter Fifteen

JONAS SAT cross-legged on the cabin floor with Bruce curled up beside him. He had his portable typewriter perched on the edge of the coffee table, and he was clacking away at fifty words a minute. The racket clearly annoyed Bruce, who every now and then heaved a sigh of exasperation and squeezed his eyes tighter, trying to sleep.

Jonas stopped typing long enough to watch Terry stomp through the front door with an armload of firewood. He dumped the logs into the woodbox by the fireplace, then kicked the door closed behind him and lowered the crossbars that sealed the door. It was coming on to evening, and the light outside was fading. With approaching night, the colder air was moving in too. The starlings blathered in the rafters, talking about it. The cacophony of their jabbering and the clatter of the firewood tumbling into the box, not to mention the blasted typewriter, was the final straw for Bruce. He dragged himself to his feet and plodded up the stairs to escape all the noise and try to get a few winks of sleep under the bed.

Jonas was as excited as the starlings about the coming cold. He couldn't wait to seek a little warmth of his own by getting naked later and snuggling with the burly redhead standing by the grate clapping the bark from his gloves.

When they were clean, Terry shed his gloves and leather jacket, then dragged the helmet off his head and tossed it on the couch. Terry might have shaved that morning, but he already had a red shadow of fresh whiskers sprouting on his cheeks. His hair was still long and frazzled. It cascaded down in a curly mass that almost reached his shoulders. Standing in front of the fire, Terry buried his hands in that lustrous red mane and gave his head a shake, combing through it with his fingers to get the tangles out and the circulation moving. With the fireplace ablaze behind him, it looked like his head had suddenly shot up in flames.

Jonas gave a soft admiring whistle. "Wow. For a mountain man, you are something else."

Terry peeked through his fanned-out hair and offered Jonas a dubious smirk. "I'm not a mountain man. I'm a substitute schoolteacher and a notary public. And you bloody well know it." He looked embarrassed as his eyes traveled to the typewriter. "Working on your book?"

It was Jonas's turn to blush. "I was. Until you decided to get sexy in front of the fire and ruin all my fantasies by telling me you're not Paul Bunyan."

Terry laughed. "If you think I'm Paul Bunyan, then you've been away from butch men far too long."

Jonas rolled his eyes in exaggerated wonder. "Boy. What you don't know about yourself is a lot."

There were two rosy splotches still burning on Terry's cheeks, so Jonas figured he had teased the man enough. He glanced into the fire for a moment to gather his thoughts. From the fire, he let his gaze travel around the cabin. The walls and ceiling were all fortified now with the galvanized fence posts sturdily nailed down with only two-inch gaps between them. Nothing bigger than a hamster would be getting into this cabin without a bulldozer. The trick for actual survival, of course, was not to be trapped *outside* the cabin when the creatures attacked. Consequently, every excursion they made from this point on, either into the tiny town of Spangle for supplies or across the mountain slopes to check out the caverns on his map, would be a gamble. It was then their lives would be in the greatest danger.

Terry plopped himself on the sofa. He uncapped a bottle of water and guzzled it, smacking his lips when he was finished like it was really what he needed. Jonas smiled watching him.

"When was the last time you saw a living person other than me?" Jonas asked.

Terry stared at him, his lips still moist from the water. He carefully replaced the cap on the bottle and set it on the table. Leaning forward with his elbows on his knees, he studied Jonas closely.

"I don't know. A few weeks maybe. But I'm sure there are still people around. They just prefer to stay hidden. Why do you ask?"

Jonas gave a shrug. "I was just wondering if we're the last two people on the face of this mountain."

"I doubt it. But what if we are?"

"I'm not sure," Jonas said. "Do you suppose the authorities know we're here?"

Terry considered that. "Maybe. Maybe not. I haven't seen any helicopters running sentry over the place. No National Guard troops beating a path through the underbrush or tearing through the houses in town, trying to scare up survivors so they can hustle them off to safety. On the other hand, they could be accessing satellites and drones and keeping tabs on the area without us knowing anything about it. Seems to me they have to know we're here."

"Then don't you think it's kind of odd they haven't tried to make contact? A lot of people have died here."

Apparently his last statement struck a nerve. Terry's eyes grew hooded. The line of his lips tightened. "First off, I never wanted to be contacted by the authorities. I have no intention of letting them decide if I should stay or go. That's why I destroyed the cell phones. Secondly, I *know* a lot of people have died here. Some were my friends. One was my husband, remember? Everybody I knew who shared this corner of the world with Bobby and me are gone. They either left while they had a chance, or the creatures picked them off one by one. So what exactly are you getting at?" He glanced down at the portable typewriter in front of Jonas. "What *are* you writing, anyway?"

Jonas's fingers slid across the silent keys. He could feel the muscles in his jaws work while he tried to decide exactly how to formulate the words to explain what it was that had started to worry him so much. Finally, he pushed the typewriter aside and leaned over the table. He reached across to touch Terry's knee.

"It's not going to go on like this, you know."

"What's not going to go on like this?" Terry asked.

"Us," Jonas said.

Terry drew his knee back, evading Jonas's touch. "If you want to leave, you can. Just because we're sleeping together doesn't mean we've made any promises of everlasting commitment. I got along fine before you came along. I can get along fine if you—"

Jonas smacked the tabletop hard enough to shut Terry up. He leaned closer and snagged Terry's pant leg again, pinching it tightly between his thumb and forefinger. Holding on. Refusing to let go.

"Please don't pull away from me again, Terry. That's not what I'm talking about. You know how I feel about you."

Terry didn't look convinced. "How am I supposed to know how you feel about me? You've been under my roof for what? Six weeks?

Going on seven? We fuck each other and suck each other's dicks, but that doesn't mean I can read your mind."

Jonas inhaled a deep breath and tried to calm himself. He forced himself to speak slowly and rationally. This wasn't the conversation he had wanted to have today. His worries lay far deeper than how the two of them were beginning to feel about each other.

"Terry, listen to me. Even I don't know how I feel about you exactly. It's confusing. I want to be with you every minute. If that means I'm falling in love with you, then maybe that's what I'm doing. In the middle of everything we're going through, is it really that important if I fall in love with you or not? Do you really think that's where our priorities should be focused right now?"

"It's never the wrong time to fall in love," Terry said stubbornly. His voice was calmer now, but his eyes reflected hurt. He stared down at Jonas's fingers clutching at his pant leg. He couldn't seem to lift his eyes to Jonas's face.

Jonas studied him closely. He could feel his heart thudding behind his rib cage. It had been a long time since a man had avoided looking at him like this. It had been a long time since any man had harbored enough feelings about him to even contemplate doing such a thing.

"You're right, Terry. It's never the wrong time to fall in love." He chewed on his bottom lip. "And maybe that is what we're doing. I *hope* it is. I like being with you. You're the sexiest man I've ever known. You seem to like me too."

Terry chuckled wryly at that. The chuckle was pretty sarcastic, but at least he managed to smile afterward, and that gave Jonas hope. But it still wasn't what Jonas wanted to talk about right now.

"Terry, listen to me. How we feel about each other will happen whether we want it to or not. But right now we've got bigger problems."

"Yes, I know, but—"

"No," Jonas said. "I don't think you do know. What do you think the authorities are doing right now?"

Terry blinked in confusion. "The authorities?"

"Yes. The authorities. The people who are trying to keep this mountain and your little hometown quarantined. What do you think they are talking about? What do you think their plans are for the long run?"

"The long run?"

Jonas huffed in annoyance. "Terry, they're not going to want these creatures to escape out into the rest of the world. You know that, right? They'll do everything they can to keep them isolated right here. So they can deal with them in a relatively confined space."

Worry wrinkles bunched up on Terry's forehead. He leaned in a little closer, allowing his own hand to brush Jonas's now. Reaching out with his other hand, he pushed the tumble of dark hair back from Jonas's forehead. The touch was gentle. It was something a lover might do, and that didn't go unnoticed by Jonas. But still it wasn't enough to steer him away from what he really needed to say.

"Terry, if the authorities think there are only a couple of idiots like us left alive on this mountain, a couple of idiots too stupid or too stubborn to leave, don't you think they'll give us up as lost anyway. And go ahead with whatever contingency plan they've decided on."

"*What* contingency plan? Spit it out," Terry said. "What exactly are you trying to say?"

"Terry, if the authorities think that most of the civilian population in Spangle and on this mountain are either dead or gone, they're going to try to destroy the creatures in the quickest and most thorough way they can. Don't you think that's what they've been waiting for? The last thing they want is for these things to break free. If they do, there will be absolutely no stopping them, no holding them back. They'll breed, they'll spread, and… they'll feed. Everywhere. No one will be safe."

Terry had unknowingly tightened his grip around Jonas's hand. Finally, Jonas had to gently extract his hand before Terry snapped his fingers like matchsticks.

"What could they do?" Terry quietly asked. "The authorities. What could they do to destroy the creatures while they're still here? What is it that's worrying you so much?"

Jonas studied his face. "You honestly don't know?"

"No. Explain it to me."

Jonas sighed but then proceeded to do exactly that. "My guess would be they would go for a single massive strike. Wipe out the whole area. It would be the only sure way to annihilate all the creatures."

Terry scooted back on the couch and simply stared at Jonas, his face blank, empty. He mouthed the word "massive" under his breath. "How would they do that?" he asked, his voice muted and numb, as if he needed to know the answer but didn't really want to hear Jonas say it.

Jonas understood that completely. He didn't want to say it either.

"They could napalm the town and mountain. Or hell, they could drop a small nuclear device and wipe everything out. It's the only way they could be sure to succeed."

Jonas watched the reality sink in as Terry turned his head and peered through the cracks between the galvanized fence posts nailed across the nearest window. At the trees outside. At the birds, still frolicking in the rafters, unaware it was their futures at stake as well. Unaware that their little lives were hanging in the balance too. Past the birds, Terry stared out farther, through the trees and across the mountain to the meadows and the valleys he loved so much.

Oh so gently, as if the words were slipping away from his lips without any forethought, Terry whispered softly, "I do care for you, you know. I've cared for you since the first time we slept together. I know we've only known each other for less than two months, but it doesn't matter. I know how I feel. I've known it since the first time you touched me."

Jonas groaned his way to his feet and stepped around the coffee table to lower himself next to Terry on the couch. He took him into his arms and pulled Terry snug against him. With his lips in Terry's hair, he whispered, "I care for you too, Terry. I've known it just as long as you have. Now the question is, what should we do about it?"

Terry pulled back and studied Jonas's face. "What do you mean, what should we do? Are you talking about leaving?"

Jonas smiled then. "You don't want to leave. This is your home. And lately, I've sort of been thinking it's my home too. I love this cabin. This mountain. And you have a house in town. I've never seen it, but somehow I know I really want to spend time in it with you, if you'll let me."

"As lovers?" Terry asked, his green eyes wide and hopeful.

"Yes. As lovers, if you want."

Terry's bottom lip gave a tiny quiver, like a wee hypodermal earthquake had shifted the layout of his chin. He licked his lips and gazed down at Jonas's hand again, where it rested under his. Jonas could see him struggling to find his voice.

"Everything I have, Jonas, everything I am, is here on this mountain, in this town. My life. My past. All my memories. Everything I own. And ever since you came along, even my future is here, I hope. You know that, don't you?"

"Yes," Jonas said. "I do know that. And it's my future too. I don't imagine either one of us wants to see it all go up in a flash of napalm or be vaporized to pixie dust inside a mushroom cloud."

Terry almost smiled, because the thought was so horrific he had to lighten it in his thoughts somehow before he could really comprehend it. "God forbid we should ever let that happen." Then his face darkened again. The worry lines etched themselves back into his forehead. "But what can we do? How can we stop it?"

It was Jonas's turn to stare through the slats at the mountain outside, at the dusk settling over the cabin, at the starlings in the rafters working their way toward bedtime, their chittering quieter now, their stirrings less frantic.

"We have to find the creatures, Terry. We have to find them and destroy them ourselves before the authorities decide to take matters into their own hands. If we *can't* destroy them, then maybe we can tell the authorities exactly where they are so they can pinpoint their bombs with enough precision not to take out the rest of the area too."

"In the caves, you mean," Terry breathed, following Jonas's gaze. "We have to find the creatures in the caves."

"Yes. In the caves," Jonas said. He leaned in and buried a kiss in Terry's hair. He inhaled the delicious scent of the man and his cock shifted in his pants. Jesus, even under the threat of nuclear annihilation, he had the energy to erect a boner. *If that isn't love, what is?*

"That must be where they are," he said, ignoring his dick for once in his life, or trying to. "In the caves. Where else could they be? Tomorrow we'll really start to search. We've concentrated on reinforcing the cabin long enough. We checked out the one cave you knew about. Now it's time to check out the two on my map." He gripped Terry's shoulders and pushed him far enough away to look into his eyes. "You and me. We'll do it together."

"Of course," Terry whispered, nodding. "We do everything together, don't we?"

At that, Jonas almost smiled. "We do indeed."

Once again, Jonas's heart gave a leap. He leaned in closer, dragging Terry into his arms. They sat like that, staring into the fire, enjoying the silence, watching the darkness close in outside and thinking their own thoughts.

Later that night, after they made love, after the sparrows and the finches had settled down for the night and the fiery embers on the grate had crumbled to ash, Jonas lay naked with Terry in the bed at the top of the stairs. As the stillness gathered around them, he couldn't help wondering if the creatures were outside waiting. Growing hungrier now as their food supply dwindled. Desperation settling in. Longing for the scent of blood. The taste of flesh.

Aching. *Aching* to feed again.

And maybe, like Jonas and Terry, contemplating a search of their own to find it.

Chapter Sixteen

THE MOUNTAIN was small. Terry supposed if a person wanted to be technical about it, it might not truly qualify as a mountain at all. Just a mishmashed pyramid of boulders and trees and seams of granite bulged up into a heap by some long-ago terrestrial upheaval of earthquake, volcano, and converging tectonic plates. The landscape was peppered with wildlife, but there was humanity in residence too, or had been before the trouble started. Vacation homes were sprinkled here and there inside the piney woods, tucked in among copses and up against cliff faces. Alongside game trails, hiking paths and dirt roads for motorcycles and ATVs crisscrossed the terrain. One rutted lane, broad enough for vehicles, gave Terry's Jeep and the other residents' vehicles access up and down the mountain. The backbone of the mountain reached a height of less than 2,500 feet, even at its tallest point. It covered a grand total of 400 acres from the beginning of one rising slope to the conclusion of the other, yet it didn't have a name. To Terry it was just his mountain.

The town of Spangle, nestled at the foot of the mountain on the opposite side from where Terry's cabin sat, encompassed an even smaller landmass. Perhaps eighty acres, tops. No major highway connected Spangle to the rest of the world, only two-lane blacktops and a scattering of gravel roads. Once you were off the mountain and in the middle of town, you were in what could best be described as backcountry desert. The land was flat and hot and sandy. Rattlesnakes flourished in the summer, and every third or fourth winter, it might snow enough to draw the tourists from San Diego, many miles to the southwest.

Real estate wasn't as expensive on the mountain or in the town of Spangle as it was in the tonier California cities. Yet the mountain cabin and the little clapboard house in town where Terry had lived with Bobby, and from where he worked as a notary public, constituted the bulk of Terry's financial worth, and he would sorely hate to lose it.

If the authorities decided to blow the area sky-high in an effort to wipe the creatures off the face of the earth, they would pretty well wipe

Terry out as well. He would be left with nothing. And if he was still on the mountain when they dropped the bombs, he wouldn't even be left with his life. Nor would Jonas. They would be as dead as the creatures.

And that was unacceptable. Jonas loaded all the equipment into the back of the Jeep. They were both decked out in their modern-day coats of armor, as they were every time they went outside. Jonas had the .38 strapped to his waist in the holster they'd swiped from the sporting goods store in town, and Terry had his 16-guage shotgun dangling off his shoulder. Both guns were loaded, with the safeties on, and since neither man really knew much about firearms, Terry's greatest fear was they would accidentally shoot each other before the authorities had a chance to blow them up or the creatures got around to consuming them.

Equipment loaded, they angled their long legs into the Jeep and buckled up: Terry behind the wheel, Jonas in the passenger seat. Bruce stood on his back legs on the console between them, peering over the dash to watch the trail unfold before them. The little pug had howled his head off, refusing to be left behind this time, so Terry had him tethered to his leash, determined to take him along wherever he and Jonas decided to go.

They had lingered late in bed, then dawdled over breakfast, so part of the day was behind them when they started out. The late morning was crisp and nippy. The sky, a smudgeless blue bowl above their heads, was on full view through the mangled remains of the Jeep's canvas roof, that reminder of the creatures dragging Bobby through it to his death. The remaining tattered canvas was still discolored with Bobby's blood. Terry tried to keep his eyes turned away from the unintended skylight whenever he drove the Jeep.

Jonas clearly had no similar compunctions. He eyed the shredded canvas warily. "It's gonna be cold in this Jeep if the temperature drops much more. Maybe we should car shop the next time we go into town. Even if there aren't any car dealers, there must be a vehicle parked somewhere we can confiscate. Preferably something with a metal roof. Not a Ferrari. They're snazzy but too low-slung. They'd bottom out on the trails. Might make for a fast getaway, though, and God knows we'd look sexy sitting in one." He offered up a sneaky grin to show he was kidding.

"Funny," Terry sniped. But he shot Jonas a friendly wink nevertheless. "We'll check it out next time we're off the mountain."

Jonas rubbed his gloved hands together. "Goody. I love car shopping."

Terry clucked his tongue. "Don't give yourself airs. What you're talking about isn't car shopping. It's actually grand theft auto."

Jonas grinned. "Now, now, Bwana."

While Terry drove, Jonas unfolded the United States Geological Survey map and spread it out in front of him, holding it flat to the dash and away from the wind whipping through the cab. Ever since Jonas brought it with him to the cabin, he'd spent long hours in front of the fire studying the map. They had concentrated their first efforts on securing the cabin, but now that was out of the way, and it was time to get down to business. That business was called survival. And the only way for them to truly survive was to locate the creatures and destroy them before the authorities took it into their heads to blow up the whole frigging mountain.

The two cave entrances were clearly marked on the USGS map. Located by satellite Infrared Thermal Detection, or IR, they showed up as dark shadows opening to the mountain's surface. The maps only showed the cave openings, not the depth to which the caves descended or how far beneath the mountain's surface they spread.

From the corner of his eye, Terry watched Jonas stare intensely at the map, like he was trying to wring every piece of information he could glean from the damn thing. Jonas had drawn from that well of intensity before. When he was writing. When he was hunting. Hell, when he was making love. Everything Jonas did, he seemed to give it his all. As if he only had one chance for success, and he wasn't going to soften his approach until he got things right. Their relationship included. Even now, eyes fixed on the map, Jonas reached across the console behind Bruce and brought his hand to rest on Terry's thigh as if determined to keep Terry in the loop, perpetuating a connection, making sure he knew he wasn't forgotten even while Jonas's own thoughts were a million miles away.

Terry liked that intensity about Jonas. He liked Jonas's need to touch, his desire to maintain a bridge between them at all times.

Raising his voice loud enough to carry over the wind and the roar of the old Jeep as it grumbled its way up the side of the mountain, Terry said without taking his eyes off the road, "I'll still want to be with you, you know. Even when this is all over."

Jonas didn't appear touched by Terry's statement. He didn't appear moved or surprised. Continuing to stare at the map, he simply answered, "I'll still want to be with you too."

Terry placed his hand over Jonas's and pressed them both against his belly while with the other hand he steered the Jeep up the potholed lane. "If there's a mountain left standing, will you live with me here? Or do you have to go back to the city for your work?"

Jonas shrugged, his eyes still on the map. "I'm a writer. I can work anywhere. How about you?"

It was Terry's turn to shrug. "This is my home. I'd like to stay here. Being a substitute teacher, I'm used to commuting. I'm on call with six different school districts, some as far away as San Diego. The notary work I do out of my house in town is my bread and butter."

"So we'll manage, then," Jonas said.

Terry smiled. "Yeah. If we find the creatures and destroy them, and we don't go to prison for looting, and if we can avoid getting nuked by the Feds, and you don't wrap our stolen Ferrari around a tree with us in it, then I suppose we'll manage."

The Jeep hit a rut, and all three occupants bounced skyward. Bruce gave a startled yelp and scrambled to keep his back feet beneath him. Jonas howled, "Ow!" when he came down hard and drove his asscheek into the pistol strapped to his hip.

Terry reached over and scratched Bruce's ears. Bruce gave him a grateful lick in return, then continued to cling to the dash and eye the road ahead. His little tail whipped back and forth in anticipation. Christopher Bruce Columbus, pug dog extraordinaire, eyes on the horizon, worlds to conquer.

"Do you know where we're headed?" Jonas asked, rubbing his butt.

"I think so. I'm still cross-eyed from studying that damn map for hours last night, but I think I've got it all figured out."

"Have you been in this cave before?"

"No, but the map is pretty clear. I can find it without too much trouble."

They rode on in silence. The day was coming awake, the sun clawing its way toward the top of that vast blue bowl of sky overhead. The surrounding trees were bristling with wildlife—birds, squirrels, and chipmunks galore. In no hurry whatsoever, a skunk and its three young ones waddled across the trail up ahead. Terry slammed on the brakes and waited patiently while the animals meandered one by one into the underbrush, leaving the scent of ammonia behind.

Terry downshifted to low and goosed the Jeep up the last steep incline. Wheels spinning, throwing up dirt and mulch in their wake, the vehicle topped the mountain's crest and began descending the other side. In the distance, they could see the town of Spangle sprawled out below. The buildings looked deserted. No smoke rose from chimneys. No vehicles moved along the dusty streets.

"Ghost town," Jonas whispered, as if in wonder.

"There are a few people there," Terry answered. "I'm sure of it. All of them wouldn't have fled. And all of them can't be dead either. Maybe they're hiding out in the school auditorium or the public library. Someplace big enough where they could all be together."

"Why wouldn't they leave?"

Terry shrugged. "Same reason I didn't, I suppose. It's their home. And a lot of people around here have a sort of frontier mentality. Stubborn. Antiestablishment. Liking a good fight and deathly determined to hold on to what's theirs."

As if to prove his point that there were still people in residence, Terry pointed. "See? There. Look!"

A lone figure, an older man by the way he moved, was running along the sidewalk in front of the town's one and only movie house, which had been closed and boarded up for years.

Jonas gave a soft whistle. "Wow. He's really moving. Is he being chased?"

Terry shook his head. Sadly. "I don't know." As if suddenly wearied by what he'd seen, Terry slipped the Jeep into gear and trundled forward, riding his brake down the steep incline, descending the mountain slowly. He'd traveled less than three hundred yards when he pulled off the path, tucking the Jeep into a bank of shadow from an ancient pine tree that had probably been on the mountain longer than the two of them had been alive. The bright sunlight blinked out as if someone had flipped a switch. Under the pines it was forever dusk, an inch away from night. The birds in the branches fell silent, watching them. Leery. Waiting to see what they were going to do.

Terry lifted his chin, indicating the hazy tangle of trees ahead. "According to your map, the cave is right in there," he said. "Maybe a hundred yards into the woods."

Terry popped his door open and set a single foot onto the mulchy ground. Before he could set the other foot down, a woman's scream echoed across the mountain. The cry was so sharp, a flock of starlings exploded from the trees. Goose bumps popped up on the back of Terry's neck, and he damn near lost his balance. Jonas was rattled too. He came scurrying around the Jeep to grab Terry by the arm and hiss in his ear.

"Who was that? Where did it come from?"

Terry grabbed the shotgun from the back seat and flipped the safety off. "Arm yourself," he whispered.

With shaking fingers, Jonas released the .38 from its holster and tripped the safety. He held the gun out to his side, pointed up. With his other hand he clutched at the back of Terry's jacket.

Terry tied Bruce's leash to the steering wheel to assure he wouldn't follow, then stooping low, he and Jonas headed into the trees.

Chapter Seventeen

ANOTHER SCREAM of terror rolled over them. It was definitely a woman, and she was definitely close. There was an echoing quality to the scream, like it had come from the bottom of a well.

Or the depths of a cave, Jonas suddenly realized.

Jonas was so unnerved by the woman's tortured wail he could barely catch his breath. He crept along through the trees at Terry's back, chewing his bottom lip, looking in every direction at once. Imagining threats that weren't there. Hearing noises that didn't exist. His muscles were so knotted up he could barely walk. It was a chore to put one quaking foot in front of the other without falling flat on his face. The gun was dead weight in his hand. He pointed it straight up into the air now for fear he would stumble and shoot Terry in the back.

He hooked his chin over Terry's shoulder and whispered, "Shouldn't we be running the other way?"

"Hush!" Terry whispered back. He lifted his shotgun higher, calmly pointing it straight ahead. The barrel wasn't shaking at all. Jonas had to give Terry credit for all that composure. He certainly wasn't showing much himself.

By the time they slipped from between the last of the trees, the screaming up ahead had stopped. The silence left behind was even more nerve-racking than the scream. They stepped out onto a small bald. The bald, or meadow, was located at the base of a steep cliff that looked to Jonas's untrained eye like a sweep of sandstone rising up from the face of the mountain. Parts of the cliff face had only recently broken away, perhaps due to the rain, and avalanched down the hill, gathering into a mound of debris at the foot of it. Streams of mud, great boulders as big as automobiles, and a lot of cliffside foliage, including a few fallen trees, had been swept down the hill in the collapse.

Off to the side of the mess, Jonas could see a smudge of black between two vast heaps of scree and stone. The smudge was clearly a blob of shadow. And the shadow clearly led into the very cave they had been searching for.

Of the woman who had screamed, there was no sign.

Terry stepped closer to the cave entrance. He placed his feet carefully among the loose rocks, probably to avoid losing his footing, to say nothing of trying to keep his approach silent. Jonas, still clutching at the back of Terry's jacket, stuck to him like glue. His little .38 was still pointed skyward where he couldn't kill anybody if it accidently went off.

The opening to the cave was far larger than the last one they had entered. This time there was no need to crawl at all. The entrance was pretty much the size of an ordinary door, without the smooth edges, maybe seven feet high and three across at its broadest point.

To Jonas's dismay, Terry didn't hesitate. He switched on his Maglite and slipped through the entrance. Reluctantly, Jonas followed. He still had his face mask down, as did Terry, but once they were inside Terry lifted his so he could see better in the dark. Jonas left his face covered, unsure what he was about to find. In other words, unsure if some of the flying creatures were in here waiting to suck his face off.

Another scream erupted, this time far closer and far louder. It came from somewhere ahead of them in the shadows. The sound was so piercing and startling, Jonas jumped and almost dropped his gun.

The next sound they heard was even more startling. It was the full-throated growl of a cat. Not a house cat. A *large* cat. Like a mountain lion. In fact, Jonas quickly realized, it wasn't *like* a mountain lion at all. It fucking *was* a mountain lion.

The animal was hidden behind a mound of shattered rocks, scree, and shale-like spears of stone. The mass in the middle of the cavern came from a rockfall that had collapsed part of the roof. Jonas could see the scar in the light of Terry's flashlight beam. Like outside, this fall looked to be fairly recent. Standing on the opposite side of the heap from Terry and Jonas stood a woman and a young girl of about eight, visible from the waist up. The child had hair even redder than Terry's. She was clutching at the terrified woman—who, judging by her own flaming red hair, was the child's mother—beside her. They were both staring goggle-eyed in horror at whatever had made the growling noise on the other side of the rocks, where Jonas couldn't see.

Once again, Terry's calm astounded him. He slowly, step by careful step, moved around the mound of fallen stone, easing closer to the woman and child. And to the hidden menace lurking on the other side.

He spoke quietly, as if sharing confidences over a cup of tea. "There's nothing to be afraid of," Terry told the woman as he kept moving closer, craning his neck, trying to see what the threat really was. "My friend and I have guns. We'll protect you. I need to know. Are there any of the flying creatures in this cave?"

The woman remained staring straight ahead, speechless with terror. The child looked up at her mother, then squinted into the beam of Terry's flashlight. "We haven't seen any," she said, her voice quivery but steady enough under the circumstances. "We were trying to get off the mountain when our car died. Mommy said we ran out of gas. She was afraid to stay outside, so she brought us in here to hide." She raised her arm and pointed to whatever was invisible to Jonas thanks to the heap of rocks. "Then we ran into *that*."

"Mountain lion?" Terry quietly asked, still unable to see what was hidden behind the rocks.

The girl mutely nodded. "A big one," she said on the back of a sob. "I think it's mad at us for being here."

"Are either of you bleeding?"

The girl shook her head, finding her voice again. "No. We aren't hurt. But daddy was killed yesterday. Th-those things. They took him. One minute he was there, and the next minute he… wasn't." The child bit back a sob while trying to stand up straighter, trying to show her courage. "That's why we're leaving. Mommy said there's nothing to keep us in Spangle now." She edged closer to her mother, then trained her eyes back into the beam of Terry's light. "Can you shoot it, please," she asked in a little-girl voice. "It's starting to wiggle its butt like our kitty cat does. That's what happens when she's getting ready to pounce on a mouse."

Jonas could hear Terry's voice soften as he tried to calm the child's fears. "So in this case, you'd rather not be the mouse?"

The girl nodded, although the feeble attempt at humor seemed to be lost on her. No surprise there.

"Yes, please," the girl whispered anyway. And turning, she buried her face in her mother's hip.

It was only then that the mother seemed to snap out of her trance. She splayed her hand across the back of her daughter's head and turned to Terry for the first time.

"Should we come to you?" she asked, struggling to find her voice.

"No," Terry said. "Don't move. I'll come to you."

Casting a glance back at Jonas, he said, "You stay here and cover me. If you have to shoot, don't hit the woman or the kid. Or me. Aim for the cat if it attacks."

"I can't *see* the cat!" Jonas hissed.

"Neither can I," Terry said. And with that, he moved farther around the mound of rock, seeking a cleaner line of sight. Before he found it, he looked back at Jonas one more time. "Keep your face mask down. If anyone gets hurt, the creatures will be on top of us in seconds."

"What about you?" Jonas all but accused, and Terry reluctantly lowered his visor.

Jonas's gun arm was starting to cramp up. After all this time, the stupid .38 felt like it weighed ten pounds. Jonas was pretty sure if he did have to shoot, he couldn't hit an elephant. Let alone a charging mountain lion.

He took a step forward.

"Stay!" Terry snapped, like Jonas was a misbehaving cocker spaniel.

So Jonas stayed. But he wasn't happy about it.

Terry turned back around to face the problem. He edged deeper into the cavern, skirting the heap of rocks and approaching the mother and child. They hadn't moved, and they were no longer watching him. Their eyes were frozen on the cat that was still hidden from Jonas's view.

But not from Terry's. "I see it," he quietly said. He forced up a smile for the girl's benefit. "It's a big one, just like you said." Jonas could hear the tension in Terry's voice even while he was trying to stay calm for the benefit of the young woman and her daughter. Of the two of them, Jonas decided, it was the daughter who was holding it together best. The mother not so much. There were tears streaming down her horrified face, and she was clutching her daughter so tightly that the kid was starting to squirm under the mother's mindless grip.

Jonas froze when Terry lifted his shotgun, aiming it at the big cat Jonas still could not see.

"Don't move," Terry told the two yet again. This time as soon as the words were out, he took a shooter's stance and propped the shotgun securely against his shoulder, ready to fire if he had to.

Jonas saw a mere glimpse of a tawny tail whipping back and forth above the rocks. Apparently, Terry had its attention now, and the beast wasn't happy about it. Jonas cringed every time he heard a *chuff* of expelled air or the *sccritchh* of claws raking hard stone. The cat was furious.

"Ease back into the shadows," Terry calmly ordered the woman. "I'll try to drive the cat outside."

Jonas realized suddenly that if the mother and daughter were blocking one escape route for the big cat, and Terry was blocking the other, then the damn thing would have to fly straight at him if Terry did actually manage to scare it away.

"Wait!" he started to call out.

But before he had a chance, a horrible caterwauling rose up behind him. It was so unexpected, Jonas almost keeled over in a dead faint, thinking there was another troop of lions bearing down on him. But when he spun around to face this brand-new terror, all he saw was a tiny shadow whipping past his feet, trailing a bright blue leash behind it.

It was Bruce! The little pug! And he looked really pissed.

Without hesitation, Bruce flew around the edge of rocks on his short little legs. He ignored Terry altogether and planted himself smack in front of the big cat. Bruce stood there, trembling in fury, hopping up and down like an irate Chihuahua. He growled and snapped and barked and yipped and made enough noise for ten dogs. His hackles rose on his tawny back, making him look considerably larger than he actually was, which was still pretty damn small. Fearlessly, he bared his little teeth at the cat that weighed about twenty times more than he did. In all the confusion, the mountain lion lost a bit of its bluster. It took a step back, clearly confused. When Bruce growled deep in his throat, the cat shuffled back a little more.

"Bruce, no!" Terry cried. He lunged forward to reach for the pug to yank him out of danger, but Bruce danced to the side, eluding his grasp. Still trailing his blue leash, the little dog snarled like a grizzly and launched himself straight for the lion's throat. Caught totally off guard, the mountain lion defied gravity completely. It sprang straight up into the air like it had been shot from a catapult. The lion pounced to the top of the mound of stones. From there, it gave a leap and sprang out over Jonas's head—who almost had a stroke—and flung itself through the cave door. With a clatter of stones and final roar of fury, it disappeared into the trees.

Jonas stood there stunned, his heart stuck in his throat. Not really thinking about what he was doing, he felt his crotch to see if he'd wet himself. He hadn't. But then the day wasn't over yet.

He turned back to face the interior of the cave and followed the beam of Terry's flashlight. It was casting a perfect circle of light on the mother and child, both of them looking shell-shocked by what had transpired. The mother was clearly struggling to pull herself together as she aimed terrified eyes at the two of them.

"Help us get down off this mountain," she pleaded, still clutching her daughter close. "Please."

Only then did Terry and Jonas exhale. And a moment later they were shaking themselves to action.

Chapter Eighteen

"Do you need food or water?" Terry asked.

The woman and daughter were standing at the side of the trail, about a quarter mile up from where Terry had parked earlier. Jonas was in the act of pouring gasoline into the tank of the woman's bright yellow Camry at the spot where it had run out of fuel. There was a large smear of dried blood on the car's front fender, which Terry thought it best not to ask about.

It was only after they were out in the sunlight that Terry recognized the woman. He didn't know her name, but she was one of the town's librarians and worked in the public library. He remembered she had helped him find a book on Thoreau once.

If the woman recognized him, she didn't let on. In fact, she didn't let on much of anything. She looked like she had been through a lot, and it had left her dazed. Her eyes were a little crazy, and they kept shooting back to her daughter to make sure the child was safe.

"We're sorry about your husband," Terry said softly, not wanting to draw the attention of the girl, who was sitting on the ground petting Bruce.

The woman nodded. She opened her mouth to speak, decided those weren't the words she wanted, then weakly admitted, "He didn't stand a chance."

"No," Terry said, flashing back on Bobby's death. "I don't suppose he did." He watched Jonas fiddle with the gas can for a minute, then turned back to the woman. "Will you drive down to the foot of the mountain where the authorities are and turn yourselves in?"

She nodded. "There's nothing left for us here. We have to leave. I have to get Jilly out." Again she turned her eyes on her daughter. The woman's face was dirty, her clothes streaked with clay from the cave. The child was even dirtier, but at the moment she seemed okay. She was humming softly to herself while she patted Bruce.

The mother showed no interest in who Terry and Jonas were or what they thought they were accomplishing by staying on the mountain. She didn't seem aware that the two strangers had saved her and her daughter's life. She was concerned with getting away and nothing else. Terry suspected she was about one more surprise away from a nervous breakdown, and Terry couldn't blame her. Sometimes, at least before Jonas came along, he used to think he was at that point too.

He let his gaze fall on the girl, who was still humming and cradling Bruce in her lap. Bruce was looking very pleased with himself, Terry thought. And for good reason.

The girl's eyes were wide and bright as she tore them from the pug and centered them on Terry's face. "You should give him an extra treat tonight," she said, indicating the dog. "For saving our lives, I mean. He was very brave."

Jonas and Terry both smiled. Jonas said, "He was, wasn't he?"

The girl nodded, and then a tear slid down her cheek. "I'm sorry we're leaving. I'd like to be his friend."

Terry moved to the girl and knelt beside her. He ruffled Bruce's ears and offered a gentle smile to the girl. "When this is all over, you can come visit him anytime you want. You and your mom both. Okay?"

The girl nodded, then gazed up at her mom standing over her. Her mother didn't seem to have heard anything that was said. She simply stood there, watching Jonas pour gas into her tank. Looking impatient. The car keys tinkled in her hand as she turned them over and over, obviously eager to leave.

Jonas and Terry both studied the woman. It was Jonas who finally spoke the obvious.

"Are you sure you can drive?" he asked gently. "Terry and I can drive you down off the mountain if you like. We'll have to bow out before you actually make contact with the authorities. Otherwise they may not let us return."

The woman's eyes were empty and cold. She appeared almost angry at the men when she said, "Why would you want to return? There's nothing here but death." Jonas didn't seem to have an answer for that. He turned from the woman's glare and jiggled the last few splashes of gasoline from the five-gallon can into her tank. "Just be careful," he said, skirting his eyes to the girl. "Take care of your daughter."

The woman didn't respond.

The girl was watching them all. Her innocent gaze traveled from Jonas to Terry to her mother. When her eyes reached her mother and settled there, the fear came back into them. With a sigh, she reached up anyway and took her mother's hand.

"We'll be okay," she said, as stalwart and strong as her mother clearly wasn't. "Mommy's a good driver."

"Jilly's a pretty name," Terry said.

The girl simply nodded. "I like it." With that, she stared back down at Bruce in her lap and smiled. She pressed her face into the pug's neck and closed her eyes. Bruce licked her ear. At that moment, Terry could see how frightened the child really was. He toyed with the idea of taking the two down the mountain whether the mother wanted him to or not but quickly decided it wasn't his place to demand it. The woman had been through enough. He didn't think she could take much more drama. Truth be told, neither could he.

He turned to the mother to ask a question, and at the last moment, shifted the question to the girl. "How long were you in the cave?"

She thought about that, glancing only once at her mother, who didn't seem to have heard what Terry said. "Maybe a couple of hours," the girl said. "It was scary and dark. I was just starting to get cold when the mountain lion came crawling out of the back. I guess we woke it up."

"And you didn't see any of the flying creatures while you were in there? No sign of them? No sounds? No droppings."

The child shook her head. "Mommy wouldn't have stayed if we had. She hates them."

Jonas stepped in on that one. "We all hate them, honey."

The girl only nodded. "I know."

"Do you have a place to go when you get off the mountain?" Terry asked.

"Mommy has a friend in San Diego. I guess we're going there."

Terry turned to the mother once more, gauging her ability to drive, her ability to protect her daughter. "Go slow," he said. "The trail is rough. When you get through town and reach the highway on the other side, stop when the cops flag you down. Don't try to drive away from them. They may be authorized to shoot. You'll be okay once they realize you're only trying to find safe haven." At least he hoped they would.

"Do you need money?" Jonas asked.

The mother rested her empty eyes on him. "For what?"

Jonas was obviously taken aback by the blankness of her stare. He cut a glance to Terry, before turning back to the woman. "I-I'm not sure. Food maybe. More gas."

"He just wants you to be safe," Terry interjected. "We both do."

"We'll be fine," the mother said. She waved impatiently at the gas can in Jonas's hands. "Aren't you finished yet?"

Jonas looked so startled to be snapped at that Terry almost laughed. He stepped forward and screwed the gas cap back on the woman's car while Jonas set the empty can aside to be taken back to the Jeep when they were ready to leave.

Terry studied the woman yet again. She yanked her daughter to her feet, dumping Bruce in the grass. "We're leaving now," she stated flatly.

Jilly tore free and rushed to Terry. Wrapping her arms around his legs and looking up into his face, she said, "Thank you for saving our lives." Her eyes, bright with tears, wandered to Jonas. "Both of you." Releasing Terry's legs, she stepped back and surrendered her hand back to her mother. She stared down at the little pug and said, "Bye, little guy."

Bruce wagged his tail in response, and Terry and Jonas mumbled, "You're welcome."

Terry reached out to the mother, then just as quickly withdrew his hand. Her attitude wasn't exactly pleading for physical contact.

"Be careful," he said. "Don't stop for anything until you reach the highway. Let the authorities take care of you from there. I'm sure you'll be fine."

The mother stared at him without emotion. If his words soaked in, she didn't let on. She merely pushed her daughter through the Camry's rear door and slammed it shut behind her. The mother climbed into the front, checked to make sure all the windows were up, then turned the key in the ignition. The engine roared to life.

Without a glance at the men watching her, the woman slipped the car in gear and took off, spitting out a spray of pebbles in her wake.

Terry saw a tiny hand appear in the back window before the dust on the lane rose up to erase the yellow Camry from view.

Jonas stepped close and tucked his hand in Terry's jacket pocket. Leaving it there, Terry dropped his head to Jonas's shoulder and watched the car disappear down the mountain.

"I guess this cave is clean," he said.

Jonas looked down at himself. Like the mother, he was covered in clay and muck. "Wish I could say the same for me."

Terry smiled. "A shower will set us right. Let's go home. I'll wash your back."

Jonas lifted his head and studied Terry's guileless expression. "Nothing much rattles you, does it?"

"Losing you might do it," Terry answered.

They both let the silence reclaim them. With Bruce sitting at their feet, they all three stared down the path to where the Camry had disappeared in the distance.

"I guess we saved their lives," Jonas mumbled. "Cue the ticker-tape parade." He said it as a matter of irony, clearly not trying to hide his disappointment at the woman's lack of gratitude.

Terry lifted his head and brushed a kiss across Jonas's cheek. "Don't worry. One of these days she'll wake up and realize what we did. She'll thank us then." Again Terry stared down the trail to where the car had vanished. "Poor kid," he said as a shuddery afterthought.

"Yes." Jonas sighed, his eyes worried, his voice sad. "Poor kid indeed."

Chapter Nineteen

KNEELING IN the shower spray, Jonas stroked his soapy hands over the back of Terry's pale thighs. Terry's legs were heavily muscled and beautiful. Tree trunks. The pelt of ginger hair that covered his legs was swept into dark rivulets by the rushing water. Unable to restrain himself, Jonas pressed a kiss through the streaming water sluicing down Terry's back, dragging his tongue south. With his heart thumping in his ear like a tom-tom, he burrowed into the crevice of Terry's ass and lapped at his opening, smiling to himself when Terry gave a groan of pleasure from on high. When Terry's hand came down to cup the back of Jonas's head and hold him in place, Jonas figured he was getting the go-ahead, so he gleefully burrowed deeper with his tongue.

Terry trembled in pleasure and opened his legs even more, giving Jonas all the access he could offer. In appreciation, Jonas reached down to touch his own erection, so filled with blood it ached. He gave his own ecstatic shudder, really starting to get into it, when Terry spun around and tugged him to his feet.

Under the warm spray, Terry wrapped him tightly in his strong arms and brought their mouths together. Terry's long cock, lathered with Ivory soap, slid across Jonas's stomach, causing both men to buck. When their tongues touched, Jonas almost came. He opened his mouth wider into the kiss and gave himself up completely to this towering man who was everything he had ever hoped to find.

If only it hadn't been at the tail end of the world when he found him.

"Fuck me," Jonas gasped into the kiss. "Right here. Fuck me."

Terry reached down and wrapped silky fingers around Jonas's dick, began gently stroking the hardness he found. Jonas's legs turned to rubber, and his knees almost buckled. He clung to Terry to keep from collapsing at his feet.

Terry laughed quietly through the spray and eased Jonas around to face the shower wall. With his soapy hand, he opened Jonas up, one finger at a time. Gently, but persistently.

Loving every second of it, Jonas stood shivering, his cheek splayed flat against the wet tile, his eyes squeezed shut in bliss, drooling in anticipation. Terry eased three fingers into him and gently massaged his prostate. The enjoyment factor ratcheted up exponentially. Jonas cried out because he couldn't seem not to, but his cry was mixed with a laugh. Jesus, it felt so *good.*

"We're wasting water," Terry said, his voice husky with need.

"So turn it off," Jonas almost wept. "Just don't stop doing what you're doing."

"Bossy," Terry grunted, sliding the head of his cock over Jonas's opening. Teasing. Offering up a preview of coming attractions as it were.

How he did it with one hand directing his dick and the other clamped across Jonas's belly, Jonas wasn't sure—elbow maybe—but the shower spray instantly stopped. He was about to comment on Terry's dexterity, when a rod of steel slid effortlessly into his butt. It inserted itself all the way up to his diaphragm, or so it felt, and whatever Jonas had been about to say was lost in the moment. He couldn't have made a coherent statement if he'd tried.

Neither man seemed prone to conversation anyway.

Terry's cock was fat with hunger, and Jonas happily accepted every millimeter of it.

Terry buried his face in the back of Jonas's soap-drenched hair and grunted unhappily, "I'm afraid this'll be a quickie."

Jonas shuddered as the massive cockhead slid so deep into his ass it tickled his throat. At least that was the impression he got. "W-why?" he managed to stutter, reaching behind him, trying to drag Terry deeper.

Terry's breath caught and his dick swelled up even more. "Because I'm about to come!"

"*Already?*" Jonas gasped.

"Some people are never satisfied," Terry carped. In the same moment he arched his chest against Jonas's back, and to Jonas's full-throated delight, drove his cock into Jonas's innards to the deepest point yet.

Both men bellowed with glee as the juices exploded from their bodies. Terry's, thanks to a quick withdrawal, exploded in a solid stream across Jonas's back clear up to his hairline. And Jonas's splattered in white blobby smears across the shower-stall wall.

When he was certain his heart wasn't going to pump him into an early grave, Jonas slipped around in Terry's arms and faced him. Their mouths came together in a gasping kiss as Jonas clutched Terry to him as tightly as he could.

"Wow," he managed to mutter within the kiss.

"Wow," Terry muttered back, a grin creeping into his voice.

Jonas blinked his eyes open and tried not to slobber. "Feeling funky. I think we need to shower again."

"Good idea," Terry said, and again without any seeming action on Terry's part, the showerhead burst back to life and both men bellowed yet again, this time because the water that cascaded over them was icy cold.

"You need a b-bigger water heater."

"B-blow me."

They made quick work of their showers, then dried themselves off. Still naked, Terry banked the fire in the fireplace while Jonas cooed over Bruce, who was looking offended that he had been left out of the lovemaking.

With the fire safely managed, the dog placated, and the last of the day's sunlight streaming through the slatted cabin windows, Terry and Jonas climbed the stairs hand in hand and slipped into bed. Immediately Jonas rolled into Terry's arms. The action was as natural as breathing to Jonas now. Terry seemed to accept it as the proper order of things as well. And that pleased Jonas very much.

He opened his eyes to study Terry's face. He saw worry there, and he knew immediately what it was about.

"You're thinking about the girl and her mother," Jonas said, his voice soft, still ragged around the edges from what had taken place in the shower.

Terry gave a faint nod. "I hope they made it out all right."

"We did everything we could."

Terry's eyes found Jonas and a little of the worry left his face. He slid his thumb across Jonas's bottom lip, then leaned in to lightly kiss the same spot. "I know we did," he said. His gaze slipped to the window, so Jonas's did the same.

In another thirty minutes it would be completely dark. As usual, the starlings and the wrens were chittering in the eaves outside the window. Once in a while, a pair of wings would thud against the glass, smearing the dust and leaving a feathery imprint.

Bruce took the opportunity to burrow under the blankets at the foot of the bed. He emitted a great sigh, snuggling happily between their four feet, sharing his warmth like a hot-water bottle. He instantly fell asleep. Jonas tucked his toes under the little dog, enjoying the heat. For even more enjoyable heat, he snuggled close to Terry, pressing his face into his furry chest.

"I'm glad I'm here with you," he whispered. "I'm glad you let me in."

"Into the cabin?" Terry asked. But he was smiling when he said it.

Jonas rolled his eyes for effect. "You know that's not what I meant." He tapped a fingertip to Terry's chest, right over the spot where his heart should be. "I meant I'm glad you let me in *here.*"

Terry grinned. "Oh, that. Yes. I'm glad I let you in there too."

"You were more romantic when you had me nailed to the shower wall. I can still feel you inside me."

Terry's eyes grew bright in the fading light. Sweetness seemed to radiate from them. "Can you really?"

"Yeah."

Terry's eyes softened even more. "You were incredible." Heat rose to Jonas's cheeks, but he didn't respond. Not in words, at any rate. Inside, his heart ramped up to a flurry of tiny beats, and Jonas figured that was response enough. He stroked a hand across Terry's cheek. Terry was clean-shaven at the moment, but that wouldn't last long. He'd have a ginger-colored five-o'clock shadow before the night was half over. By tomorrow morning he would be back to being a Yeti, or close to one.

Their eyes remained locked on each other.

Again Terry slid his thumb across Jonas's bottom lip. He opened his mouth to speak, then appeared to think better of it. He simply quieted, pulling Jonas closer against his chest.

"I can hear your heart," Jonas whispered.

"Good," Terry whispered back. "I want you to hear my heart."

They fell silent then. Jonas concentrated on the thudding of Terry's heart and the cacophony of birdsong outside the cabin window. He wondered what Terry was thinking, but since he had no way of knowing and was too lazy to ask, he tried not to worry about it. Even if it was about the two of them, Jonas felt sure Terry wasn't about to throw him out on his ear. Not if the elongating dick brushing Jonas's thigh said anything about it.

Both men tensed at the distant thump of helicopter rotors, throbbing in the evening sky. It didn't sound particularly close, but it wasn't that far away either. Terry was the first to climb from the bed, still naked and aroused, and patter down the stairs. Jonas traipsed along at his heels, enjoying the view of Terry's bare ass descending in front of him.

Without hesitating, Terry flung open the cabin door and stepped out onto the porch.

The cold evening air struck Jonas's naked body like a splash of ice water. It was the first time either of them had been outside in the open air without protective clothing since Jonas came to the cabin.

Unsure they should be doing it now, Jonas reached out and laid a tentative hand on Terry's shoulder. Terry seemed to understand what Jonas was silently asking.

"It'll be okay, babe. We'll go back inside in a minute."

Jonas stood at Terry's side. They lifted their heads and gazed over the treetops to the south. Terry could see the helicopter perhaps half a mile away, its port and starboard lights blinking. It was making back-and-forth sweeps across Terry's side of the mountain. They could see a flurry of white stuff fluttering in the sky in the helicopter's wake, slowly sifting down through the air to land among the trees.

"What the…?"

"They're dropping flyers," Terry explained. "I have a bad feeling about this."

Jonas gave his head a shake. "I don't understand. What do you mean, you have a bad feeling about this? Why? What's the problem? Why are they dropping flyers?"

"Just wait," Terry said, the muscles in his jaw working, his eyes riveted on the reeling helicopter in the distance.

The helicopter was drawing closer now. Unless it veered away entirely, it would be over the cabin in less than a minute.

Terry clamped a viselike grip around Jonas's wrist. "Let's go inside. I don't want them to see us."

"Why?"

"Just do it!" Terry snapped. Without waiting for a response, he pulled Jonas back through the cabin door and slammed it shut. He moved immediately to the little window beside the door, while Jonas pressed his nose to the glass on the other side. Their vision was impeded by the metal slats Terry had nailed across the panes.

Outside, the throbbing of the helicopter grew louder.

"They'll know we're here anyway," Jonas said quietly. "They'll see the smoke from the chimney."

Terry nodded, still peering through the glass. "I don't care. I want to see what the flyers say."

The men stood naked, one at either window alongside the cabin door. The room was cold, and a rash of goose bumps crawled up Jonas's back. He could hear Bruce growling from the bed upstairs.

The throb of the distant helicopter became a sudden roar, and Jonas knew it was directly overhead, buzzing the cabin. He waited. Breath held. Wondering what would happen next.

He moved to Terry's side, figuring he would much rather wait there. Terry accepted him into his space with a worried smile. He reached out and tugged him close. Together, cheek to cheek, they stared through the same window.

In the waning light, specks of shadow skittered across the ground beyond the cabin porch. Hot in the shadows' wake, like great, fat snowflakes, white sheets of paper wafted down to pepper the yard, rustling and fluttering as they came. Catching in the trees. Settling on the porch steps. Sailing past the windows all around.

While the sheets of white paper still drifted down, the scream of the hovering helicopter rose to a fevered pitch. The machine tilted off to the south, rotors *blatting*. In moments it had disappeared into the southern sky, back toward the tiny town of Spangle. Back from where it came.

Without waiting any longer, Terry pulled open the cabin door and stepped outside, Jonas at his side.

Flyers were everywhere. They still danced across the ground, tossed in the wind, drifting against the cabin walls, fluttering through the hole in the Jeep's roof. The trees surrounding the cabin were decorated with them.

In a single motion, Jonas and Terry knelt down and scooped flyers off the ground. One for each of them. They stared at the words written on the paper.

Then they turned and stared at each other.

This time when Terry looked worried, Jonas understood why.

Chapter Twenty

"THREE DAYS!" Terry spat. "Three fucking days! Then they're going to blow everything sky-high. The town, the mountain, everything!"

Jonas pawed at Terry's arm. "How can they do that? What about your house and the cabin?"

Terry gave his head an angry shake. "I guess they figure we're dispensable. They're determined to keep the creatures contained no matter what."

"You mean wipe them out."

"Yes. Wipe them out. I have no problem with that. What I do have a problem with is the fact they don't seem to mind wiping the rest of us out with them. Or blowing up our homes."

Jonas stared down at the flyer in his hand. "They don't call them creatures. They call them parasites."

"Can't argue with them on that point."

Terry had read the flyer a dozen times already, but he still couldn't believe it. "They don't say what kind of weapons they're going to use."

"No. They don't," Jonas said.

Terry could feel his face getting hotter by the minute. Everything he owned was here. On this mountain. Back in town. And it wasn't only Terry who had something to lose. Terry planned on Jonas playing a part in his future life. He planned on making this place a home for both of them.

His heart climbed into his throat when he uttered the words for the first time. "We love each other. We both want to stay here. We can't let them do this."

Quietly, Jonas said, "You really do love me, then."

Terry's anger softened. "You know I do," he said, his eyes distracted now, studying Jonas's face. "And you love me, right?"

Jonas swallowed hard and said, "You know I do."

They shared a look for perhaps three seconds, then Terry crunched the flyer into a ball and flung it to the ground. Reaching out, he raked his fingers through Jonas's hair, soaking up the warmth of his skin. The air was cold. He could see the goose bumps across Jonas's chest and feel them across his own. After all, as cold as it was, they were still buckass naked. He massaged Jonas's ear with his thumb. Even with the world about to fall apart around them, he bit back a smile when his cock began to fill with blood. When Jonas glanced down at it lengthening in front of him, and his own cock began swelling in response, Terry smiled even wider.

Jonas didn't stare at Terry's dick for long. He looked back at the flyer in his hand, then lifted his gaze to Terry's face. "We can't let this happen. We have to find the creatures first and destroy them before they do."

Terry blinked. Incredulous at what Jonas had said. "How are we supposed to do that?"

Jonas shrugged like the answer was simple. "They must be in the last cave. It's the only place we haven't searched."

Terry frowned. His mind on other matters, his dick beginning to wilt. "So we just storm in and kill them? You don't really think it'll be that easy, do you?"

Jonas shrugged again. A stubborn light ignited his eyes. Like the fuse on a firecracker, they started spitting sparks. When the sun began to dip below the horizon, Terry noticed that Jonas's eyes had gone a deeper hazel. The cognac color had mellowed. The whites gleamed astonishingly white. Shimmering with health. So fucking beautiful.

A grin played at the corners of Jonas's mouth. His very posture seemed to resonate with hope as Terry witnessed a new determination taking hold of him. A new confidence.

"We'll find them, Terry. I know we will. And we'll figure out a way to wipe them out."

Terry cupped his hand around the back of Jonas's neck and pulled him close. He pressed his lips to the soft skin under Jonas's ear and breathed in his scent. His dick started rising again. And once again, it wasn't the only dick on the move. Jonas was getting hard too.

"We have to do it," Jonas whispered, his lips now in Terry's ginger mop of hair, their bellies pressed together. "We don't have any other options. We have to find them, and we have to destroy them."

Terry listened to the words, but he had trouble matching Jonas's moxie. To think they could actually kill the creatures. Save the town. Preserve the mountain.

Live happily ever after.

The very idea of accomplishing all that made Terry so tired he wanted to sit down and cry. Then he saw the hope in Jonas's eyes blossom again, and he decided on the spot that he at least had to try.

"What makes you so sure we can find them?"

Simple," Jonas said. "Because we have to. And because failure isn't an option." His hand came to rest on Terry's stomach, burrowing through the fuzz to reach the skin. The tip of his fingers pointed south, bristling through Terry's thatch of pubic hair, nudging the base of his cock. Terry figured one more nudge and he'd be on his knees taking Jonas into his mouth. Jesus, he had no self-control at all where Jonas was concerned.

"How will we kill them?" Terry asked, trying to concentrate on the problem at hand. The *real* problem.

Jonas's teeth nipped at Terry's collarbone. It tickled.

Jonas spoke calmly, like he was planning dinner. "Wherever they're hiding we'll set an incendiary bomb."

"Huh?"

Jonas sighed. "We'll burn them out. I reported on an arsonist once. Interviewed him through prison bars. He set some amazing explosions. Firebombs from hell, he called them. I know exactly how he did it."

"Using what for fuel?"

"Gasoline."

"We'll blow ourselves up."

"Better than the government doing it."

Terry stood there while their two hard-ons bumped against each other down below. It was a pleasant sensation. Heavy rods of flesh poking straight up into the air, swollen heads bumping together, making both men's knees begin to quiver. Bruce came padding down the stairs to join them finally. Terry thought about what Jonas had said. What it would all entail, finding and killing the creatures. Except for his dick, which wasn't tired at all, a bone-crushing weariness settled over him again.

No, it was impossible. They probably *would* blow themselves up.

"Maybe we should just leave," he said. "Let the authorities do what they have to do."

Jonas pulled back far enough to study Terry's face. "But you'll lose your house. This cabin. Your whole life, everything you've acquired, will all have been for nothing."

"I'll still have you," Terry said. "You won't be a charcoal briquette. Neither will I for that matter. Or Bruce."

They looked down. Bruce was licking his butt. His priorities were simple.

Jonas leaned his head in and laid a kiss to Terry's forehead. With his mouth still on Terry's skin, he whispered softly, "Inside my head, I can see us together. It's like an eight-millimeter home movie scrolling past my eyeballs on a continuous loop. It's the future I see for us. It's the future I want us to share."

"We can't share it somewhere else?" Terry asked, biting back a smile. For a minute there, he could almost see the home movie too. He swore he could.

Jonas shook his head. "No. That future takes place here. In the cabin on this mountain, and in your house down the hill in town. I want a return address with "Spangle" on it. I want a wedding ring on my finger. And I want the ring to look exactly like the ring you'll wear on your finger. I want to be married to a notary public with red hair who part-times as a substitute schoolteacher and has a dick like a telephone pole. And I want to win a Pulitzer."

Terry grinned. "That's a really imaginative movie you're watching there."

Jonas blushed. "I've had it for a while. I worked out all the kinks and supplemented some other parts with wishful thinking."

"So I see."

"You wouldn't leave this place anyway," Jonas said. "You know you wouldn't. Not unless there was no way around it."

Terry sighed. "No, I guess I wouldn't." He cocked his head and studied Jonas closer. "So you really think we're getting married, huh?"

"Even if I have to trick you into it. Yes."

Terry laughed. "What if I don't need to be tricked?"

"All the better." Jonas smiled, a wicked, sexy glint in his eyes.

Terry brushed a kiss across Jonas's mouth. Pulling back, he stared off through the trees. Out to the horizon. In his mind's eye, he skimmed along like a drone, analyzing the terrain. The mountain. The town. The surrounding desert. Seeking the place where the fucking "parasites" were hiding. Searching. Trying like hell to sniff out their location in his mind's eye.

Perhaps Jonas thought he saw doubt on Terry's face. Or perhaps he just wanted to have the last word.

"We have to at least try," Jonas said, his voice solemn and determined. "I'm not taking no for an answer on this. We can't let the frigging government blow up our future. And we can't let the monsters win either. Sorry, the *parasites*. We have to stop them both right here."

Terry scraped a hand across his face, trying to wipe away his own doubt. Wondering what the hell he was getting himself into. And yet, strangely enough, eager to begin. "And we've got three days to do it."

Jonas's gaze softened. "Did you say you don't need to be tricked?"

"What? To marry you?"

"Yeah. To marry me."

Terry pretended to think about it. "Well, I haven't had any better offers lately."

"Asshole," Jonas mumbled.

Terry glowered theatrically. "See how verbally abusive you're going to be as a spouse?"

"Yeah, well, it's part of my charm."

Terry wrapped his fingers around Jonas's cock, loving the way it twitched in his hand.

"One of many," he said with a smile, snuggling close.

Chapter Twenty-One

JONAS WOKE with the light of a foggy dawn throwing gray shadows across the room. He extended his arm, groping across the mattress all the way to the farthest edge. Terry and Bruce were both gone. He flung the covers aside and groaned when the cold air hit him. The room was like ice. Shivering, he threw a shirt around his shoulders and tugged on his jeans. With his shoes and socks in hand, he tromped down the stairs.

He found Terry in his bathrobe, bare knees poking through, sitting on the couch with the USGS map of the mountain spread out on the coffee table in front of him. He was studying it and nursing a cup of coffee at the same time. His red hair screamed Wild Man of Borneo. He had bags under his eyes that Samsonite might actually consider patenting. A well-tended fire burned on the grate, and down here the cabin was starting to warm up. It would take a while for the heat to reach the loft.

Jonas stopped on the bottom step. "Let me guess. You've been up all night."

Terry offered him a grimace in return. "Close enough."

Jonas eyed the map. "What are you doing?"

"I think I know where the last cave is. It's misleading on the map. It's not really on the mountain at all. It's down on the flatlands at the edge of town. There's an arroyo there that floods sometimes when the rains are heavy."

"Do you think we'll be able to find the entrance and get inside?" Jonas stepped into the kitchen to pour himself a cup of coffee. He added brown sugar and cream, then ran a hand through his hair trying to wake himself up. Blowing on his cup, he parked himself on the couch next to Terry. He sipped at his coffee and pulled his socks on. His feet were like blocks of ice.

"Heard any more helicopters?"

Terry frowned. "No."

They both sat quietly, sipping their coffee, staring down at the map, bumping knees now and then to show camaraderie. Bruce was scratching himself in front of the fire. His scratching caused his back leg to thump against the floor like Poe's buried heartbeat. It was creepy.

"Stop it," Jonas told the dog. Bruce lifted his head for a second, then went back to scratching.

"Your pet has fleas," Jonas groused.

"Oh hush." Terry grinned.

They settled back into silence—except for the thumping. After a couple of minutes, the room appeared a bit brighter. The sun was rising outside. A new day was coming.

"What are we doing, then?" Jonas asked.

"Waiting for daylight," Terry said. He tapped the map, and added, "Then we're going here."

"Do you think the creatures are there?"

"I don't know. If they're not, we'll be back to square one."

"What would that mean?"

Terry turned, studying Jonas's face. "It means we'll have to rethink our plan not to leave the mountain. If we can't *find* the creatures, we can't *kill* them. If we can't *kill* them, the authorities will drop bombs on our heads and kill *us*. I've grown fond of seeing your puss in the morning. Consequently, I think it would be in my best interest to keep us both alive. Even if it means losing everything I own in the process."

Jonas's heart squeezed inside his chest. "I'm more important than the stuff you own?"

"Except for Bruce, yes."

Jonas blinked. Then his eyes crinkled into a tiny smile. "Ass."

Terry snickered and reached for his coffee.

Jonas sat contentedly sipping his own. He listened to the fire crackle on the grate. Shot the little dog a wink by way of companionship when he saw him watching. He found his eyes continually drawn to the hard nub of Terry's knee pressed against his own. He laid his hand there, stroking the knee and enjoying the sensation of bristly ginger leg hair tickling his fingertips. When Terry leaned into him and they casually bumped shoulders, a tiny smile lit Terry's face.

"I know you'll keep us safe today," Jonas said, his voice still rough from sleep. "I trust you completely."

"I'm thinking about locking you in the blood room while I check out the cave."

Jonas arched one eyebrow and smirked. "That's not going to happen, you know."

Terry frowned and stared down at the map. "I know. It's a nice thought, though."

"Whatever happens, we're in this together. Promise. Don't try to hold me back. And don't try to keep me safe at the expense of yourself."

Terry lifted his head. For the first time that morning, Jonas saw fear in Terry's eyes. Fear and something else. Something sweeter. Something that came from a deeper, warmer place.

"I promise," Terry said, although it seemed to hurt him to utter the words. A moment later, his expression changed. He edged closer on the couch and wrapped Jonas's fingers—the ones resting on his knee—carefully in his fist. "I've been asking myself what I would do if you weren't here. If you hadn't stumbled into my life."

Jonas watched him, waiting for what was to come. He finally urged Terry on, saying, "And what did you decide?"

Terry closed his eyes, then rested his forehead on Jonas's shoulder. His grip on Jonas's fingers tightened. He sighed, and Jonas smelled coffee on his breath. It was a manly smell, and Jonas liked it. He waited patiently while Terry tried to put his answer together.

"I think I would have stuck a pin in my foot and called the creatures to dinner by now," Terry said. "I didn't have much of a life to look forward to anyway. I honestly didn't know how lonely I was before you came along. I didn't realize how empty I had become. And I didn't care enough to try to figure it out."

Jonas nuzzled Terry's mop of red hair and laid a tender kiss to the top of his head. "And you don't feel empty anymore? Or should I hide the pins?"

Terry squirmed closer and, ducking his head, placed a return kiss to Jonas's throat. "There's not an empty place in me. Not a square inch. Every day when I wake up, it's like I'm brimming over with so many different emotions I don't really know how to cope with them all. I loved Bobby for a long time. I know what old love is like. But it's been years since I suffered through the *beginnings* of love. The *falling in* part. Old love is comfortable and unhurried and safe. New love is something else entirely. It's worry and want and desperation and danger and second-guessing yourself. It's wondering if you're good enough. It's wondering if the other person is really as good as they seem. It's daring to trust." He lifted his head and stared into Jonas's eyes. "It's being scared to death every minute of every day. And then you're faced with lying awake all night worrying about the same stuff all over again."

Jonas pushed the hair from Terry's face so he could see his eyes. "Wow," he said. "I always thought falling in love was the best thing ever."

And at that, Terry frowned. "So did I. Once."

"So what changed?" Jonas asked. "Why is falling in love with me any different?"

"Because not a minute passes that I don't worry about losing you. I have nightmares of you being pulled into the sky. Like Bobby. Out of nowhere, little scenarios pop into my head of you standing beside me staring down at a sudden scratch on your hand, seeing a tiny drop of blood appear on your skin, and hearing the horrible thunder of meaty wings crashing through the trees."

Jonas glanced at the two helmets sitting side by side on the kitchen table. "We're well-protected. We're careful. That's not going to happen."

Birdsong erupted outside the cabin window. They both peered out at the morning growing brighter in front of them. Jonas plucked the map from Terry's lap and neatly folded it before setting it aside. "You've stared at this long enough," he said.

"Tell me you love me," Terry whispered, watching him.

Jonas gave him a hurt little smile. "You don't know it already?"

"I want to hear it from your lips."

"I love you," Jonas said, and the ache in his heart told him he meant it.

Terry nodded. "Now tell me you'll be careful today."

"You know I will." He laid a hand to Terry's cheek and leaned in until their foreheads touched. "Let's get through today, and then I promise I'll tell you everything you want to hear for the rest of your miserable life."

"Somehow it sounded better when I said it."

"I paraphrased. Let's eat. Then we'll be on the road."

Terry gave his head a shake. "God, you're bossy."

Jonas beamed. "Just a boy in love."

Terry rolled his eyes. "Charmer."

Chapter Twenty-Two

IT WAS another brisk day on the mountain. Terry could see his breath in little puffs behind his drop-down face mask. They were in the Jeep. They had crossed the mountain's crest and were descending the other side. Both men were decked out in what Terry considered their battle gear. Heavy leather jackets, leather gloves, motorcycle helmets with visors down. On this day, they each wore two pair of denim jeans to better protect their legs. Even in the nippy morning air, Terry was already perspiring. Thank God the creatures weren't lured to the smell of sweat, or they'd be goners.

Bruce was back at the cabin, locked in, safe and sound. He had howled in protest when they drove away without him. Terry had to steel his heart not to feel guilty about it.

Over the rumble of the Jeep engine and the roar of the wind whipping through the torn canvas roof, they had to yell to communicate, their voices further muted by the face masks. After a while, they both flipped the masks up out of the way, too annoyed to scream any longer.

"Why would a cave be on flat land?" Jonas asked, sucking in his first breath of fresh air in a while.

Terry shrugged. "Unless your map is wrong, it just is."

"I've been thinking."

Terry groaned. "Uh-oh."

Jonas dug a finger in Terry's side and made him yelp. "Just listen to me. If this cave is where you say it is, right outside of town, smack in the middle of the quarantine zone, then the creatures have to be there."

"Explain."

To face Terry, Jonas twisted sideways in his seat as far as he could without strangling himself on the seat belt. "The creatures have to be close. I mean, really close. They show up in a matter of seconds when they smell blood, so they couldn't come from very far away."

"Agreed."

"They also have to be protected from the elements. A cave would be perfect for them. They're shielded from the weather. There's water available in the caves we've seen so far, and no mammal can survive without water."

Terry grunted. "If they're mammals."

Jonas waved Terry's statement away. "What else could they be? Fish?"

Terry tilted his head as if to say *Okay, I yield on that point.* "Go on, professor."

The Jeep's front wheel hit a particularly deep pothole, and the whole vehicle bucked and shuddered beneath them. Terry cringed, half expecting the engine to fall out. He eased up on the accelerator.

Jonas seemed not to notice. "The way I see it, the creatures have to be limited in number."

Terry turned to look at him. "Why do you think that? I've seen them in swarms, you know. When they carried Bobby away, they…." But he couldn't continue that line of thought. He just couldn't. "I mean to say, I know there were a score or more of the fuckers that attacked Bobby. They feed like sharks in a feeding frenzy. Moving in packs. Drawn by blood. Tearing their prey to shreds. They don't circle. They don't stalk. They don't piddle around planning their attack. They close right in and start eating."

Jonas laid a hand to Terry's arm as if imploring him to listen. "But a score isn't that many, you see. Not in the grand scheme of things. And their numbers have to be limited because their food source is limited."

"It's limited because most of the residents either left or they've already been eaten."

"Exactly! So where does that leave their food source now? Depleted, that's where."

Terry considered what Jonas was saying. "If what you say is true, then they'll be leaving the quarantine zone soon. They'll have to if they want to survive."

Jonas's fingers tightened on his arm. Terry liked feeling them there. Jonas's next words were a little less enjoyable.

"Yes! And once they leave the mountain, they'll be unstoppable. They'll regenerate and spread, and the next thing anyone knows, they'll be everywhere. In a few years, they'll cover the planet."

That rationale left them both speechless for a minute. The ramifications of the creatures escaping the mountain were truly horrifying. With unlimited feeding came the natural progression of unlimited breeding. And mankind would be in a world of hurt.

"So they have to be in this last cave, Terry. They *have* to be. Because we have to stop them now while there aren't that many of them."

It wasn't hard to get a handle on where Jonas was going with all this and extrapolate it forward to its obvious conclusion. "And if we don't find them in this cave, and if we don't destroy them ourselves, we have to leave the mountain and let the authorities follow through with their bombing raids. Because that's the only way the creatures will be stopped."

Jonas nodded somberly. "That's exactly right. Either we succeed, or we let the authorities drop their fucking bombs and disintegrate everything you own into pixie dust." Terry heaved a long sigh. Jonas had been right in everything he said. It was only common sense. Still, convincing Terry didn't seem to have given Jonas much pleasure. For now Jonas had settled back in his seat and closed his eyes as if the whole explanation thing had exhausted him. Terry was pretty sure Jonas was also wondering what would happen when they came to the last cave.

And wondering what they would do if there was nothing there to find.

Terry drove carefully. This stretch of mountain road was rough. He didn't dare go more than fifteen miles an hour. Jonas opened his eyes and leaned forward, peering through the windshield. Up ahead, where the rutted lane followed a curvature of rock, twisting around to the left, they both spotted a splash of color at the same moment. The color was bright and unnatural, and it scared Terry to death the moment he saw it.

"Oh no," Jonas whispered, clutching Terry's arm. "It can't be. Stop. Stop!"

Terry slammed on the brakes. A moment later, he refocused on the spot where Jonas was pointing. Fear rose up inside him as soon as he realized what it was.

The splash of color was actually a scream. A scream of canary yellow. It stood out on the arid landscape like a smear of blood on a clean linen sheet. It was the color of the Camry belonging to the young girl and the mother they had freed from the mountain lion back in the second cave.

The kid's name was Jilly, Terry remembered with a sinking heart.

He and Jonas approached the car on foot. Carefully and quietly, with guns drawn. It was fairly evident what had happened. The mother had lost control on the turn and driven the Camry into a deep patch of sand at the edge of the lane. The wheels were mired all the way past the hubcaps.

Or maybe the mother lost control when the attack came. Maybe that's what drove her off the road.

Whatever led them here, and whatever drew the creatures to them, the results were the same.

The windshield was shattered from one side to the other. Smears of blood and ribbons of flesh were stuck to the sharp edges of glass where the creatures had battered themselves inside and claimed their food, dragged it back outside.

Both mother and daughter were gone. Yanked away into oblivion.

"Jilly…," Jonas muttered softly, his eyes misting over with tears.

Terry knew immediately what Jonas was going to say next. Because Terry felt the same way.

"We should have forced them back to the cabin with us," Jonas said. "I knew the mother was too upset to drive. She was barely holding it together when we found them. We never should have trusted her to drive away with the kid."

Terry moved closer to Jonas and laid a hand to the small of his back. "She didn't want our help. She wanted to get down off the mountain as soon as she could. We couldn't have forced them to return to the cabin with us, Terry. We're in no position to tell anybody else what to do. We're barely holding it together ourselves. That woman had to follow the path she thought was right for herself and her child."

But Jonas wasn't listening. Terry knew that by his faraway look. By the way the muscles in his cheeks worked. The way his Adam's apple bobbed up and down as he continually swallowed back his grief and guilt.

Jonas turned away from Terry then. Tired, maybe, of Terry's eyes on him. He moved to the edge of the trees. Standing there, he cupped his hand around his mouth and roared "Jilly!" as loud as he could.

Terry stared down at his feet as Jonas's plaintive cry echoed off into the woods. He knew as well as Jonas that the young girl wasn't out there. The creatures had taken her as surely as they had taken her mother.

But would the creatures hear Jonas calling for her? Would they come to investigate this human voice bellowing in the woods?

He stepped forward and clutched Jonas's arm, gently coaxing him around. "We can't stop now, Jonas. We have to keep going. We have to check out the last cave. There's nothing we can do for these people. They're gone. You know that."

Slowly, Jonas appeared to calm down. He centered his gaze on Terry's face, and after a while the fear in his eyes appeared to slip away. He brushed a streak of tears from his cheek as a horrifying calm set in somewhere back behind his retinas. He nodded faintly. Matter-of-factly. Businesslike. Calm again, Terry realized. In control. Or appearing to be.

"Let's go on, then," Jonas said.

Taking one last look at the savaged Camry, he gripped Terry's hand and led him back up the lane toward the Jeep.

They were less than two hundred yards up the road when Terry spotted movement in the sky through his driver's side window. "Jonas!" he hissed, pointing.

Both men stared at the tiny drone hovering along at their side, matching the Jeep's speed. It accompanied them down the road for another hundred yards or so, then skirted off to the left, disappearing behind a wall of pines.

"It's the authorities. They're watching the mountain more closely," Jonas said. "First the helicopter and now the drone. They're gearing up for something. I wonder if we really do have two days left before they start dropping their bombs."

Terry didn't respond because he didn't know what to say.

Without another word, he drove on down the mountain.

Heading for the outskirts of Spangle to the cave they had to find. Toward the creatures they had to destroy.

Finally Terry asked the question that had been on his lips for days. "I know what we need to do, Jonas. It's the *how* I'm a little less clear about. How exactly are we going to kill these things if we find them? Do you really think your firebombs will work?"

Jonas thought about it for a long time. Finally he said in a hushed voice that barely carried over the wind, "I guess we'll find out when the time comes."

Chapter Twenty-Three

THE DEEP arroyo scarred a path through the valley floor, twisting and turning this way and that. In the rainy seasons, the water sometimes sluiced among the rocks with enough force to sweep away anything in its path, be it bobcat, cow, or automobile. When the rains were heaviest and the rushing waters climbed to a certain height, the surging torrent spilled out of sight through a crevice in the arroyo's bank, forming a subterranean river channel.

To the north Jonas could see a scattering of dusty buildings marking the outskirts of the tiny town of Spangle, California, where it rose up from the desert floor. To his back stood the beginning rise of Terry's mountain leading up into the trees. The arroyo was like the DMZ between the two. Or more precisely, no-man's-land, where, if you didn't keep your wits together, the earth might suck you down its maw before you could escape to either town *or* mountain.

The spot where the floodwaters were known to disappear was clearly the opening to the cavern they were seeking.

Jonas didn't like the looks of the cave entrance at all. It was small, cramped, and unless he was hallucinating, Jonas could swear he saw the tail end of a rattlesnake disappear down the hole as they arrived. He had been laboring for days under the assumption it was too cold for snakes to be out and about. Apparently he was wrong.

"Did you see that?" Terry asked. Obviously he had seen the snake too.

Jonas groaned. "Yes. My sphincter snapped shut like a Venus flytrap."

"Lovely image."

"I don't like snakes."

"So I gathered."

Terry poked at the cave entrance with the barrel of his shotgun, but nothing happened. No venom-slathered monstrosity sprang out to do battle. If the snake was still lurking inside, Jonas suspected it was waiting for something juicier than a tube of gunmetal to stab its fangs into. Like a human ankle. Or an unsuspecting kneecap.

On the way here, Terry had told Jonas that more than one foolish hiker had been lost trying to learn this cave's secrets. "Being an underground river during the rainy season, the cavern is endless," Terry had said. "Rumors say it goes all the way to the ocean, more than a hundred miles away, but I have a hard time believing that. However, deep inside there are subterranean pools and lakes left behind after the rains are over. Our creatures could live here if they had to. It's centrally located, which would give the bastards quick access to each and every sniff of human blood that gets spilled either in town or on the mountain. To reach their kills as quickly as they do, you said they would have to be centrally located."

Jonas hated it when he made sense. "Yeah. That's what I said."

Still rattling the shotgun around in front of him like a blind man's cane, Terry dropped to his hands and knees and crawled through the tiny entrance.

Feeling suddenly very alone, Jonas quickly but reluctantly crawled in after him.

"I love the view," Jonas mumbled, watching Terry squeeze his luscious ass between the rocks in front of him. "The destination not so much."

He had never considered himself particularly claustrophobic until he started threading himself through this inky hole, knowing there was a frigging rattlesnake in there with him.

They crawled for a good twenty feet before the opening began to widen. The minute Jonas's shoulders weren't touching both sides of the tunnel at once, he breathed a sigh of relief. He breathed even easier when the roof opened up above his head and he was able to stand erect.

He flipped his face guard up and saw Terry watching him.

"You're looking a little bug-eyed," Terry said. "You okay?"

A blush crept warmly up the front of his neck. "Don't quite know how to say this, but having your ass squirming around in front of my face for the last twenty feet gave me a boner."

"Good to know I've still got it." Terry grinned. "Ready to move on?"

Jonas tried to drum up a little enthusiasm, but it wasn't easy. He lit his Maglite and flashed the beam around the cavern. The ground at his feet was rocky and still damp from the latest rains, with little puddles of standing water sprinkled here and there. The roof above his head was tiered in sharp shelves of what looked like limestone, gleaming gray in the beam of his flashlight like a series of knife blades. Still, he didn't see any snakes lurking, either underfoot or head high, and that gave him hope.

"Lead the way," he finally said, lowering his voice because the echoes in the cave were giving him the heebie-jeebies. "Let's get this over with. For some reason this cave is spookier than all the others put together."

"It'll be okay," Terry softly said, laying his hand on Jonas's arm. And without further encouragement, he led Jonas deeper into the cavern.

Up ahead, water dripped. The air smelled damp and crystal clean, like a freshly opened bottle of Evian. With each step forward, the temperature seemed to drop another degree or two, until finally Jonas was glad for all the clothes he was wearing.

Their two flashlight beams jounced off here and there, seeking out corners and dark recesses. Everywhere they looked they saw gleaming cavern walls and reflections off water. There was none of the bioluminescent fungus they had seen in the first cave, and none of the mud and clay they had tromped through in the second. Here the floor and walls had been washed clean millennia ago. This cavern was home to no indigenous bats either. But for the rattlesnake Jonas had seen at the entrance, the environment appeared to be totally absent of animal life.

By Jonas's estimate, they walked for upward of a quarter mile, burrowing deeper and deeper into the underground chasm. He had little fear of getting lost because the channel veered neither left nor right but dug a steady path straight under the desert floor.

Terry at long last stopped in his tracks, effectively halting Jonas too. They were standing at the edge of a wide underground lake. Terry picked up a stone and tossed it as far as he could. It landed with a splash, and their flashlight beams caught the lake's surface, rippling in silver circles. The water looked pristine and limpid. They stood stock-still, listening to the *kerplop* echo off into the darkness. It stirred no answering cry from any living creature they could hear.

Terry turned and aimed his light at Jonas's feet so he could look at his face without blinding him.

"This can't be right," Terry said. "This air is too sweet and clean. Carnivores have a reek to them. Their lairs are scattered with bones and crap. If the creatures were here, they would leave a sign. We could smell them."

Jonas edged closer to Terry's side. "So you're saying they aren't here."

"Yes. They aren't here. We've failed."

"So what do we do?" Jonas sighed, suddenly exhausted. "What's our next step?"

Both men, as if by unspoken agreement, switched off their Maglites and let the impenetrable darkness swallow them whole. To his amazement, Jonas realized he felt no fear. By that, more than for any other reason, Jonas knew Terry was right. The creatures were not here.

Terry found Jonas's hand in the darkness. He clutched it gently. "We have to leave the mountain, babe. There's nothing else to do. In a couple of days, this whole place will be a huge bomb crater."

Jonas hated saying the words. "You'll lose your home."

"No," Terry answered. "We'll lose *our* home."

They fell silent, listening to the tinkle of water dripping down a limestone wall. "Would you have really wanted me to stay here with you?" Jonas softly asked.

Jonas was surprised when a hand came out of the darkness and leather-clad fingers brushed the nape of his neck.

"I'll want you with me, no matter where we end up. I just hate to start over from scratch, is all. I hate to leave my town and my mountain. My two properties. This place has been my whole life for a very long time."

"I'm sorry," Jonas said.

He heard a clacking sound and realize his teeth were clattering. That's how cold it was. Terry must have heard it too.

"Let's get out of here," Terry said with a sigh. "If we're really going to leave, I need to make a trip into town to get my papers together. Insurance forms, birth certificate, passport, all the stuff you can't live without these days. Then we'll swing by the cabin and pick up all your research and your unfinished book."

"And the dog."

"Yeah. And the dog."

"I don't want to go," Jonas said.

"Neither do I," Terry answered. "But we really don't have a choice."

Without another word they retraced their steps through the long cavern, following the little point of light that showed where the entrance beckoned. As the tunnel narrowed, they dropped to their hands and knees and, in single file as before, they crawled out into the sunlight.

When they could at long last stand, they groaned their way to their feet and switched their flashlights off.

They immediately froze.

There was a policeman with a big potbelly standing there, watching them. His khaki uniform was stained with sweat, and he had dirt on his knee like he must have slipped climbing down the rocks. That might have been enough to explain his foul mood, or maybe he was grouchy all the time. Jonas wasn't sure. What he was sure about was that the fat guy had a pistol aimed at Terry's belly.

"Drop the guns," the policeman said. "Both of you."

Terry carefully laid the shotgun on the ground, and Jonas slipped his .38 from the holster at his waist. He tossed it into a pile of bracken at the edge of the cave entrance.

The cop had a mean glint in his eye. He looked like he hadn't slept for a while, leaving his patience worn thin. He waved his gun toward the only reasonable path out of the arroyo.

"Climb," he said.

As Terry and Jonas began to clamber up the side of the gulch, the cop scooped up the two guns they had dropped. He holstered his own pistol, stuffed Jonas's .38 in the waistband of his pants, and kept the shotgun trained on his prisoners, since that was clearly what he considered them to be.

"We've been watching you fools for weeks. You and all the other idiots who refused to leave this goddamn place. If it was up to me, I'd drop the bombs anyway. A few less stupid people in the world isn't going to hurt anything."

"You're all heart," Terry said, turning a mean eye of his own on the man with his gun.

They were almost to the top of the arroyo wall. The cop still brought up the rear. He had the shotgun trained on Jonas's back now, and Jonas wasn't liking it much.

"Careful," Terry hissed in front of him, pulling himself up short.

Jonas walked into him before he could stop himself. He looked where Terry was pointing. Not two feet away from where they stood, another rattlesnake lay coiled in the dirt.

"Keep moving!" the policeman barked, clearly not knowing what was happening.

"I'll move," Jonas said on a growl.

And stepping sideways, directly toward the snake, he lashed out with his foot, scooped the rattler off the ground in the arch of his boot, and kicked it through the air directly at the cop.

The rattler was fat and long and still rattling a furious warning as it writhed in midair, sailing directly toward the policeman's face. The cop spotted it and let out a horrified scream. He threw his arms across his face, dropping the shotgun and at the same moment losing his footing and tumbling sideways into the brush.

The snake landed on his chest, and as the policeman opened his mouth to scream yet again, the snake lunged forward, burying its fangs in the cop's cheek. The policeman screamed even louder then, emitting a high-pitched wail of terror as the two of them, man and snake, rolled around in the weeds, one trying to get away, the other trying to latch on tighter.

"Oh Christ!" Jonas cried, appalled by what he'd done. He sprang forward and snatched up the shotgun off the ground. Not quite sure what to do next, he suddenly found himself yanked backward. Terry's arms came out and grabbed him, dragging him to the ground.

"Stay down!" Terry spat in his ear. "Don't move!"

A moment later Jonas heard it. Above the wailing of the policeman and the insane *bzz* of the snake's rattles came the drumbeat of wings slapping fat bodies. The concussion of those wings downstroking the air to stay aloft. The bone-chilling reedy song of the creatures' hunting cries, their bloodlust ignited by the blood leaking from around the rattlesnake's fangs still embedded in the poor cop's cheek.

In spite of Terry telling him to lie still, Jonas—and Terry too— scrambled farther away from the man and the snake. When a shadow passed over them, they burrowed flat to the ground in each other's arms, face masks down, and didn't move.

Jonas squeezed his eyes shut as he pressed his face to Terry's chest and tried not to listen to the policeman's horrified screaming.

In a flurry of wingbeats, a final scream was cut short. Jonas opened his eyes in time to see the man lifted straight up into the air, his body already being torn apart. The snake was nowhere to be seen, perhaps devoured already because it was covered in the man's blood. Collateral damage, he supposed. Tough luck, snake.

Without thinking, Jonas rose up to a sitting position and pointed the shotgun at the man hovering just above the ground, stretched wide by a dozen nightmarish creatures as they peeled the flesh from his bones and then proceeded to pulverize those bones between fangs as long as Jonas's little fingers.

"No!" Terry cried.

But it was too late. Jonas couldn't have stopped himself even if he wanted. He pointed the shotgun straight up into the air and pulled the trigger. The kick smashed him back against Terry's chest, and in that same moment, Terry wrapped his arms around him and dragged Jonas back to the ground. He covered him with his own body, and with the fury of the attack quieting behind them, waited for whatever would happen next. Either the creatures would come for them, or they wouldn't.

In less than a minute, the banks of the arroyo lay silent around them. The attack was over.

They opened their eyes, and where the policeman and the snake had fallen, there were only vast splashes of blood. He saw the snake now—a two-foot section of rattlesnake, headless, lying in the dirt, twisting in its death throes, too dumb to know it was already dead.

Beside the rattlesnake lay one of the creatures. Peppered with shotgun pellets. Its wings shattered. Long talons at the base of the wings, clenching and unclenching like the fists of a dying man. Trying to hold on to life.

While they watched, the clenching stopped, the jaws fell slack, and the creature lay still.

Slowly, with Terry's hand still clutching at Jonas's shirt, the men rose and took a step forward. Then another.

The creature lay sprawled among the rocks like some horribly mutated butterfly from hell pinned to a slab of cardboard. Its fat body was sprinkled with dark, wiry hair. Leaning closer, Jonas could see fleas squirming over the beast's flesh. He cringed and pulled back, making a face. He could smell the creature now. The gamey reek of rotted flesh wedged in razor-like teeth, the stench of old blood clotted among the hairy pelt.

The wingspan was almost five feet wide from tip to tip. In its jaws, slack with death and still smeared with the policeman's blood, were serrated teeth, inches long and gleamingly sharp. To either side of its face protruded two stubby ears, small for the creature's size. Fleshy and pale.

In the middle of the face, above the jaws wrenched open in death, a fleshy nose lay flat, spread from ear to ear below the lifeless onyx eyes. Nostrils slit. Rubbery and mottled pink, clearly riddled with nerve endings.

It was the heart of the beast. Jonas glanced at Terry, who looked back at him and nodded. They both knew immediately. That nose was the creature's greatest weapon. It could hone in on a droplet of human blood in a nanosecond from God knows how many miles away. The creatures' speed reaching the policeman proved that to be true. And it was the bloody great wings, powerful and strong, that swept the creature there.

An array of thick muscles stretched from the torso of the beast to the outer edges of the meaty wings. The muscles on the breast of the thing were thick and bulbous. Heavy sinews also stretched from the jaws to the back of the skull. Jonas tapped a fat tendon with the barrel of the shotgun, like a professor pointing out an equation on a blackboard.

"Look how strong it is," he said. "In flight and in the tearing of flesh. This thing is truly a carnivore."

"It's also huge," Terry breathed, his jaw slack in wonder. "It's not a bat at all."

"No," Jonas said. "But there are resemblances."

"What are you saying?"

"I don't know. I'm not a zoologist." Jonas turned his eyes away and scanned the arroyo, first in one direction, then the other. He was jittery, nervous. And still scared to death. He admired Terry for looking so calm after everything that had happened. "At least we now know what they look like up close. Maybe we should take this carcass to the authorities and let them study it."

"And let them arrest us at the same time? I don't think so. As cool as it is that you blew one out of the sky, Jonas, it really doesn't change things. We should still get our asses out of here, and we should elude the authorities when we do. What happened to the patrolman was an accident, but they may not see it that way. We have little more than two days left before they blow this mountain off the map, and I really don't want to be standing on it when they do. Nor do I want to be arrested for murder while trying to leave it."

Ten minutes earlier, Jonas had made peace with Terry's decision to leave his home, his mountain, his town. But now he was having mixed feelings about all of it. What the hell was wrong with him? Then his eyes wandered back to the creature lying dead on the rocks. And the spray of blood that covered the ground beneath it.

"I didn't mean to kill that man," he whispered. "I... I was just trying to scare him. It... it wasn't really murder, was it?"

Terry scooped his arms around him and pulled him close. "No, of course not," he murmured in Jonas's ear. "You only did what you had to do. I thought about it too."

"Really?"

"Yes," Terry said, a tiny smile touching his lips. "But you were quicker."

Jonas eyed Terry closely. "So you still want to go, then? Off the mountain? Abandon everything you own?"

There was deep sadness on Terry's face as he slowly answered. He couldn't seem to take his eyes off the creature at their feet. "We have no choice. These creatures could scatter themselves to the four winds if they aren't stopped here. You and I can't destroy them if we can't find them, so we have to let the authorities do it." He took Jonas's hand. "Let's get into town before a drone flies over and they start wondering where their policeman went."

Jonas eyed the sky, the reality of what Terry said sinking into him like a three-inch-long incisor.

"Town it is," he said. "Then back to the cabin to pick up Bruce and my portable typewriter. Me and that typewriter go back a long ways. I'd hate to see it blown up."

"Then we're out of here?" Terry asked, his eyes even more anguished than they had been before. But still determined.

"Then we're out of here." Jonas nodded, already hating himself for saying it, as he suspected Terry did.

Cowed by their own disappointment at abandoning everything they loved and everything they thought they could do to protect it, Jonas and Terry slouched toward the Jeep. They kept a leery eye on the sky for drones. Or, God forbid, another swarm of slavering creatures.

Guilt over the policeman's death followed Jonas every step of the way.

Chapter Twenty-Four

TERRY SAW immediately that the residents of Spangle—the ones who were still alive, at least, and too damn stubborn to leave—had been busy protesting the imminent destruction of their homes. There were banners painted on bedsheets and nailed to walls and rooftops from one end of town to the other. Save Our Homes! the banners cried. Don't Bomb! another said, and a third pleaded Drop Troops Not Napalm! One brave citizen, clearly with the heart of a rebel, had painted words directly on the street from one end of the block to the other in gleaming white. It took Terry and Jonas a couple of minutes to figure out from the ground. Dear Dot Gov, the words read. Fuck You.

They read the sign twice, then glanced at each other and snickered.

"More people stayed than we thought," Terry said.

"Yeah, and they're a little upset," Jonas answered.

As they drove through town in their battered Jeep, they could tell they were being watched. Not only by drones buzzing overhead, monitoring their movements for the authorities, but by the occasional wary face peeking out from behind drawn curtains and through dusty upstairs windows.

Terry spotted a young man scurrying from one side yard to another. He was wearing camo and toting the biggest gun Terry had ever seen in his life.

Jonas noticed the gun too. "He must be hunting elephants," he commented wryly.

"Who knew they were such a problem, elephants?" Terry sniped, and both men shook their heads in wonder.

Streets and lawns were littered with flyers dropped from the sky. Patches of blood-stained sidewalks and front walks. The stains were from older kills, and the blood had turned black, rotted in the sun. Flies had given up on the bloodstains long ago. The smell of death no longer lingered on the air as it had the last time Terry was here. The silence, however, was far more unnerving. Now a sense of looming disaster hung over the town. As well it should, he supposed, since the town was about to be bombed into oblivion.

Terry parked the Jeep under the shade of a huge pepper tree at the side of his street. He gazed across Jonas to the house with slate-gray walls and white trim that he had called home for the last seven years. It was a neat little craftsman. Single story. Three bedrooms, a breakfast nook off the kitchen, one bath, a sundeck in the back, and with more memories clinging to every room than Terry would ever be able to count.

A shingle swayed in the wind from the edge of the front porch. The shingle read Terence Jones, Notary Public.

"That's it," he said quietly. "That's my house." He glowered at the unkempt lawn. "Try to imagine it with the yard mowed."

"I like." Jonas smiled, covering Terry's hand with his. "Nice color."

"Bobby's idea. I wasn't thrilled with it at first. But now… I am." Terry's voice sort of petered out, and Jonas squeezed his hand for reassurance.

"Let's get this over with," Terry said, kicking open the Jeep's door and swinging his long legs out of the cab. Jonas followed, and hand in hand they walked up the front walk to the tiny porch with a row of untended geraniums turning to straw in terra-cotta pots lining the front door. Terry carried his shotgun in the crook of his arm. Jonas still had the little .38 tucked into the holster at his hip.

On the porch, Terry stood motionless, staring at the dead flowers. Jonas took it upon himself to pluck the key from Terry's hand and unlock the front door. He stepped back and let Terry enter first.

It had been so long since he had been inside the house, Terry sucked in his breath, almost floored by the emotional connection it still held over him. The pictures on the walls. Snapshots of him and Bobby. Photos from their simple wedding at City Hall. Bruce's toys still scattered across the floor where Bruce had left them the last time he played here.

The rooms smelled musty and stale. Terry stepped into the kitchen with Jonas at his heels. Everything was clean but dusty. Terry was tempted to open the fridge and see what he would find, but he was pretty sure he had left food in there. Milk. Lunch meat. Eggs. Stuff that would be rotten and reeking to high heaven by now, even if the power *was* still on.

He exhaled a long sigh and tried to ignore the thumping of his heart. He pointed to a room off to the left. "My office," he said. "The papers are in there."

Jonas strolled the rooms, snooping, studying everything he saw, pictures especially. Terry went directly to his desk and started dragging out all the important documents he thought he should save before the bombs fell. Social security crap. Credit cards. IDs. His diplomas from college, and the certification papers that qualified him to be a notary public. Bobby's papers, too, he gathered up, since he supposed he would need to register his spouse's death with the coroner's office at some point or other. He grabbed his address book with phone numbers of friends and family, along with email addresses and the passwords for all his computer files. From a small safe buried in the office floor, he extracted a thousand dollars he and Bobby had stashed there for emergencies—Terry suspected now would qualify.

When he'd recovered everything he thought he would need, plus his laptop, and stuffed it all into a spare accordion folder he found tucked in a desk drawer, he went in search of Jonas. He found him standing in front of the same picture Terry had on display back at the cabin. The picture of Bobby and Terry, hiking the mountain not far from the cabin during the first year they were together.

They stood silently for a long moment, Jonas and Terry, each staring at the blown-up snapshot.

"Your Bobby was handsome," Jonas said, his voice barely loud enough to hear.

"Yes, he was," Terry said, with the faintest of smiles twisting his mouth.

"You must miss him," Jonas quietly said, sidling closer to Terry.

"I'll always miss him," Terry said, laying his hand on Jonas's back. "Like I'll miss you if you ever go away."

"Thank you," Jonas said, his eyes sad, his lips a thin line.

"Just try not to go away," Terry added, his tiny smile gone.

And Jonas nodded. "I'll try."

They left the house in single file. As Terry closed the front door behind them, he reached out to lock up, then, at the last second, pocketed the key and walked away, leaving the door closed but unlocked.

"Terry?"

"There's nothing but memories left to steal. They won't do anyone any good but me."

They turned toward the Jeep. Again, as they traversed the front walk, Jonas took his hand.

"I'm sorry," he said.

Terry shrugged. "I never really thought we'd have to abandon everything. I always thought things would somehow work themselves out."

"I know." And once again Jonas said, "I'm sorry."

Before climbing into the Jeep, they looked up and down the street. At the rumpled bedsheets with messages painted on them, nailed to walls and roofs. At a tumbleweed skipping along the gutter a block down as if it, too, was in a hurry to get out of town while it still could. A stray cat observed them from the mouth of a sewer at the end of the block.

"Do you still think they'll bomb?" Jonas asked. "I mean, with people here?"

"They'll have to if they want to stop the creatures from spreading. They'll try to round up as many citizens as they can, I suppose. Like they tried to round us up. Too many civilian deaths from their bombing raid won't look good on the evening news."

"Letting the creatures swarm all over the planet won't look good either."

"No," Terry agreed, his jaws tense. "It won't."

Terry reached out and took Jonas's hand. With his other hand he tossed the accordion file containing all his papers on the front seat of the Jeep. "Drop your face mask," he said, grabbing the shotgun from the back floorboard. "Let's walk. I want to see the town one last time."

Jonas did as Terry asked. Hand in hand they strolled along Terry's street. Through his tinted visor, Terry studied the familiar houses they passed. He remembered dogs that once came out to talk to Bruce when they passed on their evening walks. Wondered where those dogs were now. Had their owners taken them with them when they left? Or had the poor family pets gone wild after their owners were killed, leaving them orphaned, set loose in the world to fend for themselves? Or worse yet, had they starved to death, locked inside the very homes that had once shielded them from danger?

"So much sadness," Terry said, shaking his head. "This used to be a happy town. I guess the happiness was the first to go."

They were in the business district now, which was only a couple of blocks from Terry's house. Terry smiled to himself, realizing how small-townish and unsophisticated it all must look to Jonas.

"Is that where you got your hair cut?" Jonas asked with a smile, pointing to a tiny storefront with a barber pole and Ed's Barber Shop painted in electric-blue paint over the front door. Through the plate-glass window, they could see two barber chairs and the row of plastic lawn chairs that constituted the waiting area.

"That's it," Terry said with a grin. "Not exactly Vidal Sassoon, I know. But Ed usually left my scalp attached."

"Well, that's the important thing." Jonas returned the grin.

They walked on. There were more tumbleweeds here on the main drag, wedged under the bumpers of abandoned cars and tucked into doorways where the wind had carried them.

Coffee shop. Thrift store. Tiny mom-and-pop market. Insurance salesman. Doctor's office with a blood bank next door. They passed a seedy beer bar, where a couple of old guys were playing pool as they waited to be firebombed. Terry knew they were playing pool by the rattle of the balls. He knew they were old because he could hear them laughing and coughing cigarette coughs while they listened to country music on the jukebox. He knew they were waiting to be firebombed because, really, what the hell else would they be waiting for?

Farther down the block on the corner stood an IGA store. There was a traffic jam of discarded shopping carts strewn across the parking area where looters had helped themselves to the goods, then abandoned the carts when the electronic brakes on the fuckers stopped them at the edge of the lot.

Across the street from the IGA stood a massive brick building that took up a quarter of a city block. The building had clearly been abandoned long ago, and there were no signs now on the outside to show what business might have once transpired inside. Terry saw Jonas eyeing it, wondering what the hell it was.

Jonas moved closer to Terry's side when they passed the brick monstrosity. He pulled Terry to a stop and flipped up the face guard on his crash helmet. Tilting his head back, he studied the somber three-story structure in front of him.

Without being asked, Terry volunteered the information he knew Jonas wanted.

"It was a research facility. They used to develop and manufacture vitamin supplements here. Shipped them all over the country until a scandal closed them down."

That caught Jonas's interest. "What sort of scandal?"

Terry thought about it. "I don't know exactly. I think a few people died taking their supplements. Lawsuits followed. If I remember right, the owner committed suicide. The factory has been sitting here in the middle of town abandoned ever since."

Jonas leaned his head farther back, studying the brick facade. He released Terry's hand and backed into the street to get a better perspective.

The building was shaped like a big shoebox. Very little imagination went into its construction. Redbrick walls had turned dark with age and muck. Built in the '70s, Terry figured, the corners were crumbled from exposure to the sun, the front doors and ground-floor windows boarded up tight. Terry had walked past the abandoned building so often over the years, he barely noticed it anymore.

Today he noticed.

"Look up there," Jonas said. "The windows on the top floor. They're all broken out. You'd think it would be the windows on the ground floor that would be vandalized, not the ones way up there."

"You've lost me," Terry said, not really listening. He was wondering if it wasn't time they headed back to the Jeep and got their asses out of town. Bruce was probably eating through a wall by now, wondering where they were. "We'd best get home," he said.

But Jonas didn't move. He was still staring at the broken windows on the third floor of the abandoned factory.

"I can see movement up there," Jonas said, his voice hushed.

"Up where?"

Jonas pointed. "In those third-floor windows."

"What sort of movement?"

Jonas hesitated. "Sort of a... *fluttering* in the shadows."

Something in Jonas's voice set Terry's nerves on edge. He glanced up and down the street. Then he lifted his chin high and scanned the sky from one horizon to the other. Checking for drones. Checking for helicopters. Almost reluctantly, he let his gaze travel back to the spot where Jonas was staring.

At that moment, in the shadows past the broken windowpanes of the research facility's third-floor windows, Terry saw movement too. And Jonas was right. It could only be described as... *fluttering*.

"Drop your mask," Terry whispered, closing his own.

Jonas's gaze skittered to his face; then he quickly did what Terry asked. Only then, through the tinted plastic of the windscreen, did he turn his eyes back to the third-floor windows. They both did.

The fluttering movement seemed erratic yet somehow organized. Like a ritual or something. Like bees, maybe. Bees communicating through movement and touch and smell and instinct.

Only whatever it was moving around behind those broken windows was bigger. Much bigger.

"Maybe someone's up there," Terry said.

"Some*one*? No. Some*thing*? Yes."

"It could be a town meeting."

"Like what? The PTA? I seriously doubt it."

Terry didn't appreciate the sarcasm, but he supposed he deserved it. His heart sank as he muttered the words, "I'm almost afraid to ask what you're thinking."

Jonas's eyes remained focused on those squares of moving shadows three floors up.

"This place is centrally located, isn't it." It wasn't a question. It was a general statement of fact.

Terry frowned. "Couldn't be more centrally located if it tried. As you already undoubtedly know."

"The creatures need to be centrally located, you know, to get where they go as fast as they do."

"So I've been told. Over and over again." *By you*, Terry didn't add. He let the silence linger a moment longer. "You wanna fuck?"

Jonas rolled his eyes. "Maybe later."

Terry nodded as if he expected as much. "Just thought I'd ask." He eyed the windows along with Jonas. "You want to go up there, don't you?"

"Does it show?"

"Yeah, it shows. And I gotta tell you something. Personally, I'd really rather not."

There. He'd said it.

Terry was about to drag Jonas back to the Jeep whether he wanted to go or not when a sliver of glass from one of the broken windowpanes high above their heads suddenly shimmered through the air and exploded on the sidewalk at their feet. Tiny diamonds of glass shot out in every direction.

"Holy shit!" Jonas exclaimed, jumping back and pulling Terry with him. "That was jarred loose. There's something moving around up there for sure, and whatever it is, it's not particularly small."

With his eyes still trained on the windows, Jonas unlatched the holster at his hip and tugged out the .38. He cradled it in his hand like a man who had never held a gun before in his life. Which, as Terry damn well knew, wasn't far from the truth.

"What are you doing?" Terry asked, his heart sinking deeper even while it started thumping in alarm. "You're not really going to do this, are you?"

"I thought we were looking for the creatures." Jonas's head was still craned back, his eyes still trying to burrow through the darkness behind those third-floor windows.

"You can't possibly think this is going to turn out well," Terry all but whined. Then he lifted his head, swallowed his fear, and really tried to see what Jonas was seeing.

"Screw it," Jonas whispered. "Let's go inside. We have to know what's up there, right?"

For the life of him, Terry couldn't think of a single argument against it.

Oh so carefully, he flicked the safety of the shotgun off.

Side by side, elbows touching, they edged carefully forward, crunching over the broken glass. Neither had a breath left in his body. Terry's heart was banging around behind his ribs like a squirrel trying to batter its way out of a cardboard box.

"I still want that fuck later," he whispered.

"If we live long enough, I'll be glad to give it to you," Jonas whispered back.

Chapter Twenty-Five

TERRY AND Jonas circled the abandoned research facility, seeking a way in. Scroll-down security screens, rusted now with age and clogged with spiderwebs and leaves, had been placed over the windows and doors on the ground floor. The place was sealed up tighter than Terry's cabin back on the mountain.

Overlooking an alley at the rear of the building, they discovered a rusty fire escape that zigzagged its way up the back of the structure all the way to the roof. Shielding their eyes from the sun, they squinted upward. As at the front of the building, all the third-floor windows back here were broken out as well. They couldn't see movement inside as they had in the front, but all the glass was shattered, leaving only ragged shards here and there stabbing inward around the battered window frames.

"Something's definitely going on up there," Terry said. "Let's go home, get naked, and think about it."

"Wuss," Jonas replied, dragging Terry forward. He leaped up and grabbed the bottom rung of the pulldown ladder that extended from the bottom of the fire escape. The ladder screeched and clattered as Jonas dragged it toward the ground. An avalanche of rust and filth sprinkled down on their heads. Up above, the entire fire escape shuddered and shook as the ladder descended.

"Is that thing safe?" Terry asked, not looking happy.

"Heck yeah. What could go wrong?" Jonas tried to sound cockier than he actually felt. In fact, he was starting to wonder if this was a good idea at all.

"What could go *wrong*? Is that what you said? Geez," Terry drawled, "give me a minute and I'll make you a list."

"Kidder," Jonas said, too preoccupied to grin. He elbowed Terry again, more gently this time, trying to find his own bravery while teasing Terry into finding his. "Come on, lover. Show some cajones. Follow me where no man has gone before."

"Nor would a normal man ever want to," Terry muttered to himself.

With a mischievous leer, Jonas began ascending the rusted ladder, one dusty rung at a time. When he reached the second floor, he gazed down to make sure Terry was following. When he saw that he was, and that he had his shotgun dangling off his back by the gun strap, Jonas proceeded upward, finding some little bit of courage of his own in the weight of the .38 at his hip.

Both men moved carefully, jarring the ancient fire escape as little as possible while they climbed. As they passed the second-floor windows, they tried to peer inside, but it was hopeless. The interior was pitch-black, and the windows were so filthy from decades of neglect that they couldn't have seen anything even if there had been searchlights burning inside.

Under their combined weight, the old fire escape made some unholy noises. Rusty bolts clamping it to the wall began to squeal and complain. Trusting the damn thing less and less the higher he climbed, Jonas slowed his pace to keep the shaking to a minimum. He tried to distribute his weight more evenly and softly whispered for Terry to do the same.

Terry grumbled a response that sounded a wee bit like "Bite me," and Jonas smiled.

The moment he did, against all odds, he began to enjoy himself. The feeling surprised him, to say the least. Creeping closer to those annihilated third-floor windows, which constituted the only route he could see to get inside the building, Jonas wondered what the hell was wrong with him? One glance at Terry told him Terry certainly wasn't enjoying *himself*, so why the hell should *he*? What was it exactly that made him feel that way?

He didn't have to search too deeply to figure out what it was. It was exultation, pure and simple. Exultation at being the stalker for a change, rather than the one being stalked. The hunter instead of the prey. He was being afforded a shot at fighting back against all the misery these creatures had brought to this place. This town. This mountain. And the pain they had inflicted on the man he was now in love with. Suddenly here he was, on a mission to avenge Bobby's death. A man Jonas had never even met. How weird was that?

He hung from the ladder for a long moment while shooting a prayer skyward. It was a simple prayer. Basic and to the point. A "give me the courage to finish this shit and not get killed" sort of prayer.

When gentle fingers lightly circled his ankle—Terry probably wondering why he had stopped—Jonas muttered a hasty amen and continued to climb.

Two seconds later, he was in front of a busted-out window, and he got the first whiff of rotted flesh. The smell stopped him cold. He gathered his courage and leaned in closer to the broken window. Somewhere in the distance, down in the bowels of the building, he could faintly hear the shuffle of what he imagined to be countless wings and fat bodies scraping against one another. Worse than that, he could hear what, in his imagination, he interpreted to be the minute cries of hungry young.

Baby monsters! He swallowed a ghastly rush of fear that rattled through his body from one end to the other like some vile candy clattering around inside a piñata. The feeling left him almost breathless. Then slowly his courage began to seep back in.

"I'm going to regret doing this," Jonas whispered to himself. Shaking like he had malaria from the adrenaline coursing through his system, he climbed carefully through the broken window and disappeared among the shadows.

Startled, Terry cried out from the fire escape, "*Where the fuck are you going?*"

"I'm not going. I'm already there," Jonas answered calmly, poking his head over the windowsill and gazing out with a nervous grin. "Come join me. Don't be afraid."

Terry clambered hastily through the window in Jonas's wake, snagging his bootlace on a shard of glass and bitching and moaning every inch of the way. "Don't worry," he snapped. "I'm too scared to be afraid."

"That makes no sense whatsoever," Jonas wisecracked back with a grin.

Kneeling side by side, they stared into the gloom in front of them, stunned to horrified silence by the mind-numbing reek of decomposed flesh that seemed to reach up and grab them by the lapels, shaking them senseless.

"Whatever we find in here, it's not going to be good," Terry breathed, groping for Jonas's hand.

"Courage, kemosabe," Jonas whispered back. This time neither one of them smiled.

Chapter Twenty-Six

GLAD TO be off the wobbling fire escape but by no means pleased to be where he actually was, Terry crouched beside Jonas in the shadows and clutched his hand for emotional support. His throat was so dry he could barely swallow. Rivulets of icy sweat poured down his rib cage, and every muscle in his body seemed to be stretched to its limit, *twanging* like a guitar string. With only the feeble light spilling through the broken window at his back, Terry couldn't see two feet in front of his face. Nor did he want to. He had never been so scared in his life, and Jonas's courage in the face of everything that was happening was starting to make him feel guilty. And here he had always considered himself the butch one of the two. Hmm. Might have to rethink that.

The darkness was saturated with the stench of death, the air foul enough to strip his breath away. It was almost as if the smell of rot and corruption was so thick that it laid a physical sheet before his eyes. He imagined reaching out and pressing his fingertips to the vile reality of it like he might a putrid screen of decomposed flesh hovering there in front of his face. Behind that foul stench, *another* abhorrent smell tried to bleed its way through, to register itself on his already overloaded senses. This one was an acidic smell. Biting and sharp. More chemical than organic. A brittle ammonia that burned the nostrils. Like a festering reek of pus and putrescence that caught in the throat and made the stomach cramp up in disgust.

"Hear them?" Jonas hissed in his ear.

Terry jumped, startled. He was such a nervous wreck he had almost forgotten Jonas was there. Then when Jonas's words soaked in, he nodded. Slipping up through the filthy stink on the air, coming from somewhere down below where Terry knew he would never ever want to go, tiny voices chittered plaintively in the dark. They rose up from deep in the bowels of the building, far below his feet. Impatient, greedy, pleading voices. Insistent mewlings accompanied by the continuous *scritch* of what sounded like a thousand miniscule talons, clamoring for food perhaps, clawing for attention. Like baby birds from hell, demanding, demanding, demanding. Unholy infants of some prehistoric creature that had somehow clawed its way up from the depths of another world to gorge itself on the flesh of this one.

That was as far as Terry's imagination could take him at the moment. Craving light, he reached for his Maglite, but Jonas grabbed his hand to stop him.

"No lights. Wait a minute. Maybe our eyes will adjust to the dark if we get these sun visors out of the way."

Together, they slowly lifted their face masks, pushing them to the top of their helmets with trembling hands. When the visors clicked in place on top their heads, they lowered their hands, discouraged to find themselves still blinded by the shadows in front of them. Although perhaps not quite as thoroughly blinded as before, Terry thought, relying more on wishful thinking than actual fact.

"That helps," he lied. "I can almost see now." It wasn't true, of course. He still couldn't see for shit. Yet it made him feel better to say he could.

"It also makes the smell ten times worse," Jonas complained.

"Can't have everything."

"Thanks, Confucius. Our faces are exposed now. Try not to get a nosebleed."

Terry couldn't argue with that. Even if he bit his tongue, the creatures would be on him in a heartbeat. If it really was the creatures they were hearing down below.

Now that his face was uncovered, the fetor of decay washed over him unhindered. He slapped his hand to his mouth, trying not to retch. It took every ounce of willpower he possessed not to barf up breakfast and maybe a lung or two to boot. Swallowing copiously, he clutched at Jonas's arm until the feeling passed.

By the time he could breathe again without puking, he realized Jonas had been right. His eyes were adjusting to the dark.

The floor felt odd beneath the soles of his boots, and Terry saw now that they were crouching on some sort of metal catwalk. It seemed to be a single walkway leading in a direct line from one side of the vast building to another. As he eased forward on his knees, the catwalk groaned beneath his weight. They would have to move slowly and carefully, or whatever the hell was making those godawful noises down below would hear them creeping around. Terry was pretty sure that would be a very bad thing indeed.

"*What is that?*" he hissed. "I've heard the real creatures, and they don't sound like that at all. What is making that noise?"

"The young," Jonas whispered back. "At least I think that's what it is."

Terry didn't like the sound of that. "You mean to say the creatures are *breeding?*"

"That's what living things do," Jonas said softly, his mouth close to Terry's ear. He had two fingers stuffed up his nostrils to fight the smell.

"Maybe it's something else," Terry pleaded. "Rats, maybe. Or feral cats." He wasn't making any sense, and he knew it. Still, he wasn't quite ready to accept what Jonas was suggesting.

Apparently Jonas wasn't ready to accept Terry's suggestion either. "Yes, I'm sure that's what it is," he drawled, rolling his eyes. "Feral pussycats." He gave Terry a hooded glare, like a schoolteacher confronted with the dumbest student ever.

Terry opened his mouth to defend himself, but Jonas flapped a hand in his face to shut him up. He pulled the .38 from his holster and held it out in front of him. Still stooping low, he duck walked forward a couple of steps before Terry snagged the back of his jacket to stop him.

"Where are you going?"

"I think I see a stairwell leading down," Jonas said. "We have to see what we're up against."

Terry tried to think of a snappy comeback, but his brain was on lockdown. He merely nodded silently, as if accepting the fact that things were now out of his control and he might as well deal with it. Cradling the shotgun in his arms, he made sure the safety was still off before whispering, "Lead the way, bwana."

So Jonas led the way.

Humbly, Terry followed. Duck walking like Jonas, he stayed close to Jonas's back. "How come you're not afraid?" he whispered into the darkness ahead.

Jonas stopped long enough to look back, his face scrunched up in amazement as if he couldn't believe what Terry had just said. "Are you nuts? I'm scared to death."

"You don't act it."

"I'm determined to save your house."

"*What?*"

Jonas clutched Terry's shoulders and held him there, face-to-face, their mouths inches apart. "I liked your little house. I want to live there with you. If we find these fuckers, we can tell the authorities to pinpoint their bombing raid on this one building. Make a surgical strike. Maybe we can keep the damage minimal. Not blow up your whole town and mountain in the process. Take out the nest and be done with it."

"This is the nest?"

"I think so. Yeah. We'll know for sure in a minute."

Terry blinked, stunned. He was also trying to ignore the ache in his knees. Duck walking sucked. "When did you have time to figure all that out?"

"When we were outside hanging on the fire escape."

Terry let that soak in for a minute. Meanwhile, he enjoyed Jonas's breath washing across his face. It was sweet enough to help dispel the stench from whatever the hell was waiting for them down below.

"Do you really think those are the creatures we hear?"

"What else could it be? And don't give me that line about rats and pussycats again. I'm not in the mood."

"Well, don't get snippy."

"I will if I want."

Terry almost smiled. "So what's the plan, then?" he asked, shooting for a more businesslike tone, while deep down inside he was merely trying not to blubber like a baby. He really hated being in this fucking building.

Jonas heaved a slightly impatient sigh. "The plan is we get as close as we can to whatever's making that noise so we can see if they really are what we think they are."

"The creatures."

"Yeah. The creatures."

"That's all?" Terry asked. "That's all we're doing?"

"For now," Jonas answered. "Yeah. That's all we're doing."

"What happens later?"

"Depends on what we find. Oh, and one more thing."

"What's that?" Terry asked, his knees singing an aria now. His back aching. The shotgun weighing a ton in his cramping arms.

"Keep trying not to bleed," Jonas said, and leaning in close, he gave Terry a gentle swipe across the mouth with his lips. "Now come on. Let's finish this. I still have a fuck on hold. You promised."

Terry groaned. "Jesus, grow up!"

Jonas snickered and turned away. Both men rose to their feet, kneecaps clicking audibly. It was so painful, Terry almost cried out when he straightened his bunched-up legs. They inched forward, their racing heartbeats accompanying them every step of the way. Under their feet, the narrow catwalk squeaked and groaned and sprinkled rust flakes, like filthy snow, down through the shadows below. Clearly, human feet had not walked here for decades.

Great smears of a white, powdery substance stained the catwalk's handrails. It didn't take a genius to figure out it was some sort of fecal matter, dried to dust. Both men avoided touching it, even with their gloves on.

"Careful," Jonas said. "We're at the end. Here's the staircase leading down."

Gauging the edge of the first step with the toe of his boot since he couldn't really see it, Terry followed Jonas down the filthy stairway.

As they descended, the stench grew stronger. The mewlings louder.

Terry reached out and clutched at Jonas's jacket again. His heart was a jackhammer, and he imagined he could hear Jonas's heart jackhammering too. Together they were as noisy as a construction crew digging up a street. Gently he gnawed on his lower lip, careful not to break the skin.

Jesus, what the hell are we doing here?

At their backs, a sudden noise exploded around them. It sounded like the slapping of great fists and a gigantic rustle of stiff crepe, all at the same time. Clutching at each other, they ducked their heads.

Figuring that wasn't good enough, Terry dragged Jonas flat to the catwalk floor and covered his body with his own. Reaching up, he pulled both their face masks down as a swarm of creatures swept over them from behind. Close, too close, they battered the air above their heads. Broad wingtips fluttered against them, swatting them like velvet hands. It took Terry a long, terrifying moment to realize they weren't being attacked. Rather the creatures were swooping low and brushing against them as they passed before disappearing down the same stairwell he and Jonas were about to descend. Spatters of red from their latest kill flew from their wingtips with every downstroke, speckling the visor in front of Terry's eyes with the blood from whichever poor human they had recently feasted upon.

Both men lay still as death until the cloud of creatures swept past. They soared by so closely, Terry could feel the wind from their wings at the back of his neck, where neither the helmet nor his jacket collar covered him. When the last beast thundered past to dip below the floor of the catwalk, following the staircase into the shadows below, Terry at long last raised his head.

Jonas rolled over beneath him and pushed both their face masks up. His eyes were as big as saucers, and to Terry's amazement, Jonas was grinning like a kid. "This is the place," he said. "It has to be. We've found the fucking nest!"

Terry's voice was fluttery and weak from the pounding of his heart. "Are we positive?"

Just as Terry knew he would, Jonas shook his head and frowned. "Well, no. We have to go deeper to make sure."

Terry groaned. "I was afraid you'd say that."

He dropped his head to Jonas's chest and listened to Jonas gasping for breath for a while, sick of hearing himself do it. His chest muscles were starting to ache from trying to keep his galloping heart corralled inside his body. He wondered if he was about to have a stroke. But then even that fear left him, because he had too many other things to worry about. The renewed stench of rotted flesh and putrescent blood rose up over them once more, stirred by the flapping of all the blood-soaked wings that had recently passed over.

"They were coated with blood," Terry said, made breathless again thinking about it. "They had just made a kill."

Jonas nodded. "I know. You have spots of blood all over you. So do I." He reached over and ran a gloved fingertip along the ribbed metal of the catwalk. He held the blood-smeared finger up as evidence. "See? It's everywhere."

"Then how come they don't attack us?"

"I don't know. Maybe it's no longer fresh enough to attract them."

Terry swallowed hard before rolling off Jonas and helping him to his feet. They turned to face the stairwell down which the beasts had descended. Both men aimed their guns directly into the darkness in front of them. Two metallic clicks proved their safeties were off.

"Close your mask again," Terry breathed, determined to take control of his fear. "I've got the shotgun. Let me go first. Don't use any lights. Stay close."

He waited until Jonas took a fistful of his jacket to anchor them together before carefully stepping forward. Leading the way this time. Letting Jonas cower behind him for a change.

The stairwell opened up in front of him like a lightless maw. Far below he could once again hear the chittering of what they assumed to be the young of these horrible creatures. Reaching behind him to clutch Jonas's arm and keep him near, Terry began descending the rusty stairs one step at a time. In the darkness, their footsteps were deafening.

Terry hesitated, but behind him Jonas whispered, "Don't stop. Keep going."

Nodding silently, Terry continued descending, the shotgun heavy in his arms. It was Jonas's courage that kept him going, not his own. And Terry damn well knew it.

Slowly, step by quavering step, he descended the catwalk stairs. The man Terry loved clutched the back of his jacket, dragging along in his wake, stuck to him like glue.

The noises and the smells grew stronger as they descended. And so did Terry's sense of loss.

He knew—he absolutely *knew*—they would never be able to leave this place. Their love for each other would die right here in this stinking darkness.

It was that certainty that fed his anger.

And it was his anger that kept him going now. Not his eagerness to prove himself.

"Let's finish this," he hissed into the shadows. He almost smiled, feeling Jonas edge closer to his back, his fingers still grappling at Terry's coattail, hanging on for dear life, getting as close as he could get without crawling up Terry's ass and disappearing altogether.

After what seemed like hours but was really only seconds, they reached a landing on the staircase where the steps turned to descend in another direction. The moment they stepped out onto the landing, the noises below fell mute. Suddenly, they were bombarded with silence.

Jonas hooked his chin on Terry's shoulder and whispered in his ear, "They know we're here."

Terry nodded to show he had heard. There was a fist gripping his throat. The fist was fear. He didn't bother trying to speak because he knew he wouldn't be able to make a sound even if he tried.

A moment later, with Jonas still pressed close to his back, Terry continued descending the catwalk stairway down toward the second floor.

Chapter Twenty-Seven

JONAS'S SALIVA glands were working overtime. The farther they descended, the fouler the reek became. The last thing he wanted to do was throw up. Hurling would make too much noise. But the stench was almost unbearable. There was the added concern that if he barfed inside his helmet he would probably drown in it. Lovely.

Even worse than the smell was the continuing silence that had fallen around them. He imagined hordes of creatures somewhere down below, crouched in anticipation, waiting for the two humans to draw closer. Claws scrabbling at concrete, itching to attack. Bloody, sharp-toothed jaws salivating, gulping in anticipation, eager to rend and shred and tear, aching to consume the delicious warm blood and quivering flesh of their one and only prey. Man.

Jonas tried to shake these thoughts away. It wasn't easy, but having Terry at his side helped him maintain his courage. Or at least maintain the *appearance* of courage.

While he would never get used to the stench of this place—or the unearthly silence either—his eyes had at least grown accustomed to the dark. The shadows were still frightening, but they no longer blinded him. He knew he could see movement now, if movement occurred, and that would give him time to react. If not to save himself, at least to fight back. Blow a few of the fuckers out of the air with his tiny .38. Assuming he could hit them.

More and more he longed for the comfort of Terry's bigass shotgun. Or better yet, Terry's bigass arms holding him naked and safe in their bed, far away from this stinking hellhole and these goddamn monsters.

Side by side with Terry now, Jonas stepped off the staircase and found himself on another catwalk. From where they stood, it appeared this catwalk was different from the last. This one was not a single pathway across the building but meandered off in every direction. A metal maze of turnings and dead ends, all set at right angles. Down below he could see a warren of offices, cubicled off with movable head-high panels. Desks, chairs, file cabinets: it was all there. Everything but computers. Jonas realized that when this business was up and running—back in the '70s, was it?—computers weren't the norm for office equipment.

He and Terry gazed out over the maze of catwalks, and at the same time checked out the warren of offices down below. Still freaked out by the silence… and the fact that down here, deeper inside the building than they had ever been before, the stench of death was almost unbearable. They had the visors lowered on their helmets, but it did little to alleviate the smell. They still avoided touching the catwalk's handrails. The bleached-out remains of creature feces were splattered everywhere. It was down below too, smeared over desktops and puddled in pools of white dust on the office floors.

But of the creatures who made them there was no sign.

"There!" Terry whispered, pointing straight ahead. And Jonas saw it. Another catwalk stairwell leading downward. Past the floor of offices below to the ground floor beneath. To where the creatures must be hiding. Where they lived, perhaps. Where they did whatever they did while they waited for the enticing aroma of human blood to stir them to action, exploding them skyward in hungry, furious swarms, out through the shattered windows above to where some unsuspecting human was bleeding. Ringing the dinner bell. Just for them.

The offices down below seemed to have been quickly abandoned. Or perhaps it was the destruction of empty decades that had thrown them into such chaos. Chairs were overturned. File cabinets had sprung open, spilling pages and pages of paperwork. A lot of puddles were sprinkled about from rain that had blown through the shattered windows above.

Here on the second floor, Jonas could see nothing of the beasts. But he knew they were here, waiting farther down. Cowering for the moment. Or maybe snickering in apprehension. Eager for the stupid humans to draw closer. But how long would they really wait? What would it take to send them shrieking into the air to come tearing at them, mouths gaping, talons extended, their deathly reek leading the way?

Jonas didn't know how long he had been standing there, his imagination getting the better of him. He didn't move until Terry gripped his arm and whispered softly, "Keep going. We're almost there."

And Jonas nodded.

On rubbery legs, he took the lead once again, approaching the stairwell that descended to the floor below. The first floor. He wondered what he would find there. More offices? More overturned chairs and leaking file cabinets? Papers scattered everywhere, drenched and stained with rainwater and filth like what was on the second floor? He was such a bundle of nerves, he had to constantly remind himself to keep his finger off the trigger of the .38 so as not to blow his own foot off. And oh, wouldn't the creatures come then!

A hand at his back urged him gently forward. Comforted by the fact that Terry was there, and in just as much danger as he was, Jonas took the first step down the second stairwell.

He turned at the landing, as he had on the stairwell above, but this time as he approached the second maze of catwalks, he knew things were different. There were no offices below. Only a single reception area that stood opposite the front doors leading out onto the street. That reception area appeared more for show than actual purpose. Behind the reception desk were steel doors leading into the building's interior. Signs could still be read on the doors: Do Not Enter. Do Not Enter.

Edging farther along the catwalk, this one roofed by the floor of the offices above except where the stairwell broke through, Jonas saw the beginnings of what he knew was the source of all the trouble. He didn't know how he knew it; he just did. Terry stepped beside him and pulled him down to his knees, and together they peered down through the mesh of the catwalk floor to study the vast factory floor below. Behind the tiny reception area and the steel doors, the first floor was one vast open space.

It would almost have looked abandoned but for the scurrying of creatures in the shadowy corners. Barely seen, they lurked behind deep vats and labyrinths of stainless steel pipelines that twisted off in every direction. Great valves and wheels and dials and levers were scattered along the pipes. Some of the creatures hung upside down from the gears and tubing, batlike but unbatlike too, gripping the protuberances with the claws that extended from the underside of their wings.

As Jonas knelt above watching, he saw countless eyes, beady and black and cold, staring back. Around the eyes, still hidden in shadow, the bodies of the creatures writhed and shifted in the darkness. Clouds of fat flies buzzed around the creatures, drawn to their stench, feeding off their filth. Halfheartedly, the creatures snapped at them when they came too close.

"Why don't they attack us?" Jonas hissed.

"Remember the dead one we saw? Its nose was huge, but its eyes were tiny. I bet they are almost blind. That's why they only attack at the smell of blood. Human blood. They know we're here because they can hear us a little, but they won't know if we are food as long as we aren't bleeding."

Jonas shivered, thinking about it. It was speculation, of course, but it made sense—as much as any of this did. Then he looked around more closely.

Of the mewling young, he suddenly realized, there was no sign.

Jonas froze. From a distance across the factory floor, back in the depths of the building where he could not see without moving farther along the catwalk, he heard a loud *thump*. Then an echoing metallic *bong*. In his mind's eye, Jonas imagined a heavy body—a body far larger than the creatures they had seen—bumping against one of the huge copper vats scattered around down below. This noise scared him more than all the other noises combined. Because this noise sounded *big*. *Too* big.

"What was that?" Terry cringed at his side, his lips pressed close to Jonas's ear so his voice wouldn't carry.

In answer, Jonas shook his head. Rising silently to his feet, he tugged Terry up beside him. "Let's go find out," he muttered, much to his own surprise.

With Terry's hand firmly clenched in his, he took a step across the catwalk floor in the direction of the sound. Then he took another step. The catwalk squeaked and rattled beneath him, but he kept going, never shifting his gaze from the creatures in their pools of shadow below.

"Careful," Terry breathed in his ear.

Jonas released Terry's hand but stayed close to his side. The noxious odor around them was almost blinding. They crept forward, guns at the ready.

The factory floor below, other than the sealed-off reception area, was not divided into cubicles like the floor above. Here it was a vast hodgepodge of copper vats and assembly belts. Laboratory equipment was scattered across tabletops as far as the eye could see. Glass vials lay shattered on the floor. Everything was covered in cobwebs and dust. It was here where the acidic, chemical smells arose. Jonas breathed through his mouth to dispel the stench. Yet still, beneath it all, the reek of rotting flesh hovered over everything.

"Look out!" Terry cried.

In that instant, a mass of winged creatures exploded from the laboratory floor, swirling upward, their furious cries piercing Jonas's ears. Startled and wracked with sudden terror, he crumpled to his knees and threw his arms over his head. Terry was there too, hunkered down at his side, his strong arms holding Jonas close while they waited for the maelstrom of living, screaming creatures to disperse after rising up through the catwalk stairwell he and Terry had just descended. Seconds later, all sound of their passing ceased, and Jonas knew they had exited the building through the third-floor windows far above their heads.

The moment the creatures were gone and the turmoil over, Jonas sucked in a lungful of air, trying to calm himself. Only then did he realize how long he had been holding his breath. He turned to Terry, whose arms still circled him. Through their face masks, they studied each other's reactions, and in unspoken agreement, they rose up together on kitten-weak legs and looked around.

"They're gone," Terry said.

"Not all of them," Jonas answered back. He leaned over the catwalk railing and pointed downward at the factory floor below. In a maze of great copper vats and cauldrons, half of which had been overturned, he had spotted movement. A chill climbed up his back when he realized what it was.

There amid the vats and shattered equipment, the floor was writhing. No, not the floor. But a mass of mewling creatures intertwined *upon* the floor.

"It's their young," Jonas whispered, his voice brittle with fear.

Terry leaned in beside him. They stared down over the railing, shoulders touching, once again forgetting to breathe.

The organisms below were smaller than the other creatures they had seen. Undeveloped, perhaps. Barely past the embryo stage. White, like fat maggots, with rudimentary wings. Their tiny cries were sharp little yips of sound. They battered at one another with undeveloped wings, tore at one another with tiny claws, fighting for the food Jonas suddenly saw strewn among them. Chunks of bloody flesh, red ropes of intestine and lumps of offal. All human, no doubt. Torn from the bodies of living victims. The younglings fought one another for every bite. And during the fights, when blood was drawn from a sibling, they would turn on the sibling as well. Furious, unstoppable. The ravenous cries of the attacking infants caused Jonas's heart to clench.

Terry pointed off to the side of the writhing beasts. There, in the shadows on the edge of the mass of young, stood what seemed to be sentinels. Full-grown creatures, still bloodied from their last kill. They were herding the young, keeping them in an enclosed space between the overturned vats. Occasionally, they would reach in, pluck one of the young from the mass, and fling it to the back where, Jonas suddenly realized, something lingered.

Something large. Larger than anything they had seen so far.

"Oh my God," Terry whispered. Among the overturned vats and scattered lab equipment, barely visible in the shadows, a great wing flexed and shuddered as if stretching away the kinks. The single wing was more than eight feet long. Onyx flesh and brown fur over a huge framework of bone and sinew. At the inner end of the wing, also hidden in shadow, he spotted a plump belly coated with brown hair and smeared with filth. Blood, feces, and among it all, a smear of something white and jellylike.

While he stared at this unholy horror, Jonas clenched the catwalk railing, no longer heeding the dried feces, not caring that it covered his gloves, was sprinkled across the front of his jacket.

"What *is* that?" Terry hissed in his ear.

As if proudly answering the question for him, the creature lumbered out of the shadows enough to expose itself completely.

It was massive. Heads taller than a man. Its slavering jaws opened wide, and some sort of evil liquid dribbled out. It unfolded both wings at once and the wingspan was enormous. Eighteen feet, maybe. Or more.

Jonas and Terry both froze when the creature lifted its head as if staring right at them. The face called up every horror movie Jonas had seen as a kid. Long fangs sparkled among the filth, beady small eyes squinted upward, as if not really seeing much of anything. It was then that Jonas understood. Like the flying creatures, this beast was almost blind as well.

Most of its understanding of its surroundings, Jonas realized, came from the sprawling flat nose that lay squashed across its face. That nose, the flesh pale and puckered, quivered in anticipation as the creature breathed, sucking in the scents around it, drinking up the incoming data, analyzing everything it could learn about the two trespassers it smelled on the air.

And, Jonas was absolutely sure, homing in on them, placing them exactly where they were, these two human intruders, on the catwalk directly above its head.

Jonas was about to warn Terry that the creature knew where they were, but before he could speak, the great animal down below, which no more resembled a bat than a rhinoceros resembles a gerbil, reared its head back and open its fanged jaws. A bellow of pain or fury or bliss screamed up from its bulging throat, and from beneath its great abdomen, a bag of squirming life erupted. Spilling out onto the floor. Writhing and wriggling inside the placental sack, baby creatures, white and wormlike, tried to escape, to draw their first breath of air, to free themselves of the afterbirth. But they were too weak.

With a single claw from the end of one eight-foot wing, the mother creature tore a gash in the side of the placental sac, and a torrent of foul liquid and small pale bodies gushed out across the floor.

There must have been a dozen or more creatures inside. They crawled away on trembling appendages and were immediately lost in the sea of young already fighting among themselves on the factory floor for their scraps of human flesh.

The mother raised her head one last time, and from her vile throat, another cry erupted. This one victorious. And again Jonas knew the creature's attention was drawn back to the two humans standing on the catwalk above her head.

"Bats don't breed like that," Terry said, his voice a hush of rattled nerves and fear.

Jonas nodded. "These aren't bats."

"No, they aren't. But what the hell are they?"

"I don't think they have a name."

"Can we kill them?" Terry asked.

Jonas turned and stared at him. "We can try. But we have to get out of here first. We have to make a plan."

"Plans are good." Terry gulped, his eyes falling back to the enormous creature below. "Let's do that. And getting the fuck out of here sounds even better."

Jonas's eyes were locked on the monstrous mother. His mind raced. He studied the giant beast through the visor on his crash helmet. The visor was smeared with specks of blood from when the creatures flew over earlier. He had to squint to see through it. "That's the queen, I think. Like with bees. She's the one who breeds these things."

The queen stood among the mass of newborns spilled from the most recent placental sac. Occasionally she took a step forward, using her broad wings like crutches, and as she did, one or more of the infants were crushed beneath her weight. She didn't seem to care. Nor did the other young. They simply slithered in and consumed the body while it was still twitching, rending and gnawing with tiny teeth and claws, emitting a high-pitched whine of pleasure as they fed.

Without warning, a scream tore through the air. A *human* scream!

Stunned, Terry and Jonas spun around. From behind the catwalk staircase leading down to the floor below, a different swarm of creatures appeared. These creatures were struggling in flight. Their wings almost incapable of carrying the cargo they held aloft among them.

It was a young woman. A girl, really. A teenager. She was naked. Her clothes had been stripped away. Her arms and legs were scratched and torn, pulled wide by the claws and fangs of the creatures swarming around her. Rather than tearing her to shreds, they were transporting her. Carrying her toward the queen and the squirming mass of young.

Six feet from the floor, the hovering creatures released the girl. Arms flailing, she screamed again as she fell. The mass of baby creatures writhing below became a frenzied, hungry swarm as soon as the young woman landed among them. She tried to pull herself to her feet and run, but she slipped in the bloody mass of bodies and afterbirth. She fell, landing hard, and the instant she did, the infants closed in, climbing all over her.

"No!" Jonas cried, as the creatures tore with their tiny pale jaws at the girl's flesh. She wailed in pain and struck out in terror, trying to fight them off, but it was hopeless. For in the end, it wasn't really the baby monsters she needed to worry about. It was their mother.

The queen dragged her bloated body across her writhing young and, bending her head, jaws wide, fangs dripping, tore the life from the young girl with one horrible swipe of the dewclaw at the base of her giant wing.

The queen stepped back as her young rushed in again, smothering the girl, lapping at the fresh blood, tearing in a frenzy at the wound in her throat. In their midst, the girl's vacant eyes stared lifelessly at the two men watching in horror from above. The squirming mass of young gnawed at the flesh of the lifeless girl in tiny nips and clawings until there was nothing human left of the girl at all.

Turning away, Jonas pressed his face to Terry's chest.

"Look!" Terry whispered, his lips at Jonas's neck. "The queen is going to feed."

"I can't. I can't look."

But in the end, Jonas turned, still fighting back a sob. The scene down below was almost beyond imagining. The poor girl's flesh was ribboned and torn, the bones exposed, her organs scattered about her. She lay motionless, a pale stick figure among the slithering mass of ravenous young still squirming all over her.

The queen stepped forward toward the girl's body, her massive belly engorged with more young. She dipped her great head and sniffed at the corpse of the girl on the floor. Opening her jaws wide, she bellowed a cry that sent the little hairs on the back of Jonas's neck climbing all over one another.

Jonas realized quickly enough that Terry was right. The queen *was* going to feed. But not from the pitiful remains of the dead girl at her feet. The queen's appetite was centered elsewhere.

She stepped across the body on the floor and lumbered on her crutchlike wings to one of the great copper vats still standing upright. The vat was connected to a maze of piping that crisscrossed the factory wall. At one point the pipeline had broken. And it was from this broken length of pipe that a gelatinous white mass seeped into the vat below.

The vat was man-high, but the queen was tall enough to bend her head over the lip of the vast cauldron. From their vantage point up above, Jonas and Terry could see everything the creature did from that moment on.

Dipping her heavy head into the copper vat, she began to lap at the white substance that had gathered inside. Like a kitten with a saucer of milk, her great body trembled in bliss as she consumed the food.

Terry's fingers tightened around Jonas's arms. "That's the source!" he hissed. "Whatever that substance is, that's what created all this! It must be some sort of growth hormone, or some other weird chemical concoction they were working on here. Maybe it was innocent enough back then, but leaving it inside those pipes for all these decades did something to it. The chemicals changed." He extended a long arm to the creature below, still lapping at the cheesy, bubbling mass inside the vat. "And when a regular bat ate from the vat, it created *her*!"

"How could one breeding female create all these creatures in a matter of months?"

Terry shook his head. "Who knows? If it is a growth hormone, maybe it has some sort of accelerant in it that speeds up the process. Plus you saw how many live births can be accomplished at once. More than a dozen tiny creatures came out of that thing." To prove his point, he pointed to the infants still writhing on the floor below in the pool of afterbirth and blood.

They watched as one of the flying creatures, so much smaller than the queen, landed on the lip of the vat beside her dipping head. It leaned down to sip at the white mass too, and the moment it did, the queen roared in fury. With a swing of her massive wing, she knocked the creature across the room. It struck the wall and slithered lifeless to the floor, where more of the young slithered in to tear it apart.

"She's the only one who eats it! She guards it from the others to hoard it for herself," Terry said, tensing at Jonas's side. Terry's eyes grew bright behind the bloodied face mask. And when Terry said what he said next, Jonas knew he was exactly right.

"If we destroy the factory and whatever that white stuff is coming out of that pipe, we can kill the queen. She clearly needs it to remain what she's become. The breeder of all these… *things*."

Jonas stared down at the young girl's lifeless body. It was almost unrecognizable now, so little was left of it. Another piece of the puzzle clicked into place inside his head.

"The hunters must be drawn to only two scents," Terry added, his eyes still bright with excitement. "The smell of human blood, which sends them out to kill and feed. And the scent of their queen, which draws them back here to feed her young and to rest until they hunt again."

Jonas gripped his arm. "But there aren't many people left. For everyone but the queen, the food supply is dwindling. They'll have to move on soon. They'll have to escape the quarantine zone and find a fresh supply of humans to feed upon."

Jonas blinked, suddenly understanding it all. "The authorities! They don't have to blow up the whole town and mountain. They just need to blow up this one building. This one nest!"

Terry nodded, excitement lighting his eyes. "We have to tell them." He tugged Jonas toward the stairway they had descended only minutes before. Not caring that the catwalk was rattling beneath their feet. Not caring that the creatures below could hear them hurrying to escape.

"We have to tell them *now!*" Terry hissed, climbing faster.

Before the catwalk behind them could block their view completely, Jonas stumbled to a stop to look back. There, at the great vat with the white cheesy chemicals seeping into it, the queen stood frozen, her special food smeared pale across her jaws, her furred head bobbing high.

Her splayed nose twitched and flexed, catching every nuance on the air, as she coldly watched them leave. Something about the hateful tilt of her head and the piercing glare of her weak small eyes, made Jonas think she was imprinting their scent on her memory banks.

Sickened by the thought, Jonas shuddered and spun away.

Chapter Twenty-Eight

THE JEEP barreled through the empty streets of Spangle like a bat out of hell. And *that*, Terry reprimanded himself with a sardonic grin, was simply a figure of speech, not a reference to the current wildlife situation. Although considering what they had just seen, it certainly could have been. He clipped a tumbleweed with his front fender and sent it flying. A stray dog yelped and scurried across the street to get out of their path.

They banged into a pothole, and Terry and Jonas both had to scramble to hold on.

"Do you think they'll listen?" Jonas yelled, both hands on the dashboard, trying not to be catapulted through the windshield.

Terry had to bellow to be heard. The wind rushing through the hole in the canvas roof was deafening. "The authorities are there to keep the creatures quarantined. They must know by now they can't really do that. They have to kill them before they have a chance to escape!"

"But they already have a bombing run planned in two days' time, remember?"

"Yeah!" Terry cried, fighting the wheel and staring furiously at the road ahead. "They'll be taking out the whole town and an entire mountain when they do. I'm hoping they'll listen when we offer them a less destructive path to take, yet still get the job done."

He glanced at Jonas, who was looking worried. "Maybe we should find a landline in town and telephone it in," Jonas said. "If we show ourselves, they may not let us return."

"If they want us to share the information we have, and if they really want to kill the creatures, they'll have to let us back in," Terry answered.

With the mountain rising up at their backs on the other side of town, the two-lane highway they were traveling that led away from Spangle to the north was flat and dry and cut through desert scrubland. The wind was up, and thick streamers of sand drifted across the asphalt in front of them. The blowing sand was so deep, the yellow lines were already obscured. Route 79 had never been so deserted. There was no other traffic on the road.

Jonas leaned forward and peered upward through the windshield. "Helicopter!" he cried.

Terry craned forward to see where Jonas was pointing. It was a News 8 chopper, and it was following them down the road. He could see a guy leaning out the chopper's open side door with a big camera on his shoulder, filming the Jeep below.

Terry laughed. "We're on TV!"

Jonas rolled his eyes. "We're lucky it's a camera lens, and not a gunsight."

In the distance, Terry saw the flash of red-and-blue lights strobing atop a row of cop cars blocking the road ahead. A line of armed highway patrol officers with long guns in hand, stood in front of the cars, legs braced wide, watching the Jeep race toward them. Squinting, Terry could make out Army vehicles lined up behind the squad cars. Men in uniform—either Marines or Army; he couldn't tell from this distance—stood watching them from truck beds with binoculars. The military guys looked a little less freaked out about their approach than the cops did. Terry was glad to see them, though. It was the military guys he needed to talk to.

As the Jeep drew close, Terry eased up on the gas and laid on the horn. He traveled the last few hundred yards making as much noise as he could. He raised a white hanky through the hole in the canvas roof and waved it around as he drew near since the cops were still looking nervous. Every person on the planet knew that nervous cops were trigger-happy cops. Terry was hoping the military guys would keep the cops in line. He and Jonas didn't need to get blown away at this point in the game.

He slammed on the brakes. Jonas gave a yip of surprise, as the Jeep slued around on screaming tires to buck to a stop not ten feet away from the nearest CHP cruiser. When he turned off the ignition, every gun in every cop's hand was aimed directly at their heads.

Terry supposed they didn't like his driving.

Leaving his shotgun behind, he plucked the .38 from Jonas's holster as well and dropped it on the floorboard before he climbed out of the Jeep and walked toward the line of policemen. Jonas joined him, and not giving a rat's ass what anyone thought, Terry wove his fingers through Jonas's and hung on tight, keeping him snug to his side as they approached. When he reached the cops, he squeezed between two highway patrol guys without saying a word. With guns still aimed at their heads, he ignored the policemen completely and dragged Jonas forward until they were face-to-face with the military men in the back. They were Army, he saw now. And they looked deadly serious, if not a little curious to boot.

A lean Army man who must have been in his fifties, with far more stripes on his uniform than the others, stepped up to meet them. To Terry's surprise, the officer stuck his hand out and offered to shake. Terry accepted, and so did Jonas. After that, the cops shuffled their feet, looking disgruntled, but still kept their weapons raised. Terry didn't care about them or what they thought. After their handshakes with the officer were over, he reclaimed Jonas's hand, wrapping it safely inside his own.

Terry opened his mouth to explain what was going on, but the officer spoke first.

"We've been watching you two."

Terry looked surprised enough for the officer to smile. He pointed skyward at one of the drones hovering overhead. "Drones," he explained. "We've been monitoring everything. My name is Colonel Briggs." He eyed the two up and down, even glancing at the torn canvas roof of the Jeep. "Where's your little dog?" he asked with a smile.

"Bruce is back at the cabin," Terry said without missing a beat.

The officer nodded, as if he'd expected as much. Piercing blue eyes studied both men in turn. "I'm assuming, gentlemen, that you didn't come here to surrender."

"That's right," Terry said. "We didn't. And no matter what happens in the course of this meeting, when it's over, Jonas and I are going back across that quarantine line to our home. I just want you to know that."

"I could arrest you for your own protection," Briggs said, but he didn't appear to be inclined to follow through with that threat. Instead he asked point-blank, "So what are you here to tell me?"

"You've been watching us?" Jonas asked.

Briggs eyed him and pushed his khaki hat back off his head to rub his forehead. His hair was snow-white and cropped so close as to be almost nonexistent. He made an impatient flapping motion with his other hand, and all the armed policemen reluctantly holstered their weapons. The soldiers behind the colonel had already done so.

"Yes, son. We have."

Terry stepped closer and lowered his voice. "Then you know where we've been. In the old research facility in town."

"The abandoned brick building, yes. And the way you ran out of the place, I have a pretty good hunch that building has something to do with what you want to tell me."

Terry glanced at all the soldiers eyeballing the three of them. He saw the weapons in their arms, pointed down at the ground now, and he also took note of a variety of bigger guns mounted on Army vehicles lined up behind the police cars. He knew this was only one checkpoint in the line of defense against the creatures escaping. He didn't want to think about the bombs he couldn't see.

"We're not the only two people left in there."

Briggs nodded. "I know."

"Then you also know you'll be killing innocent civilians if you carry through with your threat to bomb the area."

Briggs didn't look happy when he said, "We're aware of that, son. But letting the creatures escape to wreak havoc across the planet does no one any good either."

"I understand that," Terry said. "But what if I can pinpoint the location of the creatures for you? What if I can tell you exactly where they'll be?"

Briggs studied him closely, shifting his gaze to Jonas for a moment, then back to Terry. "I'm afraid it won't matter," he said. "Not unless you can guarantee us that every single creature on that mountain and in that town will be in the very same spot at any given time. Can you do that?"

Terry felt Jonas's eyes on him. He stared up at the news helicopter, still watching—and filming for all he knew—as it hovered overhead. He thought of the creatures spilling out through the broken factory windows, pulled away from their nest by the scent of fresh blood. *Human* blood. How *could* he guarantee that every creature would be inside that building at the same time? And how could narrowing the bombing raid to one particular building work at all if he *couldn't* guarantee it.

His mind raced while Briggs stared. The older officer didn't look impatient; he merely looked resigned, knowing he had given Terry an unsolvable problem. And no matter what Terry thought *should* happen, there could really only be one outcome, and it was the outcome the colonel had been planning all along.

"I'm sorry," Briggs said. "I know you want to save your homes. But blanket bombing is the only way to ensure the creatures are exterminated. Unless you can think of a better plan, the bombing will begin on schedule." He glanced at his watch. "In thirty-nine hours and twenty-seven minutes to be exact."

Jonas jumped, and both Terry and Briggs turned to stare at him. Jonas grabbed Terry's arm and gave him a shake.

"I know how we can do it!" he blurted out. "I know how we can make sure every single creature is inside that factory at the same time!"

Terry opened his mouth to ask how, or to ask if Jonas was nuts, or maybe simply to ask what the hell Jonas was talking about. But he didn't get a chance.

Jonas simply lifted his head, eyeing the helicopter above. He raised his arm, extended his hand, and gave the cameraman the finger. A moment later, looking defiant and sexy as hell (Terry thought), Jonas rested his eyes on Briggs instead. His fingers tightened around Terry's hand. "It'll work. I know it will. Give us a chance, sir. You can monitor us, and if we succeed in getting all the creatures inside that building, you will know. You can launch a pinpoint bombing run, drop a shitload of bombs on that one tiny target, and if we fail, you can still do a blanket bombing run later and take out the whole town and mountain. But we can do it, sir. We can get the creatures in there. I know we can! When we've succeeded, we'll signal you from the ground."

Terry couldn't imagine what Jonas was thinking of or what kind of plan he was talking about, but he wasn't about to argue. If Jonas thought he had a plan, then who the hell was Terry to doubt him?

Terry turned to Briggs to back Jonas up, reassuring himself that the colonel knew exactly what it was he and Jonas wanted his Army to do. "When we give the signal, we want you to bomb the old deserted factory. The building you just saw us leave. Don't take out the rest of the town. Don't bomb my mountain or my house or the Tastee Freez on the corner of Tenth and Juniper. I love that Tastee Freez. Just annihilate the one single abandoned fucking building we're telling you about. That's where their nest is. That's where their *queen* is."

Briggs's eyes popped open wide. "What do you mean, their queen?"

"It's how they breed, sir," Jonas explained, "and it all takes place inside that building."

"Take out the queen," Terry explained, "and you take out their ability to reproduce. Take out the building and you take out the workers and all the freshly spawned young that can't fly yet but one day soon will. This is your only chance to get them all together and wipe them out in one big kablooey."

Colonel Briggs was clearly biting back a grin. "In military parlance, we don't really call it that, son."

It was Jonas who leaned in and tapped Briggs's chest with a fingertip. "We don't care what you call it. Just so long as you *do* it. All right?"

Briggs laughed out loud. "Jesus, boys, go round up your monsters. You get 'em in one place, and I'll tear them a new asshole. Believe me. I can send a single napalm-tipped SSM and hit a spot six inches in diameter within five minutes of your signal."

"What's an SSM?" Terry asked.

"Surface-to-surface missile, son."

"Oh."

"What kind of signal should we send?" Jonas asked.

"I don't know. Hell, son. Wave your little white hanky again. Seemed to work the last time. Just make sure you get yourselves to a safe distance away from that building before you call in that strike, or it'll be your own assholes that go up in smoke."

Jonas grinned. "Well, that's descriptive." He turned to Terry. "Wasn't that descriptive?"

Terry laughed. He shot an apologetic wink at the colonel. "My friend gets a little excited. Bear with him. It's been a hell of a few weeks. What with falling in love and everything."

Briggs eyed them each in turn. He was still looking fairly amused, Jonas thought. And a little confused.

Without commenting on the "love" remark, Briggs pointed skyward at a tiny drone, humming about forty feet up. "We'll monitor you with that. When you wave your white hanky, the one you were waving when you barreled through our quarantine line, then we'll know we have a confirmation that the creatures are inside the building. We'll give you five minutes to get away before we strike. And trust me. It'll be a big, hot kablooey when it comes. So get yourselves to a safe distance. Understand?"

"Yes," Jonas and Terry said in unison. "We understand. And thanks."

The smile faded from Brigg's face. His eyes grew serious. "You realize that if we think we missed even one of these critters with this pinpoint bombing strike you're asking for, the original plan will go back into effect. We'll blow the whole town and the whole mountain right off the map. Is that understood?"

Before either could answer, Colonel Briggs turned away and started yelling orders. Soldiers jumped to attention, then scurried away like ants.

Jonas stared at Terry for a long somber moment before heading for the Jeep.

Terry shook his head and followed, hoping to hell Jonas knew what he was doing.

Chapter Twenty-Nine

ONCE AGAIN, Terry manhandled the Jeep along the same route they had taken to talk to the colonel. With their face masks pushed up and out of the way, they had to squint against the wind rushing through the torn canvas roof. Spangle was coming up fast, and Jonas knew Terry still had no idea what his big plan entailed. Terry didn't know because Jonas didn't have it all figured out yet either. He sat hunched over in the passenger seat, mumbling to himself, trying to lay it all out inside his head before explaining it to Terry.

But Terry wasn't looking particularly patient. Obviously, he wanted to know *now*. After all, a big chunk of the United States Army was back there waiting for them to do whatever it was Jonas had promised they were going to do. Who could blame Terry for wanting to know *how* they were going to do it?

Terry tried for the third time to worm it out of him. "Just tell me this," he demanded. "How are we going to account for every single creature and make sure they are all inside that building at the same time?"

Jonas snuck him a glance. Suddenly he didn't seem as sure of himself as he had back when he was poking his cocky finger in the colonel's chest. "I do have a plan, you know."

Terry's knuckles were white on the steering wheel as he plowed into another tumbleweed. It flew back over the roof of the Jeep like a gigantic soccer ball. "Yes, dear, I *know* you have a plan. But what the hell is it?"

"It's sneaky," Jonas said.

Terry heaved a sigh. "Sneaky's good. Can you be a little more specific?"

They were speeding down Spangle's main drag now. Two blocks up, they could see the stained brick walls and shattered third-floor windows of the bankrupt and abandoned supplement factory. Hovering alongside the factory walls, Jonas pointed to the tiny drone that Briggs had sent to keep an eye on them.

Terry nodded to indicate he had seen it already. "Plan," he growled through clenched teeth. "Tell me your *plan*."

Still two blocks away from the factory, Jonas cried, "Stop!" and Terry slammed on the brakes. The Jeep lurched up onto the sidewalk and took out a parking meter. Nickels and dimes rolled off in every direction. The guns in the back seat clattered to the floor.

"Oops," Terry said.

He gazed questioningly at the storefronts nearby. Doctor's office, hobby store, small appliance repair shop. Blood bank. Ice cream parlor. They were two blocks short of the research facility where the queen resided, and Terry clearly still didn't know what was going on. "What the hell are we doing here?"

"I love you," Jonas said, his eyes as big as he could make them. Puppy-dog eyes, he hoped. Because frankly, if Terry didn't like his plan he suspected the big burly redhead was going to wring his neck. Puppy-dog eyes might be Jonas's only avenue of defense. He brought out the big guns as well, laying a gentle hand on Terry's muscled thigh, which, in spite of everything happening around them, still made Jonas's dick give an anticipatory twitch inside his pants.

Good to know that in spite of it all, the testosterone was still pumping.

He slid his hand to Terry's crotch and felt a definite shift of priorities there as well, as some sort of intriguing bulge began growing beneath his fingertips.

Terry narrowed his eyes and glowered. "As you can undoubtedly feel, I love you too. Now what's the plan?"

Jonas pointed to the storefront closest to the Jeep. "*That's* the plan."

The store sitting next to the doctor's office had a big red heart painted on the window. Terry blinked, staring at it.

Jonas grinned, watching him. "I can hear the wheels turning inside your head. You're starting to get the picture, right?"

Terry tore his eyes from the storefront window and focused on Jonas with serene blankness. "It's the blood bank," he said. "So what?"

Jonas gave a cluck. "Maybe it wasn't your wheels I heard turning after all." He jabbed a thumb through the open Jeep window at the building Terry was still gaping at. "They store blood in there. Human blood. We swipe it, haul it into the bat nest, and use it for bait. The smell will draw every creature within a dozen miles, if there are any that far away. When the creatures are all there, slurping up the blood, presto!" And he hauled out his little white hanky and flapped it in Terry's face.

Jonas was pleased to see a little more life pop into Terry's eyes. "Now the wheels are turning," he said, with a wily squint. "I can hear them creaking."

Terry eyed him warily. "You really think it'll work?"

"Got any better ideas?"

Terry frowned, licked his lips, scratched his ear, and finally smiled a cagey smile. He slapped open the car door and leaped out. "Excellent plan!" he cried, grabbing the shotgun. "Let's do it!"

"Really?"

"Yeah. Really. Besides, what else have we got?"

Jonas shrugged. "Nothing."

"Exactly."

Jonas mumbled to himself in relief that Terry had accepted his plan so easily. It still sounded a little goofy to him. He reached down to the back floorboard, grabbed the .38, and stuffed it into his holster.

Two seconds later, Terry was smashing a hole through the blood bank's plate-glass window with the barrel of the shotgun. He diligently knocked a few leftover shards out of the frame and climbed inside with Jonas at his heels.

Terry scratched his head, looking around. "Now what?"

Jonas pointed to a Medical Personnel Only sign on a swinging door at the back of the room behind the reception desk. They skirted the desk and banged their way through the door. Inside they found two reclining chairs with IV stands alongside where the blood was donated. Past the chairs, another set of swinging doors led farther into the interior with more signs telling nonmedical personnel to stay the hell out. Only nicely.

Jonas and Terry poked their heads through the second set of doors together. "Bingo!" Terry laughed.

Beaming proudly, Jonas followed him into the lab. Three large stainless steel refrigeration units stood in a row along the back wall. They looked like gigantic refrigerators, but Jonas knew better. He had given blood a few times in college to finance the occasional drunken weekend. He knew how blood banks worked.

The refrigeration units weren't locked. He yanked the door open on the first one and there in front of his eyes hung row after row of clear plastic transfusion bags filled with blood. Jonas didn't know if this was whole blood or not, and he wondered if it would be enough to attract the little bat fuckers and keep them in the research building long enough for the Army to light them up. Now that he was here, he seemed to find a few unexpected holes in his plan. Platelets, plasma, red blood cells, who knew what really drew the creatures in? Or what would work best for bait.

Terry tapped one of the bags. "RBC. Red blood cells," he said. "It's labeled right here. This is close to whole blood. At least I think it is. We'll use these."

He started yanking the red IV bags off the hooks and dumping them on a tabletop nearby. Jonas found a cardboard box and, handling them carefully, stacked the bags inside. It wouldn't be prudent to tear the bags open before they get to where they needed to go. Otherwise the creatures might think they were offering *themselves* up for bait.

When the box was full, Terry shot him a wink and said, "Let's go."

Jonas nodded, all businesslike even while taking a brief moment to slide his hand along the bristle of Terry's five-o'clock shadow, which he loved to touch.

Terry kissed his hand with a teasing glint in his eye, then tugged him toward the door. Once outside, Terry ordered, "Wait here."

To Jonas's surprise he disappeared into a thrift store on the other side of the doctor's office, once again smashing his way through a plate-glass window with the barrel of his shotgun. Looter extraordinaire. He was in and out in seconds, and when he did return he had two brand-new backpacks, one blue and one yellow, draped across his shoulders. Two minutes later, Jonas was back in the Jeep, cradling the backpacks stuffed with infusion bags filled with human blood in his lap while Terry gunned the Jeep down the street and swerved around to the alley at the back of the research facility.

They climbed out, staring upward at the rusty fire escape attached to the wall above their heads. As they gawked, a swarm of creatures tore through the broken third-floor windows. Jonas and Terry ducked, but the creatures ignored them, winging away to the south where somebody was about to have a very bad day.

"Let's climb," Jonas whispered, and without waiting for an answer, he began scaling the fire-escape ladder, one backpack dangling off his back. Terry gave him a friendly pat on the ass and mounted the ladder to follow, the second backpack, the yellow one, hanging from his shoulders.

Jonas paused below the shattered third-floor windows and scanned the skies around him, praying he wouldn't see any creatures returning.

And he didn't. But from below, Terry tapped him on the ankle and pointed to the north. Jonas saw it then. A tiny drone, hovering about fifty feet away, monitoring their movements with its small but efficient camera.

Jonas shot the drone a thumbs-up and could have sworn he saw the tiny rotors dip in response. He scooted the rest of the way up the ladder to tumble through the broken third-floor window. Terry landed in a heap beside him. There they were once again bombarded with the reek of death and rot and corruption. Both men immediately lowered the visors on their crash helmets, but it didn't help much. The stench was too powerful. In the distance, the mewling of the infants, slithering around in their placental slime, could be faintly heard rising from below.

Where the queen was, Jonas didn't know. Nor did he really want to.

Moving carefully now, Jonas led the way. He edged along the catwalk toward the first staircase leading down. By the time he got there, as he knew they would, his eyes began to adjust to the dark.

Moving as quietly as he could, Jonas headed down the metal stairs, one squeaking step at a time, clutching tightly at the backpack on his shoulder. The sound of Terry's boots and the swish of Terry's clothing assured him Terry was trailing along behind.

The familiar, frightful smells brought an all-new flood of terrors rushing over him. He tried not to think about what lay in the shadows below. Or the girl the creatures had torn apart only an hour before. He hesitated, stumbling to a stop, his heart hammering a mile a minute.

"Keep going," Terry whispered when Jonas paused. Determined, but scared out of his wits, Jonas finally did as Terry insisted. He kept moving forward.

A moment later, they stood side by side at the head of the last staircase leading down into the depths of hell. Jonas clutched the backpack in his sweaty hand, uncertain how to proceed.

"How do we do this?" he hissed.

At that moment, they heard a soft, whimpering cry coming from below. A human cry. A *child's* cry. "Help me!" the child sobbed. "Please!"

"Oh shit," Jonas gasped. "It's a kid!"

Thrusting the backpack filled with blood into Terry's arms, he vaulted down the last flight of stairs. Straight into the creatures' lair. Beneath his pounding boots, the metal catwalk rattled loudly enough to wake the dead.

Chapter Thirty

"NO!" TERRY screamed. But it was too late. Jonas was too far away to be snatched back.

Terry knelt at the top of the staircase. He watched as Jonas splashed through the pool of placental slime with the mewling, maggotlike infants still feeding on what was left of the teenage girl the creatures had dropped before. There was almost nothing left of her now, and the babies were clamoring for fresh meat. Their mewling intensified as Jonas hotfooted it through and around them, heading for the mess of upturned vats lying in a tumble by the back wall. The disgusting infants snatched at his ankles as he passed, but cussing up a storm, Jonas shook them off as quickly as they latched on.

Looming ahead of Jonas, the queen appeared, her white-smeared jaws oozing the chemical concoction she had been devouring earlier. She opened her gaping mouth wide and roared in fury at the intruder. Around her, the flying creatures, her workers, her drones, trembled and scuttled in the shadows, aching to swoop in and tear Jonas limb from limb. But they were clearly afraid of the queen and refused to draw any closer than they already were.

Regally, the great creature ignored her underlings, as queens are wont to do. Her beady eyes, black and fearless, were centered solely on Jonas. When he slipped in the placenta at his feet, the queen raised her broad wings as if preparing to attack. But Jonas reclaimed his footing and kept running.

"Where are you!" he cried, scurrying through the shadows, searching for the child.

Up ahead, both Jonas and Terry heard a plaintive plea. Terry tensed at the top of the stairs while Jonas shifted course immediately, hustling through a tumble of old barrels that must have once held chemicals for the production of whatever the hell it was they had been making here. Supplements, supposedly. *Growth* supplements, no doubt, judging by the size of the queen.

Jonas disappeared behind the barrels, and at the edge of his sight, Terry could see the workers shuffling closer. They were preparing to attack Jonas now that he was farther away from the queen.

But before they could swoop in, Jonas reappeared. He popped out from behind the barrels and into the dim light so quickly that Terry heard himself shouting a cheer before he even knew it was coming.

His jubilation died quickly enough when he saw what Jonas was carrying in his arms. It was the little girl from the yellow Camry. The one traveling with her mother. The one he thought had been slain with the mother back on the road when they found the abandoned car with the shattered, bloodied windshield.

As if he didn't have enough to worry about, Terry still took a moment to wrack his brain, trying to think of the girl's name. Jenny…? Jackie…?

Jilly! That was it. The kid's name was Jilly.

Grabbing up the shotgun and the two backpacks filled with infusion bags, Terry stormed down the stairs to help Jonas. Not caring about the noise he was making now, he danced through the placental pool as gamely as he could, kicking the young fuckers out of the way like fat squishy footballs. In their midst he dropped the two backpacks and left them in the writhing mass of infants. Slinging his shotgun back over his shoulder, he tried to take the girl from Jonas's arms, but Jonas shrugged him away.

"I've got her," Jonas cried. "Let's get out of here! Where's the blood?"

Terry pointed to the backpacks on the floor. The embryos were crawling all over the two bags, trying to find a way inside. Even the flying workers seemed to have taken an interest in the bags. They were edging closer to them, less afraid of the queen now than they had been before. Terry wondered if they could smell the blood.

Well, if they didn't now, they would in a minute.

"Get up the stairs, then!" Terry yelled. "I'll be right behind you! I've got one more thing to do."

Jilly lifted her head to stare at Terry, her eyes wild and terrified. She wore only a filthy pair of cotton underpants. The rest of her clothes had been ripped away. Her frail body was coated with filth, although she seemed to be unhurt. She flung out a tiny hand and grabbed Terry's collar. "I remember you," she said. "You saved me and mommy from the lion in the cave."

Terry tried to smile, to comfort the girl. "That's right, honey. Now we're here to help you again."

She blinked as if accepting his words as utter truth. She glanced back at the place where Jonas had found her. "I'm the only one left," she said. "The others are... dead."

"You mean there were others with you?"

Jilly nodded. "They were feeding us to those white things, one at a time."

Jonas and Terry both looked back in the direction where Jonas had found the girl.

"Are you sure you're the last?" Terry asked, fighting the urge to weep at what this child had gone through.

Jilly nodded. Then biting back a sob, she squeezed her eyes shut as if trying to block it all from her mind. Everything. The creatures. Her mother's death. All of it.

She began to sob quietly in Jonas's arms as Terry pushed them both toward the stairs.

"Go," Terry ordered. "Get her out of here! I'll be right behind you."

Jonas turned to run but stopped when a large shadow fell over the three of them. It was the queen. She lumbered toward them on her crutchlike wings. She trembled and flung her massive wings wide as if daring them to pass. A whining tremolo of fury erupted from deep inside her furry throat. It was a wail of anger and ferocious hatred. With the scream came a fresh spate of foul air rising up from beneath her broad wings, like the stench of corruption at the opening of a sodden casket. The smell brought tears to Terry's eyes, and again he pushed at Jonas to get him moving toward the stairs.

The queen shuffled closer, and as before the workers retreated, drawing back into the shadows. As Jonas and Terry slid and stumbled through the placental slime and the maggotlike creatures wriggling in it, snapping at their shoes and cuffs as they passed, the queen bellowed in fury once again.

Terry chased Jonas across the factory floor, slipping and sliding through the filth. He clambered up the catwalk staircase hot on Jonas's heels. As Jonas continued racing upward with Jilly weeping in his arms, Terry turned at the first landing and stared down at the writhing creatures below. At the maggoty babies, blind and disgusting, slithering in the slime. At the winged workers—the drones, the *killers, like the ones that took Bobby*—hesitating in the shadows as if afraid to move without the queen's permission. Then there was the queen herself. Her wings spread wide, her vast corrupt body pulsating with hate and bloated conceit, offended to the core that these paltry human beings had invaded her domain.

It was toward the queen that Terry focused his purest rage. The ugly bitch.

And it was that final thought that made him laugh out loud.

He raised his hand and shot her the finger, then lifted the shotgun and aimed it at the two backpacks on the factory floor. They were all but buried beneath the crawling bodies of the newborn young, their greedy voices and fat white bodies still clamoring to be fed, still scrabbling for flesh to rend, for blood to drink.

"I'll give you blood." Terry smirked. And sighting carefully, he pulled the trigger.

The shotgun kicked and the noise was deafening, echoing between the factory walls. He recocked and fired again. Down below, first the blue backpack, then the yellow one, exploded in a mist of red as pints and pints of blood splashed out in every direction, splattering everywhere.

The winged workers immediately billowed out from every shadow, every crevice. The queen roared in anger. The fat younglings mewed and slavered and squirmed over the remnants of the shotgun-shattered bags, fighting one another to feed, relishing the fresh bounty. And over it all, an influx of winged workers swarmed into the building from outside, drawn by the smell, pushed to ravenous insanity by the spicy scent of fresh human blood. Swarm after swarm, creatures roared through the windows above, drawn by the scent radiating up from the factory floor. They swept down through the catwalk staircases, a solid stream of hunger and fury.

As the creatures spilled into the building from outside, Terry spun and threw himself up the staircase, batting the flood of beasts aside as he climbed. Jonas was already out of sight, around the staircase bend on the flight above. He could hear Jonas's boots clattering across the catwalk. He was speaking softly, crooning almost, trying to calm the girl in his arms. At the sound of Jonas's voice Terry's heart swelled to twice its size and he admitted yet again how much he loved the man. How much he wanted to be with him for the rest of his life.

But first they had to get away from this building and give Briggs the signal to attack!

"Look out!" Jonas yelled from above.

Terry looked up just in time to see another swarm of creatures swooping down from the floor above, dipping in a cloud down the staircase in front of him like a tornado of flesh and claws and teeth. Whirling and corkscrewing, they funneled their way toward the factory floor below… homing in on the smell of food. Behind them, in swarm after swarm, more creatures kept coming.

Unable to move forward against the flood, Terry hunkered down while the beasts swooped over him in a steady stream. When the last of the creatures had finally passed, he allowed himself a second to chuckle maliciously at how stupid they were. Then he took off running to catch up with Jonas and the girl.

It was time to get the hell out!

Chapter Thirty-One

JONAS FLIPPED the face mask back out of the way and sucked in a great mouthful of clean air. Sunlight had never felt so welcome against his skin.

His shoulders ached with the weight of the girl clinging to his neck. He kept one arm around Jilly's waist as he clamped her to his chest, and with the other arm he climbed carefully down the fire escape at the back of the building. Off to his left in midair, he saw one of the colonel's drones monitoring his descent.

Even as he climbed down, his whole body shaking with fatigue and adrenaline, Jonas kept staring upward, waiting for Terry to exit the building too. Wondering what was keeping him. Wondering what he would do if Terry didn't come out at all.

Their plan had worked. He knew that much. Scattered creatures were still flitting through the shattered third-floor windows from God knows where. They were homing in on the scent of blood exactly as Jonas thought they would. Amazingly, his plan had worked far better than he ever hoped.

But he knew damn well he wasn't going to let Briggs blow the place up if he didn't get Terry out first.

Jilly sobbed softly in his arms, and he gently shushed her, telling her everything would be all right. "Just hold on. We're almost there." The child buried her face against his neck and squeezed her eyes shut, her own small body trembling as much as Jonas's.

He craned his head back and stared upward again while he continued to descend. The creatures had all gone inside. No others were entering now, flapping their way between the shattered panes. He could imagine them all in there, swooping down toward the factory floor, lured by the scent of blood. He had heard the gunshots. He knew what Terry had done to release the blood. But now it was time for Terry to leave! *Where the hell is he?*

"Terry!" Jonas bellowed toward the windows above.

The girl clutched him more tightly, startled by his yell, and as he shushed her again, he spotted a weary face poking from the window above, wearing a grin.

"Keep your pants on!" Terry sputtered. And clambering through the window frame, into the sunlight and out of the gloom, he began scrambling down the fire-escape ladder. He moved quicker than Jonas because he didn't have a kid around his neck and had both arms free. Soon Terry had caught up, and the rest of the way down, the three descended together.

In the sky beside them, the colonel's drone descended too. His strength almost drained, Jonas gratefully set a foot to the ground and stepped back out of the way so Terry could leave the ladder too.

He looked down at the young girl in his arms and realized she was asleep. Poor kid. What she must have gone through!

Jonas breathed a sigh of relief when Terry stepped close and wrapped his arms around the two of them, Jonas and the girl.

Jilly opened her eyes, and Jonas could see in their gentle depths that she knew she was safe. A weary smile twisted her mouth as she looked at her two rescuers. Slowly she closed her eyes, her face at peace. With both arms free to hold her, Jonas realized the kid weighed practically nothing. Heaven knew how long it had been since she had eaten. He had to get her to the authorities and let them take care of her.

"Send the signal," Jonas said, slipping free of Terry's arms. "Send it now while the creatures are still inside."

Terry nodded, all business. It took him a moment to locate the drone hovering overhead, but when he did, he snatched the white handkerchief from his coat pocket and flapped it furiously in the air. To Jonas's surprise, the drone immediately sent a signal of its own in the form of a fine line of infrared light, aimed directly at the building at their backs. He and Terry gaped at each other with quizzical expressions on their faces.

Then both men seemingly realized simultaneously what it meant.

"That's the homing beacon for the missile!" Terry cried out. "We have to get away. Five minutes, Briggs said! We've only got five minutes!"

Clutching the girl tightly to his chest, Jonas took off running at Terry's heels. They raced for the Jeep half a block down and flung themselves inside. Staring up through the windshield at the brick building in front of them, they saw the infrared beam of light centered directly on the shattered third-floor window they had escaped through. In his imagination, Jonas saw what a napalm-tipped surface-to-surface missile would do when it struck its target. It wasn't a pretty picture. Then again, maybe it was.

Banging his fists on the dashboard, he yelled, "Drive! Drive! Get us out of here!"

Jilly popped her eyes open, terrified all over again. Jonas shushed her back to silence while Terry cranked the engine over, slipped the Jeep into gear, and scattered rocks in his wake as he floored the accelerator and fishtailed out of the alley toward Spangle's main drag.

Moments later, they were passing the Spangle city limits sign and headed for the open highway. Terry's hand came across the seat and Jonas took it, tucking it under his chin. Nestling against Jonas's chest, Jilly's eyes slipped open, and she saw the two holding hands. Once again she smiled.

"Boyfriends," she whispered sleepily. And Jonas and Terry smiled too.

Jonas squirmed around in the seat and looked at the tiny town retreating behind them.

"Pull over," he said. "Let's watch the fireworks."

Terry did as Jonas asked. Leaving the girl sleeping in the seat, Jonas pulled Terry out onto the road. He pointed to a small hillock only yards away, and they climbed it side by side to get a better vantage point.

The day seemed like any other day. Birds were chirping in the desert underbrush. Off in the distance, Terry's mountain rose up in the sunny haze. But here, closer at hand, the scent of honeysuckle washed over everything, drowning out the memory of other smells. Other smells if not other images. Jonas stood there blinking, trying to wipe them from his thoughts. Hoped he'd never think of them again.

Terry stood close at his side. He leaned in and whispered, "We're safe," and Jonas nodded. Jonas heard footsteps behind them and turned to see Jilly treading carefully with her bare feet on the stony road. Terry took pity on her and scooped her into his arms. Jonas edged close again, and the three of them stood watching the town's meager skyline in the distance.

A sound that might have almost been imaginary began to make itself heard in the distance. A soft whooshing sound. But in seconds, the barely perceptible whooshing became a screaming roar.

All three humans ducked as the SSM screamed past, seemingly inches above their heads but actually far higher. Was that the shock wave of its passing Jonas felt, or was it an illusion? Jilly let out a tiny cry, but Jonas and Terry both cuddled close, coaxing her to silence, letting her know yet again that she was safe.

Jonas lifted a hand and pointed off in the distance. He aimed a fingertip at the spot where he could see the roofline of the brick factory they had recently left.

"Watch," Jonas whispered in Jilly's ear, still pointing. "Watch."

The three of them froze. Waiting.

The fireball came so quickly they barely reacted. Only the girl let out a whimper. Jonas merely stood and stared, Terry tense beside him, as a gigantic eruption of flame blossomed in the middle of town. The sound wave from the exploding inferno hit them a second later. Thick black smoke billowed skyward, darkening the desert around them. The flames swelled outward into a cloud, as red as the rising sun. Jonas thought he could hear the fury of the flames eating at the building from where they stood. The last remaining windows in the research facility exploded in the heat. Jonas lifted his hands to his face, fearing the heat would blister his skin, the fingers of flame reach out and singe his hair.

The great fireball swelled high in the sky, then as quickly subsided. The explosive sounds quieted. But the flames remained.

Jonas and Terry and the girl stared for long minutes, made speechless by the destruction they were witnessing.

"They killed them, didn't they? The monsters?" Jilly softly asked, her head at rest against Terry's chest.

"Yes, honey," Jonas said, aching to take a wet cloth and wipe the filth from her face. "The creatures are gone now. The soldiers burned them up. They won't bother us anymore."

A tiny rivulet of tears slid through the dirt on the girl's cheek, and Jonas carefully wiped it away with a fingertip. She grabbed his hand and held on, her tiny fist clutching his thumb.

Terry and Jonas stood silently with Jilly in their arms. Together they watched the flames billow and roil in the distance.

Overhead, the skies were empty. No swarms of beasts closing in. No deadly shadows soaring high. Jonas closed his eyes and breathed in the day, enjoying the sense of peace that suddenly hovered over the little town.

Cupping the back of Jilly's head to hold her securely, he slipped his arm through Terry's, and together they walked slowly toward the Jeep.

Chapter Thirty-Two

"STOP WORRYING. Jilly is fine," Terry said. "She's being well taken care of."

He and Jonas were sitting on the sofa in front of the fireplace in Terry's cabin. Logs crackled on the grate, warming the room. Bruce was on his doggie bed, snoring away like a power saw, haughtily unconcerned that his two masters had spent the day saving their little corner of the world from creatures that best belonged in a horror movie, not real life.

The front door was slung wide to let the honeysuckle-laden night air waft over them. Night birds chortled in the pines, and a moth had slipped inside to flutter about the room, scoping things out. Terry figured it was only a matter of time before the moth discovered the fireplace and lit itself up like a roman candle.

Outside, a spray of early moonlight bathed the front steps in a pretty silver glow. Up above, the moon was fat and round, climbing lazily in the star-studded sky, taking its sweet time. The air was alive with the promise of rain. Wisps of fog were gathering in the ravines.

Not that Terry cared about the weather. For one thing, he didn't have a muscle that didn't ache. He suspected Jonas didn't either. It had been a long and most remarkable day.

The saddest moment for Terry had been watching Jonas hand Jilly over to the soldiers and the EMTs. It was sad because he knew it was breaking Jonas's heart. By the time they exited the Jeep at the quarantine line, a connection had been made between Jonas and the girl, and now Jonas wasn't wanting to let her go. Jilly didn't want to be let go either. There were tears in Jonas's eyes when he gently peeled the crying girl's arms from around his neck and relinquished her to the paramedics. This all took place at the same spot on the desert highway where, earlier that day (although it seemed a week ago), they had come face-to-face with Colonel Briggs for the very first time.

Briggs was there this evening too. Clapping them on the back and thanking them for their bravery. The colonel seemed truly touched that they had found a child inside the building and risked their lives to rescue her before the missile struck. As the EMTs hovered over Jilly, taking vital signs and coaxing her to silence with gentle words, Briggs had slipped in and brushed a paternal hand over the child's forehead, softly welcoming her back to the world.

Jonas had leaned sideways at that moment and whispered to Terry, "He's an old softy. Look at him. Sure glad I'm not that way."

Terry shot him an amused glance, not mentioning the fact that Jonas still had tears in his eyes and a shiver in his chin. "Oh no. You're not that way at all."

Briggs had insisted they get checked out by the EMTs as well, but Terry and Jonas declined.

"We're going home now, Colonel, and nothing short of another missile is going to stop us."

Briggs merely nodded as if he understood. He made little shooing motions with his fingertips as if to say "Fine, then. Go," and Jonas and Terry took off before he changed his mind.

At the Jeep, Jonas turned back and called out, "Take care of the girl."

Briggs gave him a thumbs-up and bellowed back, "We will, son. Don't worry!"

Now here they were, Terry and Jonas, back in the cabin together. The evening was peaceful and soft around them but for the night noises, Bruce's snoring, and the occasional roar of a helicopter passing overhead. Apparently Briggs was tidying up the ravages of his napalm attack on the heart of a small American town. The Army guys, and probably every fire brigade in San Diego County, were still fighting the raging fire and trying to prevent it from spreading and burning every square inch of Spangle to the ground. Soon the citizens who had fled the area when the trouble started would begin returning. Reclaiming their homes, rebuilding their lives. The ones who had died—what was left of them—would be laid to rest in some fashion or other, supplying closure to the survivors. Before you knew it, Spangle would be just another tiny Southwestern town once more. Strangers would look at it and think nothing exciting had ever happened there and never would.

A few people, of course, would know better.

Terry trusted Briggs now. He didn't doubt the colonel would succeed in doing what he needed to do. He also knew that Jonas had reluctantly accepted Brigg's promise to see that the girl was taken care of. And God help him if he didn't follow through on that.

Terry gave his head a shake. Enough about Briggs and monsters and conflagrations. His eyes lit up as he turned his attention to Jonas instead.

They had showered, so the muck of their adventures was washed away. Still there was a weariness in Jonas's cognac-colored eyes that Terry suspected was duplicated in his own.

Jonas had been staring into the fireplace, watching the orange flames nibble at a log. The firewood was pine, and the cabin reeked of it. It was a nice reek, Terry thought. Smelling Jonas beside him, fresh from the shower, was nice too. Really nice.

Terry stretched out his long legs and dangled them over the end of the couch. He lay back with his head in Jonas's lap and gazed at the echo of flames from the fire dancing across the cabin's ceiling.

Jonas grinned down at him and brushed his red mop of hair back out of his eyes. Jonas's hair, as black as night, was still damp from the shower, hanging straight down over his forehead. There was a scratch on Jonas's cheek. Another on the back of his hand. Terry wasn't surprised. He had tiny wounds everywhere too. It really had been a most unusual day.

As Terry watched, Jonas's face grew somber. Jonas glanced at the flames again, fumbling for the right words. "Do you really think she has family somewhere that will take her in? Jilly, I mean. After everything she's been through, I can't bear to think of her ending up in foster care with a bunch of strangers. Tell me she has family somewhere."

Terry smiled up into Jonas's fretful eyes. "I'm sure she must. And if she doesn't, we'll do what we can to take care of her ourselves."

Jonas blinked down at him, and Terry knew immediately that was what Jonas had been hoping to hear all along. "You'd do that?" he asked gently, his eyes bright and childlike.

"Of course," Terry answered.

Relief washed over Jonas's face. His gaze settled on Terry where his head rested snugly in Jonas's lap. He slipped a hand under the collar of Terry's shirt and caressed the red pelt of hair covering his chest. He licked his lips as one of Terry's two dimples tweaked a hole in his cheek. Jonas's fingers moved slowly over Terry's chest, a prelude to exploration.

"Careful," Terry muttered. "You don't want to start something you can't finish."

Jonas's eyebrows crawled together into a single line, punching downward in the middle. "What makes you think I can't finish what I start? I'm tired, but I'm not *that* tired." A wicked grin twisted his mouth, and he bent low to press the very same grin to Terry's lips. They kissed for a long time while the flames in the fireplace crackled and snapped and the night birds out in the trees sang a syncopated aria to the night closing in.

Jonas finally had to break the kiss because of a yawn. "Well, maybe I *am* a little tired."

Suddenly too weary to tease, Jonas settled back, his fingers still nestled in the hair on Terry's chest. Terry lay there, his head remaining in Jonas's lap, fighting sleep, as comfortable and as weary as he had ever been in his life.

"We've saved our home," Terry said and sighed. "And a lot of other people's homes too. I guess that makes us heroes."

"I guess it does." Jonas shyly grinned, gazing around the cabin. His eyebrows beetled again.

Terry frowned. "What's wrong now? Why are you looking like that?"

Jonas waved a hand at the walls and the ceiling. "It's all these metal fence posts you've nailed over everything. One lightning strike will cook us."

Terry laughed. "You're right! I never thought of that." It was his turn to grimace at the metal posts he had nailed everywhere. His heart sank, thinking of the work it would take to remove them. Then he shrugged. "I guess you'll have to help me take them down. We'll start tomorrow."

Jonas rolled his eyes so far up into his head that he looked like a zombie. "On second thought, I think I'll move back to the city. Living with a mountain man who teaches school and plays at being a notary public was never high on my bucket list of things to accomplish anyway. Plus I hate hammers. They cause blisters and they're just so damned... *butch.*"

"I'll show you butch," Terry said. He twisted his head around, lifted Jonas's shirttail, and blew a raspberry on Jonas's bare belly. Jonas jumped and howled and tried to squirm away. That didn't work, so he doubled over and stuck his tongue in Terry's ear. Then it was Terry's turn to howl.

Laughing like fools, they threw themselves into each other's arms and wrestled around on the couch for a while. When they came to rest,

Terry had Jonas trapped beneath him, Jonas's face cradled between his hands, and their crotches smashed enticingly together. He planted a kiss on Jonas's mouth. In response, Jonas closed his eyes and gave the perfect imitation of a melting ice-cream cone, softening luxuriously in Terry's arms. Well, *most* of him was softening.

When Terry spoke, their lips were still touching. "I don't care how tired you are. It's time to get naked."

Jonas's hand slid down and found a perfect handle to hold on to. It was hot and hard and throbbing. Just the right size for his fist, apparently, considering the look of satisfaction that suddenly lit Terry's face. "I almost forgot," he said, leering up into Terry's eyes. "You still owe me a f—"

Jonas's mouth fell open as the words died in his throat. Wide-eyed, he snapped his head around and stared across the cabin. Terry followed suit, turning to see what Jonas was gaping at. It was Bruce. He had left his bed and now stood in front of the fire, his eyes trained upward, straight at the ceiling. A snarl had formed on his face, and every tooth in his head was on full display. His tiny back legs were trembling, his curly tail quivering. The hair on the scruff of his neck had gone bristly, sticking straight up into the air. A growl welled up from the depths of his throat.

Terry snorted back a laugh. "What in the world is the matter with him?"

He was about to tell the dog to shut up when the cabin gave a massive jolt around them. The entire structure shuddered on its foundations. One of the cabin windows shattered, and shards of glass rained inward, exploding through the fence posts nailed across the panes and spilling out across the floor. A set of canisters tumbled off the counter in the kitchen, spilling flour and sugar everywhere. A floor lamp toppled over, its knock-off Tiffany lampshade shattering into a rainbow of colored pebbles. Terry threw his attention skyward when something heavy dragged itself across the roof. He heard shingles being ripped away. They slid and scraped along the slanted roof to topple off the eaves and land in the dirt at the edge of the cabin with dull, fluttering thumps. The cabin bucked again, and this time it got Terry and Jonas moving.

They flew off the couch and stood in the middle of the room, staring up. Confused, his mouth hanging open in shock, Terry couldn't imagine what the hell was going on.

His eyes met Jonas's, and a terrible understanding suddenly flowed between them.

Jonas shot a terrified glance at the door. "Close it!" he cried. "Close the front door!"

Terry didn't need to be told twice. He vaulted over the couch and slammed the door shut with a bang, dropping both metal crosspieces into place to seal it closed.

Bruce went crazy, howling and barking. Jonas scooped him into his arms. Bruce struggled, but Jonas held on tight.

A tremendous crash jarred the roof above their heads. The light fixture in the ceiling swayed, and dust sprinkled down on top of them. Terry raced back to Jonas and wrapped his arms around both him and the little dog. Jonas was shaking like a leaf and Bruce was still baying and squirming and yowling like a rabid hyena. The wash of moonlight visible through the slats over one of the cabin windows blinked out as something large passed by behind it. A loud thump hit the ground outside, shaking the cabin again. The familiar squeak of the front steps made Terry take a step back toward the kitchen, dragging Jonas and Bruce with him. At that very moment, the front door shuddered and rattled and banged as if a battering ram had struck it.

Whatever had been on the roof, was now standing on the front porch. It was seeking a way in. And both Terry and Jonas knew exactly what it was that was out there.

"IT'S THE fucking queen!" Terry breathed. "How the hell did she escape the fire?"

"She was smelling us back in town," Jonas whispered. "Memorizing our scent. She must have followed us here."

Jonas stood shivering, his eyes wide. He spun and clutched at Terry's arm, almost spilling Bruce onto the floor. He gave Terry a shake to get his full attention.

"Light her up!" Jonas cried, pointing to the metal fence posts covering the walls. "Throw the switch! Electrocute her ass!"

Terry gaped at Jonas like he had suddenly forgotten the English language. Then Jonas's words started sinking in. Of course! The generator! The metal posts were hooked to the generator! That was the whole idea of the fucking things! To electrocute whatever was trying to get inside!

Jonas held on to Bruce while Terry raced toward the generator against the back wall. Before he got there, the queen once again battered her great body against the cabin. This time she hit it with such force, the entire cabin shifted. With a lurch and a groan, the structure slid completely off its foundation. Windows exploded everywhere. Terry stumbled and crashed into the kitchen table when the floor suddenly tilted.

The power went out and the cabin was thrust into darkness.

Terry wrestled around in the dark, untangling himself from the chair legs. "The blood room!" he yelled, finally freeing his legs and clambering to his feet. "Get inside the blood room!"

Jonas was all but weeping in frustration. Terry could hear it in his voice. "I'm not leaving you here by yourself!"

"I'll be right behind you!" Terry bellowed. "Now go!"

Jonas's shadow moved quickly through the darkness. Still clamping Bruce to his chest, he raced across the cabin and flung open the trapdoor leading into the cellar. Terry heard him clattering down the steps with Bruce still yipping in his arms. Outside, the queen crashed into the front door again. This time one of the hinges popped off the doorframe and shot across the room like a bullet. The television exploded. A sliver of moonlight slipped into the room where the door separated from the wall. Terry stared at that little wedge of light, his heart racing, his breath ragged with fear. One more hit and the damn door would come down altogether!

Terry shot a glance at the generator against the back wall. With the power out, it was their last line of defense.

He threw himself at the generator, groping for the rope pull. He had started the thing enough times in the past to know he could do it in the dark. It was simply a matter of pulling the rope hard enough to crank up the engine. There wasn't time to light one of the propane lanterns anyway. He could see what he was doing by the light of the fire on the grate.

He found the rope and took a firm grip on it, bracing his knee against the generator for leverage. He yanked on the rope as hard as he could. Other than almost tearing his shoulder from its socket, nothing happened. The generator gave a feeble, mocking grunt and went dead silent. Shit! Then Terry remembered he had to prime the damn thing. He smacked himself in the head and with trembling fingers, pumped the little red primer button a few times to send fuel surging through the fuel line.

"Don't touch the metal fence posts!" Jonas yelled from down below. "Stand in the middle of the room away from the walls!"

"I know, goddammit!" Terry bellowed back. "Just stay where you are."

"Where else am I going?" Jonas shot back. "Vegas?"

Terry spit on his hands and this time when he yanked the rope pull, he did it with every ounce of strength he possessed. The generator sputtered and wheezed and finally coughed to life like a recalcitrant lawn mower. Terry screamed in jubilation. He stood there for a second, his heart in his throat, listening as the motor settled into a sustainable hum. When he was sure it wouldn't peter out, he all but fainted with relief. The exhaust pipe he had rigged to carry the exhaust fumes outside did its job, and the air inside the cabin stayed clear. The generator was so loud he could barely hear himself think, but at least he could breathe.

The queen roared through the broken front window as if infuriated by the noise. Terry could hear the creature's breathing and the snap of her jaws as she tried to peer through the slats and get at him. The carnivorous stench of her fangs filled the cabin and Terry almost barfed. The stink of her filthy body drifted through the posts, carried by the night wind behind her. And here he had thought he would never have to smell the bitch again!

"Fuck you!" he screamed at the uglyass face in the window. It was childish, he knew, but by now he didn't much care. As if mortally offended, the beast reared up to her full height and roared again. She battered at the door, and the cabin shook and rattled. The light fixture on the ceiling tore loose and crashed to the floor, barely missing Terry's head.

"Hunker down!" Terry cried. "I'm gonna throw the switch."

He knew Jonas was safe in the cellar. If everything worked as it was supposed to, the switch on the generator would electrify the metal posts on the outside of the cabin, including the front door. A separate switch downstairs lit the posts protecting the blood room alone. He would throw that switch after the drop-down door was locked behind them both and they were safely sealed inside the cellar.

Again, the cabin gave a massive shudder as the queen battered the outside wall. She had worked herself into a real fury now. The front door all but danced in its frame. Floorboards cracked and rolled beneath Terry's feet, and the staircase leading up to the loft ripped free from its moorings with a horrendous screech of tearing nails and snapping lumber. Billows of dust flew up when the staircase crashed to the floor below. Another window shattered, and shards of glass sprayed the room like buckshot.

Barely able to see or breathe, Terry threw the switch on the generator. The walls around him and on the ceiling above, lined with metal posts, all connected by a maze of wire, sparked to life. Tiny blue flames danced from post to post, circling the room in a heartbeat.

Terry dove for the cellar door, leaping down the stairs below. He spun around with his feet on the bottom step. With his head poking up through the hole in the floor, he looked out one last time. He was staring right at them when two of the posts used as crossbeams to seal the front door suddenly bowed inward. One snapped free with a *twang* and clattered to the floor while the other gave a metallic scream and shot across the room, impaling the couch like a lance. A second later the front door came off its hinges and went spinning through the air. The queen stooped her great head through the empty doorway to peer inside, her massive body framed by moonlight.

She gave a victorious roar and lumbered inside, squeezing through on her crutchlike wings. The metal posts around the door sparked and crackled, carrying electricity to every square inch of the cabin walls. The queen brushed against the doorframe, and the electricity flowed from the jamb to the fragile black flesh of her vast wing. As the current struck her skin and burned its way through her, her beady eyes opened wide and her teeth and dewclaws flared in blue flame.

The queen threw her head back and keened a piercing, mournful wail of pain.

And at that precise moment, the generator died. The metal slats around the cabin walls ceased to glow. Terry blinked, staring at them.

"Fuck!" he screamed, still cowering inside the trapdoor with his head poking up through the cabin floor to watch. "*Fuck, fuck, fuck, fuck!*"

The queen gave herself a shake and stepped the rest of the way through the front door, having to stoop to do it. Once inside, she unfolded her broad tarpaper wings, satiny black, and stretched them wide as far as they would go. Giving her head a shake, she looked at each wing in turn as if wondering where the pain had gone. Her vast wingspan dwarfed the room around her and blocked the moonlight behind.

Her flat, moist nose squelched and flexed, and her black eyes immediately focused on Terry peering up through the floor, staring at her. She bellowed in rage and Terry ducked below, slamming the trapdoor shut behind him as he went. Blinded by the darkness, he groped around and slid the metal posts across the trapdoor, sealing it shut above him.

The bars hadn't worked on the cabin door, and Terry suspected they wouldn't work on the trapdoor either. Not for long anyway. The queen was too strong and far too motivated. But what the hell else was he supposed to do?

"This is a pickle," Jonas muttered from the shadows.

"No kidding," Terry muttered back.

"Where's the shotgun?"

"Upstairs," Terry said. "Where's the .38?"

"Upstairs," Jonas said.

So there it was, Terry decided. He and Jonas were trapped, they were unarmed, and the generator was dead. They still had their sense of humor, but that wasn't going to help them much. There was a five-hundred-pound something-or-other wanting to gobble them up for dinner, and here they were stuck in a hole in the ground with an enraged pug who was still barking his brains out and giving Terry the biggest headache he had ever had in his life. For all the work he had done to make the cabin secure, they weren't any safer than they would have been upstairs, facing the queen head-on with maybe a flyswatter and a can of Raid. On the bright side, even if they did survive, the cabin was pretty much a wreck, so he wouldn't have to worry about removing all those stupid fence posts. Heck, they were probably the only thing holding the cabin together.

The cellar was pitch-black. Dust sprinkled down as the creature crashed and banged around above their heads, still bellowing in impotent fury. She must have been swinging her great wings about, using them to batter Terry's belongings to pieces, flinging them everywhere in rage. The sound was deafening.

"The generator died, didn't it?" Jonas quietly asked.

Terry could hear the fear in his voice. It was almost drowned out by the great beast tearing the cabin to shreds above their heads.

"Dead as a doornail," Terry answered. "I'm sorry."

To Terry's surprise, Jonas stepped close, still unseen in the shadows, and squeezed himself into Terry's arms. Terry clutched him tight, with Bruce in between. All three heads swiveled up to the trapdoor. Waiting for what they knew would come next.

As if Bruce wasn't making enough noise already, he launched into an entirely new set of barking. This time it was even louder than before. Unable to hold him, Jonas set the little dog on the floor before sliding back into Terry's arms.

"Hang on, baby," Terry murmured, fearing what was about to happen.

Jonas nodded, pressing his face to Terry's chest.

Judging by the sounds upstairs, the queen had at long last focused every ounce of her attention on the trapdoor. As she pummeled it, it rattled and banged above their heads. Bruce was howling and spitting and snarling, and up above the queen was smashing and stomping and squeaking in fury.

Somewhere in the midst of all that racket, another sound emerged.

It was a thumping sound. Like percussive smacks of wind in the night sky outside. It drew closer and seemed to hover directly over the cabin.

Terry and Jonas both lifted their heads and stared upward. Terry was still shaking, but not as much. He was starting to wonder if he was imagining things.

"Is that what I think it is?" he hissed.

"Sure sounds like it," Jonas hissed back.

Bruce wailed and howled and snapped and snarled. His little toenails tippy-tapped their way up the cellar steps like Fred Astaire on meth. They could hear the dog repeatedly banging his head against the trapdoor now, trying to barge through it so he could get at the creature outside and show it who was boss. If Terry hadn't been so terrified, he might have laughed at the little dog. As it was, he could only salute the pug's courage. Misplaced as it was.

"Listen!" Jonas snapped.

Terry froze. He had heard it too. Voices. Human voices. One particular voice stood out among the others. It was Colonel Briggs. He was yelling into the cabin through a bullhorn from somewhere outside.

"Anyone still alive in there?" he boomed, his voice loud enough to wake the dead.

Terry and Jonas started screaming and hollering and dancing around like Bruce, as happy as they had ever been in their lives. "Yes! We're here. We're trapped in the cellar. Help! Help!" Even Bruce got into the act, yipping and yapping and bouncing up and down.

Their laughter died the moment the trapdoor received a horrible whack from above, bursting into splinters and shattering in front of their eyes. Light poured into the cellar, and Terry realized the helicopter was hovering overhead, shining a great floodlight down through a hole in the cabin's roof.

Directly above, they saw the queen turn away from the trapdoor and focus her attention on the shattered front door instead. The human voices were closer now. Just outside, Terry thought. A lot of them.

Then he knew it beyond all doubt as Colonel Briggs called out from what sounded like the front porch, or what was left of it. His words were distorted by the bullhorn he was yelling through. Above and behind and around him, the helicopter's rotors thumped, and its engines wailed. The wind from its blades tossed tree limbs and roofing shingles everywhere. There were other machines out there too. Terry could hear their engines rumbling. Troop carriers or something. Briggs must have brought his whole Army with him.

Terry later speculated that the queen at that moment decided to ignore the soldiers and go with her original plan of eating the two gay guys who blew up her nest. Big mistake.

She poked her huge head down through the shattered hole where the trapdoor had been. Opening her great jaws, she emitted a horrific scream of outrage. Terry and Jonas stumbled back to a distant corner, still holding on to each other for dear life, and snatching the dog out of harm's way at the same time. The queen's foul breath filled the cellar, and Terry retched, tasting bile. Jonas railed at the beast to go fight the Army and leave them the fuck alone.

The queen seemingly didn't like that idea. She dropped her crutchlike wing down through the cellar opening, groping in the dark for the prey she knew was cowering there in the shadows.

Outside the cabin, Colonel Briggs, without his bullhorn now and far closer than he had been before, was bellowing orders left and right. Even to the creature upstairs. He sounded like a man used to being obeyed, when he screamed, "Leave those boys alone, you fucking cow!"

A second later, the night exploded in a storm of gunfire.

The queen, halfway through the trapdoor, trembled and danced and squawked and shook as the bullets struck her fat, fetid body. Her death wail ripped through the night. Around her, a thousand pinholes of light sprang through the cabin walls as bullets came from every direction. Above it all, the floodlights from the helicopter lit the scene below.

Terry shrank farther back into the cellar corner, dragging Jonas and Bruce with him. Blood from the dying creature above spilled down the stairs, dribbling to the cellar floor.

In one last burst of anger, the creature reared upright, propped erect on her black pterodactyl-like wings. She flung her head back and screamed in futile horror as bullets ripped broad swaths of flesh from her face and chest. Her nose erupted in a spray of blood. Her bottom jaw tore loose, dangling uselessly, torn apart by gunfire. The bones of one wing snapped, and losing her balance, the creature shifted to the side, landing pitifully on the cabin floor. From her throat erupted a faint mewling sound that sounded remarkably like the cries of her fat, white young before the napalm lit them up like roasted marshmallows.

Even after the queen went down, the bullets kept flying. Briggs wasn't taking any chances. Terry and Jonas crouched in the shadows, smelling the blood and the cordite and the carnivorous stench of the queen's foul organs as they spilled out of her dying body and crept across the cabin floor.

Terry held his breath and kept a death grip on Jonas and Bruce until the shooting stopped.

When it did, he opened his eyes and saw the floodlight shining unimpeded through the trapdoor in the cabin floor. Motioning for Jonas to stay where he was, Terry crawled up the blood-spattered steps and poked his head through the opening.

The first thing he saw was the bloated, savaged body of the queen filling practically every square inch of the room. The second thing he saw was Colonel Briggs, with a smoking AR-15 still clutched in his hands. A chewed-up cigar was poking out of his mouth, and he was grinning through the cabin door at the destruction he had wrought. Behind the colonel, lit up by the floods from the hovering helicopter, a line of soldiers in tactical gear stood waiting. They hadn't just been enjoying the view. Their guns were smoking too.

When his eyes fell on Terry, the colonel laughed out loud. The moment he did, the front porch roof behind him collapsed in a cloud of dust. He ducked through the front door just in time to avoid being beaned on the head by falling timber.

He shot Terry a friendly wink, as if it was no big deal.

"H-how did you know?" Terry asked, eyeing the huge blood-soaked body that dominated the entire interior of what was left of his cabin. Which wasn't much.

Briggs smiled. "How did I know she was coming for you, you mean? Simple. We've been monitoring her with drones ever since she escaped the fire and left the research facility through a basement tunnel. Wasn't sure what she was up to at first. Thought maybe she'd lead us to some more of those flying fuckers. But she didn't. That's when we realized she was coming after you. Where's your buddy?"

Jonas popped his head through the trapdoor alongside Terry's. "I'm here, sir."

Briggs gave him a grin. "Your friend keeps asking for you."

Jonas tore his eyes from the dead queen and stared at the colonel. He looked confused. "Uhh. That's good. But which friend is that?"

"The little girl," the colonel said. "Jilly. The one you rescued."

Jonas's hand tightened around Terry's arm. "She's okay?" he asked, his voice suddenly weak with emotion.

The colonel spit out the remains of his cigar, nudged the queen's dead body with the toe of his boot, and grinned. "Okay doesn't quite cover it," he said. "I saw her eat most of a meatloaf and three baked potatoes not an hour and a half ago."

"Well, that's good, isn't it?" Jonas smiled, every tooth flashing white in the floodlight's beam.

"That's good indeed," the colonel said, a proud glint in his eye. "You did well, boys. You made a difference. I'm proud to say I know you."

Both Jonas and Terry blushed.

Between them, a third head popped up. It was Bruce. Apparently he was still keyed up. He growled at all the soldiers staring at him. Then for good measure, he growled at the colonel.

Briggs shook his head with righteous indignation, muttered "Pugs" with a grimace, then turned and walked away.

Chapter Thirty-Three

Six Months Later

THE NEWLY constructed cabin on the side of Terry's mountain was the same as the previous cabin. Only this one had an extra bedroom added on the ground floor behind the kitchen, and there wasn't a single metal fencepost in sight.

The work on the replacement cabin had been completed only the week before. Most of the labor had been donated on weekends by a long string of Colonel Briggs's men, who were still monitoring the area. Each and every one of them was a little awed, Jonas thought, to think a couple of fruit cups could be brave enough to take the risks he and Terry had taken to help wipe out the creatures and battle their queen. Not that the soldiers had anything against fruit cups, as they constantly reminded one another.

Colonel Briggs had stopped by every couple of weeks to see how the work was going on the cabin and to offer advice here and there. Since he confessed to building birdhouses for a hobby, he assumed he was qualified to oversee the construction of an honest-to-God building. The men under him usually listened to his suggestions politely, nodded their heads understandingly, saw him off with a snappy salute, then went back to doing what they were already doing anyway.

On the day the construction was finished and the last shingle nailed in place, Terry and Jonas immediately began moving in furniture. Being the romantic slobs they were, they had decided to live on the mountain rather than in town, because that was where they fell in love. Terry's notary office would remain in Spangle. Jonas was still a writer, of course, and Jonas reminded Terry that he could write up a tree if he had to. It didn't matter where he was. He had earned the right to brag a little about his chosen occupation. He was deep into chronicling the story of how they had helped slay the creatures, and at the latest count he had three—count them, three—publishers nibbling at his manuscript with interest.

At the moment, Jonas and Terry were sipping Budweiser out of a bottle at the same little kitchen table they used to sit at and drink Budweiser from before. The table was the only piece of cabin furniture they were able to salvage after the queen and the US Army converged to destroy the place. When a platoon of soldiers take it into their heads to aerate a structure with bullet holes, they don't dick around. Terry found puncture wounds in everything he owned. Even Jonas's beloved portable typewriter had been blown to smithereens. He now worked on a brand-new Mac.

With the cabin finished and a roof over their heads again, it was nice to sit and do nothing for a change. Their lives had been a whirlwind of activity since the queen fell dead on their living room floor six months before. Not to mention the months of terror they had endured before that.

Two weeks earlier, dressed in brand-new suits and as nervous as cats, they visited the Spangle courthouse. They filled out marriage papers and, shortly after that, exchanged vows in front of a guy with the worst hairpiece they had ever seen in their lives. The ceremony took place in the shade of a ratty-looking plastic arbor draped in plastic flowers in a back room behind the courthouse cafeteria, which reeked of Tuesday's meatball surprise.

They had giggled their way through the service while Jilly stood behind them in a frilly little summer dress with a gigantic straw bonnet, cradling a spray of posies and fidgeting like crazy because she was giggling, too, and had to pee.

That was another reason the last six months had been so busy. As it turned out, after the death of Jilly's parents, the child had no one willing to accept responsibility for her. Not that Jonas minded. He set about doing everything he had to do to start the process of adopting Jilly, and he knew how blessed he was that Terry loved the kid as much as he did.

The judge was leery of awarding Jilly to unmarried adults, gay or otherwise. Terry solved that problem by proposing on the spot, and Jonas accepted. Jilly was already living with them in town on a foster care basis while the other problems were being ironed out. Still the judge was not eager to permanently turn the child over to two men who had never cared for a child in their lives.

After twenty minutes in the judge's chambers with only the judge and Jilly present, the judge had a change of heart. Jonas never found out what the girl told the judge, but whatever it was, the three were pronounced a family on the spot.

Even while Jilly was living under their roof back in town, there were nights of terrible nightmares when Jilly refused to sleep alone. She squirmed in between them in the big bed and stayed there until the morning sun chased the nightmares away.

Gradually the nightmares lessened, and the constant fear in Jilly's eyes began to abate. She found a lot of her happiness with Bruce. He tagged along behind her everywhere she went. She especially loved being on the mountain, which was one of the reasons Jonas and Terry had decided to move there full-time once the cabin was finished.

And now, after everything that had happened, here they were. One small, happy family. Two daddies, one daughter, and a pug.

Jonas could hear Bruce's toenails tapping like castanets on the hardwood floor in Jilly's room. The new one behind the kitchen. Interspersed with the tapping, Jilly hummed softly to herself while she piddled around on her bed.

Jonas listened to her with a lazy smile on his face. He dragged his chair a little closer and laid his hand alongside Terry's on the tabletop. Their two silver wedding rings gleamed red in the light from the fire flickering on the grate. Their eyes met, and Jonas's heart gave a quiet little thump of contentment.

"You need a haircut again," he said.

"So what's new?" Terry answered, running his fingers through his mop of red hair.

Both men smiled.

Jonas's eyes went sneaky. "I keep thinking about Colonel Briggs," he said.

Terry looked up. "Why?"

Jonas sucked in a monumental sigh. "Because he was kind of a hottie. And I like a well-maintained older man in uniform as much as the next gay guy. Plus he killed the queen and saved our asses."

Terry frowned. "Oh, shut up. I could have saved our asses too if I'd had an army behind me. And maybe a bazooka."

Jonas arched one eyebrow high because he knew it would irk Terry when he did. Then he nudged Terry's knee under the table and grinned.

They turned when Jilly came running through her bedroom door. She had her screaming red hair, every bit as red as Terry's, pulled up in a scrunchie at the top of her head. Her hair was so long, it still cascaded down to her shoulders. A spray of freckles danced across her nose, getting all tangled up in wrinkles when she laughed.

"I'm ready!" she sang out, doing a dainty pirouette to show she had on the proper clothing for a walk in the woods, which she had been promised and wasn't about to let anybody forget. At her feet, Bruce gave a yip as if agreeing with her. He did a little pirouette too. Apparently he was ready for a walk in the woods as well.

Jonas poured the rest of his beer down his throat, and Terry followed suit. They rose from the table and stepped to the back door, where they pulled their respective jackets off wall hooks and shrugged them on after slapping baseball caps on their heads.

Terry looked down at Bruce. "What'll it be? Leash or no leash?"

Bruce glowered and gave a testy little bark.

"No leash it is," Terry said, waving his hands in mock submission.

Jonas plucked a wool scarf off another hook and draped it around Jilly's neck. He took a heartbeat to stare deep into her eyes while she adjusted the scarf across her shoulders. The melancholy that used to hover there had almost vanished. Looking at her now, one would never know the horrors she had seen in her young life or how much she had lost in living it. Her parents, her home, and for a long time, her sense of trust. But the trust was returning. Jonas could see it in the way she carried herself. The way she smiled at little things and laughed like a little girl at big things. She still demanded a night-light when she slept, but rarely anymore did she come crawling into their bed for company. In a way, Jonas rather missed that.

Too excited to wait any longer, Jilly ran toward the cabin door, dragging Jonas and Terry along behind her. All three stepped out into the dusk of early evening. The air was cool but not cold. The dark was drawing close but had not yet settled in. The mountain and the trees and the brand-new cabin stood gray in the waning light. Like a black-and-white postcard. As always, the mountain smelled of honeysuckle and pine smoke from the chimney at their backs.

Jilly and Bruce took off running down a narrow path that led into the trees. Jonas noticed that even now, she never let herself get completely out of sight. Occasionally she would glance back over her shoulder to see where they were. To know she was safe.

Jonas heard her up ahead, chattering to Bruce. God knows about what. She gave a merry cry and squatted at the side of the trail to gather a fistful of California fuchsia for the kitchen table. The narrow little flowers bloomed red all over the mountain, and it was one of Jilly's favorites.

Her bouquet to her satisfaction, she set off down the trail once more. When they were alone, Terry took Jonas's hand.

"She'll be okay now," he said softly.

Jonas nodded. "I know."

"So will I," Terry said, gazing deep into Jonas's eyes. A happy warmth burrowed through Jonas. He edged closer to Terry's side and rested his head on his broad shoulder as they walked. Terry's arm came up, engulfing him, holding him in place.

"This is better than I ever thought it would be," Terry said. "Us, I mean. You and me and Jilly."

Jonas closed his eyes, trusting Terry to lead him safely along. "You feel it too, then," he whispered, as much to himself as to Terry. As much to the mountain around them as to the whole damned world spreading out around them. "We're a real family now. I never thought I'd have anything like that. I never thought I'd be a part of anything this… beautiful."

Terry brushed a kiss through his hair as they walked. "Neither did I."

Jonas looked up ahead, and there at a turn in the path, Jilly stood frozen. The flowers had fallen from her hand and lay sprinkled at her feet. Bruce had snuggled up to her ankle. He was standing as still and tense as the girl.

They were both staring dead ahead at something Jonas couldn't see.

He and Terry took off running. They reached Jilly in seconds. She turned when they approached, gazing back at them with wide, frightened eyes.

"What is it?" Jonas asked. "What's wrong?"

Jilly turned back toward the lane ahead where it opened into a meadow. The grass and wildflowers were short, barely covering the earth, with maybe an acre of mountain landscape open to the evening sky. Jilly lifted her arm and pointed.

"There," she said. "Look."

Jonas and Terry moved closer and tried to see what she was pointing at. Jonas was the first to spot the movement. Specks of dark shadow in the gloaming sky, flitting about above the meadow. Tiny flashes of life. As black as night against the rising moon in the distance.

All three humans and Bruce stood watching the fluttering beasts dance across the evening sky. They jittered and spun and swooped and soared, as silent as a voiceless wind.

Suddenly Jilly smiled, watching them.

"They're only bats, aren't they?" she asked.

Jonas and Terry each rested a hand on her tiny shoulders and stared down at her shining face as she gazed up at them. There was no fear in her eyes now. Only a happy, innocent wonder.

"That's right," Jonas said, grinning at her. "They're only bats. They eat the bugs. They're our friends."

"Friends," Jilly said slowly, as if trying to find the proper place to store the word inside her head. Then glancing down, she saw her flowers sprinkled across the ground at her feet.

"Oh no!"

She stooped and gathered them up as carefully as she could, making sure all the blossoms were facing the same direction. When she was satisfied they were safe, she gave them a tiny shake to remove the dirt. When she glanced back at the sky and the sea of tiny bats still darting about in front of the rising moon, the corners of her mouth tipped up a little.

"They're so quiet," she said softly, still watching the bats dip and climb before her eyes. "They don't sing at all."

Without another word, she stuck the flowers inside her jacket for safekeeping and grabbed a hand from each of the two men towering above her. The one with dark hair and the one with red hair like her own. Her hands were tiny in theirs, but she didn't seem to mind.

Neither Jonas nor Terry seemed to mind either.

"Let's go home," Jilly said, "I'll make popcorn, and we'll sit on the porch!"

Laughing gaily, she gave a tug and pulled them back along the trail they had walked a hundred times before.

Toward a life they had barely embarked upon at all.

JOHN INMAN is a Lambda Literary Award finalist and the author of over thirty novels, everything from outrageous comedies to tales of ghosts and monsters and heart stopping romances. He has been writing fiction since he was old enough to hold a pencil. He and his partner live in beautiful San Diego, California and together, they share a passion for theater, books, hiking, and biking along the trails and canyons of San Diego or, if the mood strikes, simply kicking back with a beer and a movie.

John's advice for anyone who wishes to be a writer? "Set time aside to write every day and do it. Don't be afraid to share what you've written. Feedback is important. When a rejection slip comes in, just tear it up and try again. Keep mailing stuff out. Keep writing and rewriting and then rewrite one more time. Every minute of the struggle is worth it in the end, so don't give up. Ever. Remember that publishers are a lot like lovers. Sometimes you have to look a long time to find the one that's right for you."

Email: john492@att.net
Facebook: www.facebook.com/john.inman.79
Website: www.johninmanauthor.com

JOHN INMAN
THE LAST
DANCE

Martin Dance knows better than to get involved with a rent boy. After all, he's been around the block a few times. And a few times after that. Still, there's something about Johnny Cotton that catches his eye. And his heart.

When Johnny and his best friend find themselves in over their heads with the woman who owns them lock, stock, and barrel, Martin knows he has to step in.

Martin and his old buddy, Charlie Bass, might be retired from the Firm, but they still know how to manage a gunfight. And how to go underground with a couple of male hookers less than half their age. Just for the purpose of keeping them safe, you understand. No funny business intended.

Odd, though, how funny business tends to creep in when you least expect it.

It's sort of like love that way, Martin decides. One minute you're minding your own business, the next minute you're in a world of hurt. Or, if you're lucky, a world of happy.

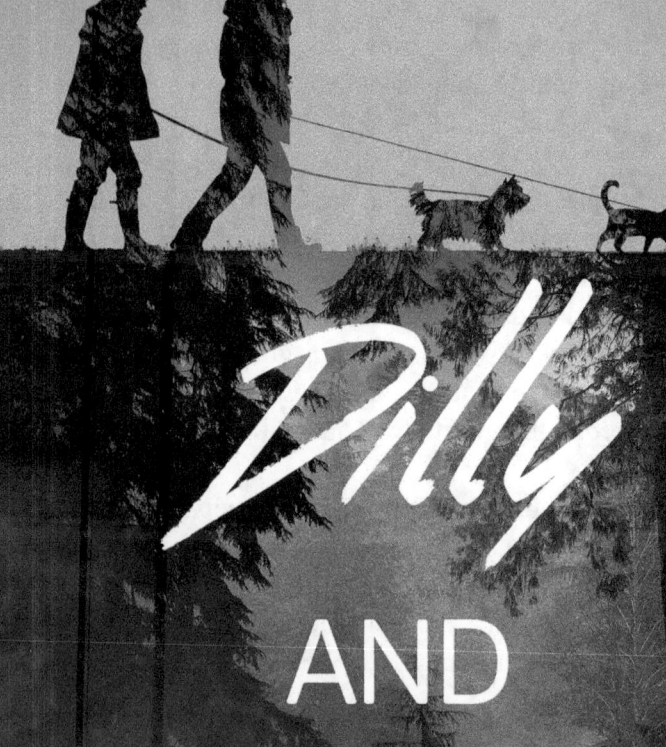

JOHN INMAN

Dilly

AND

Boz

It's funny how love nails you when you least expect it.

Dilly Jones has pretty much given up on romance ever finding him. Boz Jenkins, his neighbor, is recently out of a bad relationship but has definitely noticed the cutie across the street. When Dilly drops a bag of donuts on the sidewalk, it sets a chain of events into motion. And suddenly both men's hearts are lost.

But Boz's ex is still hanging around, and he'll do whatever it takes to get Boz back. With a brand-new romance gearing up to knock their socks off, the last thing Dilly and Boz expect is to get tangled up in a stranger's murder. Or to find themselves fighting for their lives.

Just as they finally find happiness, their love for each other becomes the thing that threatens them the most.

www.dreamspinnerpress.com

www.ingramcontent.com/pod-product-compliance
Lightning Source LLC
Chambersburg PA
CBHW070106260626
47160CB00004B/1336